ASANO NO KATANA

(SWORD OF ASANO)

ASANO NO KATANA

(SWORD OF ASANO)

*An Historical Novel Spanning Five Hundred
Years of Lord Suzuki's Family Ties to
Asano Takumi-no Kami's Clan*

GENE BROWN

In Loving Memory of my wife, Sachiko (Nina) Takahashi, to whom I never said 'Thank You' enough times.

Dedicated to my daughter, Kristina Kei, whose death in September 1993 stopped this work in its tracks.

With overwhelming thanks to my son, Richard Rei, whose daily support and encouragement helped me overcome so many of life's obstacles. Without his emotional strength, I could not have completed this novel.

A special "thank you" to author Lucia St. Clair Robson whose book, The Tokaido Road, helped me gain insight into the Asano story. Ms. Robson challenged and inspired me to write this story.

DISCLAIMER

While I have read numerous books, as noted in the Bibliography at the end, I take full responsibility for the historical inaccuracies that may appear in this manuscript. Some leeway in historical fact has been taken by the author in order to make certain progressions of the story fit.

I hope you will not think any less of history for my misuse of it.

NOTES

Japanese names are generally written, and said, with the family name first, followed by the given name.

In the story, I follow this convention in the names of the Emperors and the Shoguns. Example: the Shogun Tokugawa Ieyasu's name is written just this way, but westerners would pronounce, and write it, as Ieyasu Tokugawa.

I do use the western style with all other Japanese names in the story.

Often you will see in the story the use of honorific endings to a Japanese name. Those endings are explained when first encountered in the storyline, and proceed from 'kun' to 'chan,' used with children, and thence to 'san' and finally the most honorable, 'sama.' Sometimes the term 'chan' is used by adults as a term of endearment.

PROLOGUE

A MYSTERY UNFOLDS

A nearly six hundred year old Japanese Samurai sword speaks to a young boy, and tells him of age-old events that shaped Japan and influenced the world.

In his hands, the sword becomes an oracle of his family history, a chronicler of the relationships of many of Japan's oldest and most noble families.

This is an account of the Suzuki family, offshoot of the older brother side of Japan's early Imperial Shirakawa clan, as seen through the eyes of the samurai sword - the *katana* - that witnessed it all.

While history has recorded only some of this story, it is now up to the sword, and this young boy, to tell what may have really happened.

The story covers events beginning in 1425 and continuing uninterrupted to the present day. With history as a guide, the settings portray life in feudal Japan as lived by the noble and samurai classes.

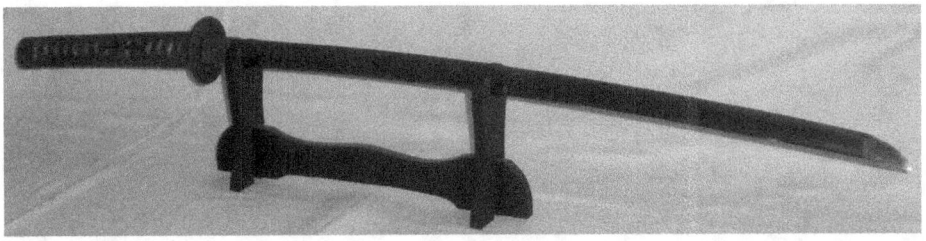

8-year-old Alexander secretly holds the samurai sword he has never been allowed to touch. The sword was passed to his grandparents for safekeeping. He has heard stories all his life from his father and grandparents about his noble Japanese ancestry. But it has all been like a fairy tale - he was fascinated by the stories but never really felt they were real.

Suddenly, while holding the forbidden *katana*, he gets the strong psychic sense of a dramatic event as told to him by the sword. The sword directs him to write this event, and he writes in a manner far advanced for his 8 years.

Repeatedly, as though obsessed, he holds the sword in secret, each time writing what the sword commands him. In time, he has written the history of the sword.

An event about which he learns and writes is of great historical significance. A Japanese nobleman, Lord Asano, drew this very sword in anger and as a result, was forced to commit ritual suicide in 1702. A year later, his masterless samurai, the 47 Ronin, took their revenge.

No one in the family knows how the Suzuki family sword came to be worn by Lord Asano, nor why it now bears his *kamon*. But *katana* tells the story as it <u>might</u> have happened, and young Alexander relates it to us as only a breathless 8 year old can do.

I

THE LEGACY MADE KNOWN

Something woke him very early, guiding him gently down the hall from his bedroom to the living room. Sleepily, he padded across the deep, gray carpet to the mantle above the fireplace and looked up. Still not awake, and not really focusing his eyes, he saw the familiar shape of the samurai sword.

Having never been allowed to touch the sword, he had longed for it from a distance. Now, he felt compelled to reach up to it, to take it down from its stand, and to hold it close to him.

This was the sword, he remembered being told, that had been in his grandmother's family for a long, long time. He had heard the stories about the sword - she called it the *katana* - all his young life, and they had filled him with awe. He had often imagined being a samurai in Japan hundreds of years ago, riding into battle carrying this sword, and fighting for the honor of his master.

But now, alone with it, he sensed more than imagination, more than just awe and wonderment. He sensed a knowledge of the life of the sword, of the battles it had seen and fought, and the men who had lived, and died, by it.

The sword was as tall as he was, or perhaps even a little taller. In its leather-bound wooden scabbard, it weighed several pounds, and he had to make a real effort to lift it ever so gently from its resting place and bring it down to his eye level.

Certainly if his father knew he was holding it he would be in trouble, for in his family only his father was allowed to touch the sword. But he was not fearful, and held it confidently in front of him. With a steady gaze, he surveyed its leather covering, and felt its weight bearing down on his arms. Slowly he brought it close and, holding it vertically, pressed it to his body. The visions seemed more real now. As he held it longer he began to feel, or sense, someone or something trying to talk to him, to tell him something.

He stood rooted to the carpet, afraid to move for fear of breaking this magical spell, yet he felt compelled to take the sword to the table in the dining room and sit with it. Slowly he carried the sword to the table and, laying it there, pulled out a chair. Without knowing why he then went to the small desk his mother had in the dining room and removed a writing tablet and pen. Getting up on the chair, he grasped the sword with his right hand and began to write.

'I am *Asano no Katana*,' he wrote, 'Sword of Asano. I will tell you my stories and you shall write them just as I speak. Do not alter a word. And do not tell of this writing, for you shall surely be scorned until the day my story is completed.

And on that day you shall proclaim my existence, and the world shall know that I have triumphed.'

Furtively he tore the page from the tablet and read it. He had never written like this before, and was surprised to see this handwriting was not like on his school papers. He wondered if Miss Haversham, his third grade teacher, would believe that he could write like this. As he reread it, he was even more surprised to see the words he had written: words that he had never written before, words that he didn't even know he knew! Could this really be his own writing, he wondered?

For a moment he sat motionless, staring first at the sword, then at the paper, and listening to see if his parents were awake. Not hearing anything, he lightly slapped himself on the cheek to see if he were really awake. He felt the sting of his hand and nodded quietly to himself: Yes, I'm awake. But I sure don't know what's happening to me.

Then, still touching the sword, he picked up the pen and began writing again. Quickly and deftly he wrote a story that was incredible and far beyond his wildest imagination. And written in a style far beyond his age or education.

I was made by Magoroku from the town of Seki. Known as Seki no Magoroku or later as Kanemoto II, my craftsman was one of Japan's finest. He made only twelve swords like me, and only I and one other still exist. My brother rests in a place of honor in the Victoria Albert Museum in London, having been given to Queen Victoria by the Shogun Iyemochi in 1860.

Seki was a small town in the hills overlooking the Bay of Ise. Surrounded by forests of pine and maple, Seki became known in the olden days as a place of peaceful worship. For this reason, Magoroku chose this place to make his swords, imbuing them with the peacefulness of the mountains and the strength of the mighty trees. The Ise peninsula on which Seki is located is considered to be the fount of Japanese culture, and is often referred to as *Uji-yamada* or Birthplace of Japan. Legend has it that the Sun Goddess *Amaterasu* lived in Ise, and the people of Japan to this day consider the region sacred.

Magoroku lived during the fifteenth century, and produced his finest dozen swords around mid-century. He was of the Mino school of sword making, and produced blades known for their sharpness and incredible strength. The practical long bladed sword was conceived in this school and many other schools of sword making copied this design. So honored was Magoroku that numerous of his students and their students took the name Kanemoto in his memory. But none produced a sword as faithful to its intent and design as did Magoroku.

Magoroku himself made the steel of my blade, using the finest, purest sand ores of the region. Afterwards, having fasted for thirty days during which time he prayed and recited Shinto scripture, and bathed in the cold mountain waterfall to obtain mental and spiritual purification, Seki no Magoroku entered a special hut - a smithy called *kajiya* - which was surrounded by special straw-rope, known as *shime-nawa*, that had been specially blessed by a Shinto priest to ward off evil spirits during the making of his masterpiece. Though not of noble birth, Seki no Magoroku would don the court noble's ceremonial costume, *kariginu* and *yegoshi*, for the final, most critical, operations. This whole procedure was steeped in mystical and etheric religious rite, as any uncleanness of the sword smith would be passed on to the sword, and it would never serve its master faithfully.

First he attached a bar of iron to the short strip of steel; this bar, called the *tang* upon its completion, served as a handle during the sword making process. He would heat the steel until it was fiery red, then beat it into a long, flat, piece. Grasping it with the tongs, he would douse it in a wooden bucket of water "the temperature of February or August". After reheating it to near melting, he would fold the steel and again beat it with his mallet, molding it longer and flatter each time. Carefully he would fold the hot metal in half, then beat it flat. Doing so hundreds of times produced a blade that has thousands of layers of steel. This is the secret of my strength.

After heating and cooling so many times, the steel is strong, yet not brittle. I can take a blow from another sword and not splinter, and I can slice through a man's body without a quiver. I have done so many times, and had to prove my sharpness and strength on the day of testing by cutting in one swoop through the bodies of five prisoners.

I was made for combat, having been forged during a time in the history of Japan when the country seemed to have gone mad; brother fought brother; family fought family; clan fought clan. I have proven myself on the field of battle many times, as I shall tell you later.

But I was not made to be alone. Only the samurai were allowed to wear the paired sword, and I, *katana*, was always to be accompanied by the short sword, *wakizashi*. So Magoroku made my mate, imbedding in our hilts the wisteria crest of our noble family, and together we were presented to our master, Lord Suzuki, in 1450.

You should know the turmoil of the age into which I was born. This portion of my tale is long, but you need to know it, so you see why I was commissioned. For hundreds of years, since the Fujiwara lost power in 1185 during the six-year war of *Gempei* in which the great Taira clan was defeated by the Minamoto clan led by Minamoto Yoritomo, there had been civil war and unrest in Yamato. Palace intrigue was a daily event as the Minamoto and Taira clans fought for supremacy. At the beginning of the twelfth century, the Taira had been pushing to dominate, to continue the Fujiwara control, and eradicate the Minamoto. Two great battles - *Hogen* in the early part of the century, and *Heiji,* fought in 1159 - changed the political landscape and led to the leadership of the Taira under the cruel tyrant Kiyomori, who had had himself appointed prime minister. However, upon his death, Yoritomo began his reign of power, easily finding enough lords and their armies of samurai who had grown weary of servitude under Kiyomori to defeat the Taira in the bloody battle of *Dan-no-ura* in 1185, the final battle of the *Gempei* war. Yoritomo was head of the Minamoto and a resident of Kamakura, a bustling village south of Edo overlooking the *Sagami* Bay. It was at this time that Yoritomo instituted the *Shogunate,* or military sovereignty called *Bakufu,* and the imperial court was established in Kamakura.

The Emperor Go-Toba succeeded his brother Antoku who was drowned in the lake on *Yashima* Island in the Inland Sea near Takamatsu, during the battle of *Dan-no-ura.* Yashima is shaped like the roof line of the Japanese house - flat on top and tapered at the edge - and from this it derives its name: *Ya* is house; *shima* is island. Yashima is a mere ten feet or so off the shore of Takamatsu and one can circumambulate on foot the perimeter of this lake in an hour's time. But on the day of this battle, this waist deep lake was red with the blood of soldiers and horses.

Antoku's family, which dates back to the Emperor Go-Shirakawa who abdicated in 1086 and ruled as a 'retired Emperor', includes the Suzuki line of court nobles who had established a southern home on Shikoku, being themselves originally from the Osaka area near Ise. Unfortunately for the Suzukis, they had fought on the side of *Heike*, the losers of this battle, and not for *Genji*, the winners. The family name and honor was maintained, however, since a member of the Suzuki family had married into the *Genji* side. From this time forward, the real power of the Suzukis had declined, although they were always considered a part of nobility.

Beginning with the thirteenth century, *Bushido*, or "Way of the Warrior", was promoted as the "common law" to keep all the clans under control. It required fealty by the samurai to his master, and laid down guidelines for action in many different circumstances, including the requirement for *hara-kiri* (sometimes called *seppuku*) or "gut-slashing" in certain instances of disgrace.

Over the years, the country saw a succession of *Shoguns* who actually ruled the country - always in the "name" of the Emperor who had no actual power and was to some degree a hostage to the *Shogunate* - and their appointed *Shugo*, the provincial constables. These *Shugo* governed each province through the services of stewards called *Jito*, whose duty it was to keep the *Shogunate* informed of plots against the government as well as to extract the taxes levied by the *Shogun*. Hence, there were two types of power during these times: the titular head of the country embodied in the Emperor, his family, and the select group of noble families that made up his clan or extended family; and the governing power of the country embodied in the *Shogun* and his *Shugo* and *Jito*.

When Yoritomo died in 1199, the Hojo family assumed the power of the *Shogunate*. A quarter century later the royal family and the *Shogunate* came the closest to reuniting when, in 1226, Fujiwara Yoritsune, a court noble, was selected *Shogun*. However, the *Shogunate* was unwilling to release its hold on absolute power, and the Hojo reign ended a hundred years later.

As the middle fourteenth century approached, the Kamakura government was losing its power. The new Emperor Daigo II, often referred to as Go-Daigo, in 1333 attempted to take back political control and re-establish imperial rule at the palace in Kyoto. Some of the Emperor's followers marched on the northern imperial court in Kamakura and burned it down. The Kamakura general, Ashikaga Takauji, sent to Kyoto to control Go-Daigo and maintain peace, defected to Go-Daigo's cause. However, General Ashikaga soon defected, and this set in motion the breakdown of the warrior class into more localized bands of lords, called *Daimyo*, and their vassals or "outer *daimyo*", called *Tozama*.

General Ashikaga set up another member of the imperial family - younger brother to Go-Daigo - as emperor in Kyoto, assumed for himself the title of *Shogun*, settled in Kyoto and tried to create a three-tiered feudal system composed of the *Shogunate, Daimyo* and *Tozama*. However, Go-Daigo and his descendants maintained a rival imperial court in the mountains south of Kyoto, and there were two imperial families until 1392.

The *Daimyo* were not contented with the limits of their domains and the requirement to serve the *Shogun* in Kamakura and gradually these great territorial lords began a fierce rivalry for power; open warfare erupted again in 1467. This new era became known as *Sengoku*, or "the country at war". Three leaders emerged victorious during this period of conflict: Oda Nobunaga who had deposed the last of the Ashikaga *shoguns* in Kyoto in 1573 and who died in 1582; then Toyotomi Hideyoshi who actually reunified Japan and who died in 1598; and finally Tokugawa Ieyasu, who defeated a coalition of his rivals at the fateful battle of Sekigahara in 1600. It was Hideyoshi, a common foot soldier and farmer, who rose to the exalted position of leader of the Minamoto clan by dint of his bravery and skill, and who in his lifetime, built the Osaka Castle. Upon his death, his five-year-old son ostensibly took control; the boy's mother was the real power.

But Tokugawa Ieyasu was fearful that the boy could not maintain control of his vast army. He feared a continuation of the long war that had just ended. Since he, too, had a vast army, he plotted to depose Hideyoshi's family from its seat of power at Osaka castle, and in 1615 tricked the boy's mother into filling in all the many moats that surrounded the castle. These moats had served Hideyoshi well, and had kept safe the castle and all its occupants. But Ieyasu convinced her that, since his army was available and two great armies were not necessary now that the country was under control, she should let her warriors go, turn the lands into farms and enjoy life in her new castle. Whereupon Ieyasu stormed and captured the castle, killed all its occupants - lords, ladies and defenders alike - and burned the structure to the ground.

With his rule undisputed, Tokugawa Ieyasu then instituted the Tokugawa *Shogunate*, which lasted until the restoration of the Emperor's powers in 1868, known as the Meiji Restoration.

As I shall tell you, *Shogun* Ieyasu distributed lands and titles upon those who had helped him win this important victory. He claimed the spoils of war for his victors, and shared his power amongst his most trusted viceroys.

Young Alexander Akira put down the pen and stared at the pages he had just written. Unbelieving that this could be his own writing, he reread it all. Many of the words were unknown to him, yet he had surely written them. He could not understand how he had written the Japanese words, although he had been taking conversational Japanese at the Saturday morning classes with the sons and daughters of Japanese businessmen living in his city. But he had never written the words before, and now they were on his pages of paper, written by his hand.

He glanced at the clock in the kitchen: it had been just over two hours since he first picked up the *katana*, and he was exhausted. Listening intently, he heard the sounds of his parents as they arose from their slumber.

Quickly, he wrote on a fresh piece of paper the one thing he knew from the story so far - the name of his grandmother's ancient relative: LORD SUZUKI, for whom *katana* was made.

Then he hurriedly returned the sword to its resting place on the mantle, folded the papers and stuffed them into the elastic waistband of his pajamas. He returned the tablet and pen to the writing desk drawer, went to the sofa and lay down. His mother entered the living room at that very moment and asked, "What are you doing up so early?"

He yawned and said, "I couldn't sleep, so I came out to the couch. But now I'm so tired I'm going back to bed."

And he did.

LORD SUZUKI, for whom *katana* was made.

II

THE COMMISSIONING
OF *KATANA*

As difficult as it was for Alexander Akira to contain his excitement, he knew that he dared not tell any of his friends or schoolmates, and certainly not his parents, about the revelation he had had with the sword.

Although he was still quite young, he had attended many meetings hosted by his grandparents at which they discussed supernatural events. Most of the people who came to these monthly meetings seemed to have psychic powers that were well developed, and some of them could even receive sensations from holding the clothing of someone else in the group. These several people could tell of events that had happened in the clothing owner's past, even though they did not previously know of these events. He was fascinated by all this talk; to him, it was more exciting than the science fiction movies on television: This was real!

He had talked to his friends about these meetings before, and they scoffed at him and said that their parents said there was no such thing as psychic powers and if Alexander Akira wanted to believe it, he could.

And he did want to believe it, because he had seen it for himself, and to not believe what he had seen or experienced was to live a lie, and he knew he did not want to do that.

So, in the quiet of his room, he read and reread the papers he had written and tried very hard to understand how he had written words he had never heard before, about events he never knew before, about people that had never existed in his mind before. It was all very perplexing, yet he felt compelled to try to fathom what had happened.

He knew this much: It was one thing to see other people doing mystical things and quite another to have a mystical experience yourself.

Over the several days since that first encounter, he had tried to talk to the sword as it rested on the mantle, asking it questions and waiting for an answer. But he had felt nothing. So he now believed that this was either some freak accident and he was a little crazy, or the sword would talk to him when it wanted to, but not when he wanted it to.

He pondered the battle scenes of which he had written. How many horses and warriors did it take, he wondered, to fill a huge lake waist deep in blood? And how many men were there in these vast armies, anyhow? At his school there were, perhaps, hundreds of students, and he imagined two or three schools of students all fighting - that would certainly be a vast army to him. But he didn't think that even several schools of students would have enough blood to fill a huge lake with three or four feet of blood.

And just how much blood would it take? He thought about asking his dad, but then he knew he couldn't, for his dad would, of course, want to know why he was asking how much blood it would take to fill a large lake with several feet of blood. His dad always asked why he was asking questions - just as he always asked "why?" whenever his dad told him something. They just enjoyed asking why and learning everything they could from each other.

But this would be a "why?" that he could not answer, so he knew he dared not ask.

Now he thought about the emperors and the battles that took place to keep them in power or get them out of power. If the emperors were descendants of the goddess Amaterasu, why would anyone want to get rid of them? Or why didn't the goddess help the emperors fight against the other armies and win? Why did everyone fight about who was emperor, if the emperor were the legal ruler? He could not fathom any of the intrigue that must have gone on, and contented himself with just believing that it must have happened the way he was told, even though he might never understand the "why" of any of it.

He looked at the last page he had written: LORD SUZUKI, for whom *katana* was made. Now he wished he knew more about this ancient relative, who he was, how he lived. Was he big and tall, or short and skinny? Had he studied *karate* like his grandfather and grandmother had done in the 1960's, and studied *kendo* and *judo* as his grandmother and namesake great uncle had done in their youth?

As he sat pondering these questions he was again urged to get the writing tablet and pen from his mother's desk in the dining room, put his hand upon the sword, and again, write the words that were quietly spoken to his inner self by *katana*.

Lord Suzuki was a grand man, a scholarly, intense warrior who loved his family, enjoyed writing *haiku*, the seventeen syllable verse written in the ancient *Kanbun* script so popular amongst the educated Japanese of his day, and riding his horse about the castle grounds as he surveyed the farmers tilling the soil - his soil - and the warriors practicing endlessly to defend the castle - his castle - and workmen laboring as they dug the moats - his moats - and fortified the parapets - his parapets.

He had been raised in wealth, surrounded by servants, tutored by nannies, trained by the finest *Senseis* in the ways of the warrior. He had never known want.

At the age of five he had begun the very strict regimen of scholastic and physical training that would prepare him to assume the duties of his noble birth. Even at that young age, his days began at dawn and lasted until he could no longer hold up his head. He never thought to complain, for he was continuously reminded that one day he would lead the clan, and one day the castle and all the land for as far as one could see would be his. So it was his duty, he was told, to be prepared. No shame must come to the Suzuki family because he was lax in practice or lazy in study.

And young Lord Suzuki listened and learned, and by the age of sixteen was an able horseman, a consummate sword fighter, and a knowledgeable patron of the arts of poetry - especially the court poetry, *Kokinshu*

- and *sumi-e* ink painting. This form of poetry, he knew, contained subtle references to ancient writings and sayings. The talented writer of such poetry made discrete reference to the sages of old. The talented reader of such poetry, he well understood, knew those oblique references and appreciated greatly their inclusion. He was even developing an eye for collecting the finest *takamaki-e* lacquer writing boxes then becoming the style of the Yoshimasa *Shogunate's* court.

But the Suzuki clan was not of the warrior class; it was of nobility, and even in 1441, when Lord Suzuki was sixteen, all the peoples bowed in respect when he passed by, for his forebears were of the imperial Antoku line whose lineage included the Emperor Go-Daigo a mere century before. As a young man, Lord Suzuki knew he would soon take his place amongst the other court nobles in the Great Hall in Kamakura, participating in the court of the Ashikaga *Shogun* Yoshimasa.

And in preparation for his assumption of power his family engaged the services of a matchmaker - a *Nakodo*. Generally, this person would be a close, trusted family friend of the groom, or a paid marriage broker. The proper bride for a court noble must also be of nobility, and their go-between, of some ranking himself, inquired discreetly of the several families who had eligible daughters sufficiently attractive and adequately tutored to take her place beside one who would carry so much power.

In time, he was introduced to the young daughter of Marquis Matsudaira, whose family castle and estate was on the northern shore of Honshu in the province of Izumo. Matsudaira was an acceptable family, as they were descended from Minamoto Chikauji some generations ago. The family of Marquis Matsudaira was one of fifty-seven noble families who bore the same family name, their clan having attained nobility and wealth centuries before and having spread across all Japan, marrying into many other ranking families or having their sons adopted into other noble families where there was no son to carry on the family name.

Both the Matsudairas and the Suzukis maintained large holdings of land in Edo; the Matsudairas owned the area known as Mita, on a hill in what is today the Shiba ward. Devout Buddhists in later centuries, the Matsudairas allowed the monk Takuwan to erect a temple on their grounds and create a now famous garden with ponds, hillocks and meandering paths. The Suzukis had property near the river Shinagawa and had a large, stately home overlooking the river and their gardens.

The elder Matsudairas and Suzukis were both members of the court in Kamakura, and spent much of each year at their Edo homes, traveling frequently between their ancestral homes and Edo throughout the year.

In his nineteenth year, my Lord was married to Toshiko Matsudaira who had just turned seventeen. She was suitably trained in the playing of the *koto* and *shamisen*, could properly dance the traditional dances and perform the ritualistic tea ceremony. And unlike many noble young women, she had been permitted to learn to read and write, and excelled in the creation of long scrolls exhibiting her precisely flowing script. She had also been raised to be a bit more independent than most other young noble women of her time, and she had a headstrong nature not befitting her birth in *Hitsuji* - Year of the Ram. Secretly, her servants called her *Hinoe Uma*, or Fire Horse - a term of fearful respect for her temper.

Her private vow at their marriage ceremony was to make the Suzuki name the most honored name in the land. Even more so than her own parents' name. For she was not only married to the young Lord out of obligation; in their few, chaperoned meetings she had grown to love this brash, intellectual young noble. And she was prepared to sacrifice herself for her marriage and honor.

No sooner had they consummated their marriage than he departed to battle. Over the next six years he was gone from the castle grounds more than he was home; when he was not in Kamakura at the *Roju* he was leading his warriors in the quelling of one uprising or another.

When he finally returned home, weary from so many years of battle - mental battle with the conniving noblemen of the Kamakura court and physical battle against the rebellious Taira-led clans - he asked his father's permission to replace the swords he had carried for so long. These swords, though handed down to him by his father who had received them from his father before him, had failed him in battle on several occasions and he felt their spirits were not attuned to his.

His father, aging and weakened by years of fighting, readily consented to the making of a new pair of swords which would carry the family's wisteria crest and become the heirloom from father to son from his generation forward.

So it was that in the year 1449 Lord Suzuki sought out my master, Seki no Magoroku, and commissioned the making of myself and my mate. The Lord specified that we should be capable of more than the normal tests for a new sword; those tests we passed easily, from the first, easiest test, the severing of a victim's hand - the *sodesuri* or 'cutting the sleeve' cut - to the most difficult test number sixteen, the slicing through of the body at the hips - the *ryo kuruma* or 'pair of wheels' cut.

The order was that I must pass the most difficult test of all: *Tameshigiri*, or the test cutting with a live blade. In this test, I should be made to cut through five men at once. And it was so: After my completion, my master placed me in the hands of a swordsman who performed the *san-no-do*, or 'third body cut' on five condemned prisoners. Then, Seki no Magoroku inscribed upon a fresh parchment the date and place of this test, and presented the certificate to Lord Suzuki, along with the two swords, on his twenty-fifth birthday in 1450.

Young Akira had now dropped his pen; beads of sweat stood out on his brow. He was sickened and repulsed by the vision he had of his *katana* - this very *katana* that was now hot to his touch - cutting through the bodies of five men. He could not imagine the terror of the prisoners, knowing they were to become the targets of the blade's keen edge. Sickened to his stomach he tried to get up from the chair to go to the bathroom, but he could not let loose of the scabbard. He felt immobile and rooted to his chair.

The sword had not finished with its story, and the boy was incapable of breaking out of its hold on him.

He wiped his forehead with his sleeve and picked up the pen. Shakily he continued to write.

If my Lord had one failing it was pride, for just as he wanted a pair of swords of his own making, so he wanted all that he inherited to be remade as he decreed. Thus it was that, during this time of unrest, he hired more workmen to dig the moats and repair the fortifications, and brought the farmers from miles around under his control to till the soil, fill his granary and provide him with the wealth his noble vanity required.

His wealth grew, and so did his family. His first son was born in 1448, when Lord Suzuki was twenty-three and his Lady but twenty-one. They had two more children, a boy two years later and a girl three years after the second son.

Upon the making of myself and my mate, life at the castle remained peaceful for some years. Lord Suzuki delighted in riding with his children, and taught each one the pleasures of their nobility: sword play, poetry, the dance. And upon his sons he lavished all the training his great wealth could buy. Teachers and tutors traveled to the castle from all across the country, bringing with them the vast repository of knowledge gleaned from scholars from such faraway places as Hokkaido, to the north, and Kyushu, to the south, alike.

And during these years of relative peace, Lady Suzuki was also occupied with family matters, having three children to care for - for although she and her husband had been raised by servants, nannies and tutors, she was determined to be an important and integral part of their early training. She had promised, it must be remembered, that she would make the Suzuki family the most respected of the court noble names.

Often, in this period of respite, Lord and Lady Suzuki took their family to the ancestral retreat in Shikoku. There, my Lord began construction of a castle that would rival the family estate in Osaka itself. Situated in Ehime prefecture with its back against the mountains and facing the Inland Sea, Tojo Izumigawa-cho soon became the family's favorite home. In Shikoku, the weather was mild in winter and near tropical in summer. Mount Ishizuchi, located partially on their holdings, was prominent in their view of the southern horizon, and provided them with an abundance of pine, Japanese cedar, cypress and bamboo for the construction and landscaping of their off-season home. The fast mountain streams that graced the slopes of Mount Ishizuchi gave them pure, cold water that made the best tea they had known.

When they journeyed home to their castle in Osaka, the family longed to return to Tojo even before Mount Ishizuchi was out of sight.

The boy sat motionless for minutes after the writing stopped; emotionally, he was drained. He was tired yet excited by all that he had been told to write.

But his sense of duty to the family name was heightened by the story of young Lord Suzuki's devotion and preparation, his seemingly unwavering determination to be the best possible noble, and most worthy Suzuki, that he could be. And he found himself understanding why Lord Suzuki, as he got older, was vain. If I'm even half as great a person as he was, thought young Alexander Akira, I'll have reason to be called vain myself.

Now, he felt, he was beginning to learn a little something about the people behind the sword, just as he had wanted to do. Perhaps the sword was listening to him, after all. Perhaps the sword was as ready to tell its story as he was eager to learn it.

However, having written all this, he was filled with even more questions than before. What had happened to the Suzuki family wealth? Who were the three children of Lord and Lady Suzuki and what would he learn about their lives? Did the Suzuki family buy the Shikoku land from someone or from the government? How much did it cost? How close were their neighbors? Did they own the mountain or did they just get to go to it like everybody else? And who took care of the house in Kamakura and the castle in Osaka when they were in Tojo? Or for that matter, who took care of all three places for them?

He laughed silently at the thought of all the warriors and farmers vacuuming the houses and washing the windows. Then he remembered: Back in those days they did not have vacuums. So just how did they ever clean up the places? What if one of the boys tracked in mud on his boots - did his mother have to get down on her knees with a sponge and wipe it up? He was very confused about what life was like at the Suzuki family castles, and was eager for the sword to tell him more about all of this.

He promised himself that, from this day forward, every time he was at his grandparents' home he would look through their extensive library of books on Japan and, even if he could not read the books, he would at least look at the maps and try to locate the towns he had written about, or see the pictures of what the nobles, the ladies, the samurai, the people in general were wearing. Suddenly he knew that he wanted very much to know everything he could about his "mother" country.

And he wanted to know what was the explanation for his being able to touch the sword and receive the sensations that allowed him to write about these marvelous events.

Tired as he was, he took out the single piece of paper on which he had written what he knew from the first time *katana* talked to him. On it he wrote what he had been told today, and then reread it. He was satisfied that the paper now looked like this:

LADY TOSHIKO SUZUKI

Born in 1427 as Toshiko Matsudaira
Father: Marquis Matsudaira
Related to: Minamoto Chikauji

Homes: Izumo, Edo

LORD SUZUKI,
for whom *katana* was made.

Born in 1425
Father: somebody Suzuki
Related to: Emperors Go-
    Shirakawa, Go-Daigo & Antoku
Homes: Osaka, Edo, Tojo

Married: 1444
Family: two sons, born 1448 & 1450;
a daughter, born 1453

III

LORD SUZUKI PREPARES
FOR BATTLE

It was not long after the boy had completed writing about the commissioning of *katana* that he and his parents visited his grandparents' home. The occasion was one of the monthly group meetings that he always enjoyed attending, but this time he had an ulterior motive for wanting to go. Often his mother had asked him if he wanted to do something else on these Sunday afternoons because she was concerned that he might be bored spending his day with "a bunch of adults." But he had always insisted that he was enjoying himself. Now, he knew that he would not only enjoy himself, but he would do more than just listen to the talk; he would ask some questions himself to see if anyone in the group could tell him what was going on with the sword, and the writing.

He also knew he had to be very careful so no one would get suspicious about his questions and begin to ask him why he was suddenly so interested in the paranormal. So he decided to ask some general questions just to get some ideas. And maybe ask his grandmother if he could also look at some of her books about Japan.

And while he was at it, maybe he could even look through his grandparents' picture albums and this time, he would pay particular attention to what they told him about who all the relatives were.

Alexander Akira usually just looked out the window of the car as his father drove them the twelve or so miles to his grandparents' home. He had been over this route so many times he no longer paid particular attention to the houses, the landscape, the shopping areas, the wooded interludes or the other vehicles on the highway. He just sort of looked at it all without seeing any of it.

But on this day he seemed to be more interested in all of it: in fact, he tried very hard to think of what all this would look like five hundred years hence, just as though he were in Japan traveling the very same roads his ancestors had traveled and wondering what those roads had been like five hundred years ago. Now he understood, without being told, the allure of time travel. What he would give to be able, just for an hour, to go back five hundred years and see for himself what it was really like then and there. But now he was in the here and now, and he was trying to imagine what it would be like here in five centuries.

As he passed the shopping areas, he pictured them with personal hover craft all parked in the parking lots in place of the cars he saw today. When they passed by a wooded area he imagined the trees hundreds of feet high, creating a tunnel of limbs and leaves through which the highway ran, shadowed constantly by the enormous forest. And as they passed by the houses he wondered how many of them would still be in use five hundred years from now - and what it would be like to live in a house five hundred years old.

Would any of the other cars he saw on the road today still be in existence in the year 2501? And if so, would there still be roads like there are today or would everybody travel in hover craft so there would be no need for streets and highways? He wondered if the people in Japan five hundred years ago ever wondered whether people, five hundred years in the future, would be living in the exact same houses that they, themselves, were living in then. And did they ever wonder whether those people, in five hundred years, would still be riding horses along the same roads that they, themselves, were traveling, or could they envision anything so extraordinary as cars and buses and airplanes and television sets and everything that is so much a part of his daily life?

He broke out in chills just thinking about how much different his life was than were the lives of Lord and Lady Suzuki. They had wealth and wanted for nothing that their money could buy, yet he had gadgets today that they could not even imagine then.

When they arrived, he sat a little closer than usual beside his grandmother. Somehow, today, he seemed to love her just a little more, and a little differently, than ever before.

As usual, the group talked about a variety of experiences, normal and other -than-normal. Edward, as always, had keen psychic insight into the experiences of the others, and with his usual loving manner, talked the group through another person's experiences so everyone understood the meaning of what happened. And Kathryn, the elderly retired nurse, asked her usual "Anything spooky happen to anybody?" question, to which others responded by telling of little incidents that had occurred during the month since they had last met.

The talk was always informal, light but serious, as can often be the way with close friends who know much about each other, and who love and respect one another.

At an appropriate moment, after everyone had gone around the buffet table to which they had each contributed some tasty dish, Alexander said, "Has anyone ever heard voices inside them even when no one was around to talk?" Conversation stopped for a moment. He had not asked questions before, and the group was somewhat taken aback by his unexpected voice. Then Kathryn said she had often felt that someone or something was talking to her - not really talking to her ears, but talking to her mind. And Bonnie said she had had some very strange experiences where she had felt the presence of another person or entity in the room with her, and had felt that person was trying to talk to her.

Edward, who had been busy eating and not participating in the general discussion, then spoke up. "Such voices," he said, "are very real. They can be friends, or relatives, or others who are trying to get a message across the divide between death and life, and are seeking a receptive person. Listening intently when you hear these voices will help you become more attuned to them. Meditating daily will help condition your mind to hear what is not spoken."

These brief comments sparked some rather intense discussion, and Alexander Akira heard many divergent views on the possibilities of past lives, future lives, other lives, and the context in which all these may occur. He heard his grandmother state that she had often had the intense feeling of being in the presence of her own grandfather. He had been a very strong personality, and his presence invoked feelings in her that she was certain could come from no one else. She had also been "visited" by her deceased father with whom she had had a difficult relationship while he was alive. Now, with the passage of many years since his death, he and she had communicated on a spiritual level and had resolved their differences. She could now take comfort in their relationship instead of feeling pain because of it.

Her comments prompted Kathryn to say that she had the very distinct feeling that she and the boy's grandmother had been close in some other lifetime. "In fact," she said, "I'm sure that we were close friends or relatives in Japan many years ago. The very first time I saw Sachiko I knew that I knew her from before. I still can't place where or when, but we have lived a life together before, I'm certain." She went on to say that her nationality mix is primarily Scandinavian, and none of her known relatives are Oriental. But despite that, she knows for sure that she has been an Oriental at some time in the past.

With that, his dad, who was usually a passive participant, soaking it all up but not generally saying much, said that he, too, had felt the presence of his maternal grandfather. In fact, in the very house where they were now seated, he and his father - the boy's grandfather - had together felt the cold chill of another's presence. They were certain that it was Grandpa Takahashi checking to make sure they were all right.

"But wasn't it a frightening experience?" he asked.

"No. There was no evil or malice in the presence we felt. It was love and light, despite the decidedly cold chill that permeated the air that night," replied his father.

Alexander felt the goose bumps running up his arms and down his back. Even though he had asked the question that started all this, he was a little frightened by all the talk of spirits making contact.

Yet, he thought, why should I be frightened? After all, what has happened to me with the sword is far more frightening that anything they talked about today.

But despite his rationalization, he snuggled just a little closer to his grandmother.

"Have you been seeing ghosts, Alexander Akira?" she asked. "What made you ask about the voices?"

"I'm just curious," he said. "Some of my friends were talking with me about voices and ghosts, and I just wanted to know if they were for real."

"They're for real, all right," his grandmother replied. "Your grandfather and I have many books about spirits and visitations, and since our own experience bears out what we have read, we are completely convinced that such things exist. But we cannot explain any of this for you. We can't tell you how it happens - only that it does."

As the meeting broke up, Edward made a special point of giving the boy an extra big hug. "Don't forget to meditate, Alexander. Do it daily, and if there are any spirits trying to talk to you they will see that you are receptive. Don't be afraid. Just surround yourself with white light and love before you begin meditating and only good spirits will be able to contact you. Tell me next meeting if you hear any voices."

All the way home he thought about what he had heard. There were real spirits that could talk to you even though you couldn't see them, and even though you hadn't asked them to talk to you. Then he wasn't crazy after all. Others had heard voices or had the feeling that something was going on that they couldn't explain.

He was comforted by the realization that he was not alone in having been touched by the mysteries of the psychic world.

Late that night, he was again drawn to the *katana*, and, taking it down, he carried it to his room. He sat on his bed, sword in his right hand, pencil in his left and tablet on his lap. He waited patiently while the images began to appear in his mind; the pencil wrote without his even thinking about it.

In the year 1467 my Lord was again called upon to fight. Armed warriors from the northern side of the mountains were threatening the fertile plains where the castle stood. They were led by samurai loyal to the *Shugo* of the area - but this *Shugo* had turned against the *Shogunate* and now this band of warriors was renegade. The destruction of the farms and villages along their path from the seacoast inward was complete; either the villagers became their allies or were massacred. Word of their conquests preceded them, and my Lord Hiroshi Suzuki was well prepared.

The nobles had often discussed the possibility of such an uprising when they met in Kamakura. The *Ashikaga Shogun Yoshimasa* had believed that the *Daimyo*, *Tozama* and their retainers, and his appointed *Shugo* and their *Jito*, would all remain loyal. But *Shogun Yoshimasa* had not been close to the people in many years or he would have known that there was much distaste for the local tax collectors - the despised *Jito* - and this revulsion had caused the farmers and merchants to turn against the *Shogunate* and its policies. In turn, the authorities had become increasingly separated from the earth and its peoples, and they had decided to vent their anger back on the very peoples from whom they received their sustenance. As their revolt gained momentum, some of the farmers sided with them, believing that the *Shogunate* was the enemy and that the local authorities, once in power, would treat them more decently.

The rabble became a force that swept the area, burning homes, destroying crops, gaining converts and killing resisters as they marched inland.

Although he was no longer a young man - at thirty-seven he was in his prime of life - he had continued his daily regime of *kendo* practice and horse riding. Now, he called together his samurai. Together, they rode to the surrounding villages and farms in a twenty-mile wide area, helping the residents to move their valuables, their families, indeed, their lives, back to the protective fortifications of the castle.

As he did this he reflected on his own father's genius. For when his father had planned his fortress he had cleared the ground for two thousand yards around the walls. In this cleared area he had dug moats; the outside walls of the moats were inclined gently, allowing an approaching enemy to march or ride into the water without fear. But the inner walls were vertical and impossible to climb. Hence, the horses and soldiers would be unable to breech the moats. Their heavy armor would sink them into the deep water and make them easy targets for the archers high up in the parapets of the castle walls.

Outside the cleared area was thick forest. His father had cleared three small roads through the forest, giving an approaching enemy three easy entrances to the castle area. Their mounted warriors and foot soldiers alike would be able to race towards his ramparts, unhindered by trees or undergrowth of any kind.

Except that in these deep forests his father had stationed more archers. As the enemy passed by on the narrow roads the archers would cut them down, shooting from their protected vantages high up in the trees or from behind berms he had made along the roads. It was a good plan, and my Lord would not deviate from it.

Lord Suzuki allowed himself a chuckle as he awaited the battle that was sure to come. He detested fighting, but if he must fight, then he would do so from a position of strength and power, and would surely prevail.

In the space of several weeks all the neighboring areas had been cleared of inhabitants. Daily he sent out scouts who brought back information on the number, discipline and weaponry of the approaching men, and how far away they were. He was now ready, and eager to test his new swords in battle.

The boy dropped his pencil and sat quivering with excitement. He could see it now: Hundreds, or perhaps thousands, of armed warriors riding through the villages, some of them perhaps yelling "The rabble is coming! The rabble is coming!" just the way he had envisioned Paul Revere riding through his own village yelling "The British are coming!" His young mind could not grasp the historical impact of what was happening in Japan at that time, but in his boyish way he could well imagine the bustle of activity as the castle's occupants prepared for battle.

He remembered what *katana* had said before, that it had tasted a lot of blood. Would he soon be told about this? Was the blood of the battle for which Lord Suzuki was preparing still on the sword that he grasped in his hand at this very moment? He understood the significance of this question, and of the answer. He was holding not just an antique. He was holding a part of history. How many of his friends could match that?

The sword had not talked much about the different family members, and he was getting anxious to know it all - not just the battles but the people: His ancient relatives.

What had he learned this time? Only the name of that great man, Lord Hiroshi Suzuki.

He again laid out the single sheet of paper on which he was keeping track of the family's chronology and inserted the additional information.

Now his page looked like this:

LADY TOSHIKO SUZUKI

Born in 1427 as Toshiko Matsudaira
Father: Marquis Matsudaira
Related to: Minamoto Chikauji

Homes: Izumo, Edo

LORD HIROSHI SUZUKI
for whom *katana* was made.
Born in 1425
Father: somebody Suzuki
Related to: Emperors Go-
    Shirakawa, Go-Daigo & Antoku
Homes: Osaka, Edo, Tojo

Married: 1444
Family: two sons, born 1448 & 1450;
a daughter, born 1453

IV

SENGOKU BEGINS

The boy awoke in a sweat: He had been dreaming the most horrible of nightmares. In the dream he saw great armies clashing in the fields; he heard the neighing of terrified horses and the cries of dying men; he saw the moats around Lord Suzuki's castle red with the blood of the dead. As he lay in the darkness, his heart beating so loudly he feared his parents would hear it, he imagined the sweaty dampness of his bedding to be, instead, the sticky gore from his dreams.

And he marveled at the change that had taken place - for he was sure he had been led through the battle scenes by *katana* even though he was not holding or touching it. In fact, he was certain he had heard the same faint inner voice telling him the story of the raging conflict that he had heard as he held the sword on earlier occasions.

Was he now able to take the story from the sword without having to touch it? Or was this simply a dream like many other dreams he had had after watching a scary movie on television?

He tried to clear his mind and meditate as Edward had told him to do. But there were too many thoughts, too many images, too many sounds all going on in his brain at once and he could not control it. Sweaty, tense and frightened, he slowly got out of bed and made his way to the bathroom. Without turning on the light he dampened a washcloth and wiped his face and neck. The coolness of the wet cloth refreshed him and he relaxed a bit. With it still dark, he returned to the bedroom and took out his pad and pencil. Although it was too dark to see to write, he knew that it was time, and that he could put the words on paper without looking if *katana* wanted him to.

It was the Year of the Wild Boar - *Inoshishi* - and my Lord deemed it appropriate that the swine from the coast should invade his homeland during this year. Historians mark this year, 1467, as the beginning of the great civil war - *Sengoku* - after which the political makeup of the country's leadership was forever changed.

For my Lord and his family, the war began at dawn on a cool September day. His runners had brought him information the night before of a great army of men marching through the forest, nearing the castle compound. He had then stationed his archers in the woods and behind the outer castle walls, poised to shoot upon the enemy as they passed along the roads or got mired in the moats. His foot soldiers he divided into two masses; one group he spread out in the forests just along the clearing surrounding his fortress and the other he kept hidden behind the castle walls.

They waited through the night, hearing the sounds of the marching army approaching along the narrow roads. Tension filled the night air; fear and excitement filled each warrior's heart.

Their battle began as the archers in the forests fired their deadly missiles into the great marching mass. The attackers broke into pandemonium, with some at the rear of the units turning and fleeing the rain of wooden shafts. Those who survived raced along the paths towards the clearing ahead, hopeful of escaping the range of the arrows that fell on them.

Of the thousands of soldiers who entered the woods, many hundreds were killed in this first defense. The remaining army, now in total disarray, ran into the clearing towards the seemingly unattended castle. The first ones into the moats waded bravely forward, sinking deeper and deeper into the water, heading towards the opposite bank. As the moats filled with men, the archers above them opened fire, again raining arrows upon the helpless men.

Now half the invading army was gone, killed by the hidden defenders without having gotten to use their swords against their foe. In confusion, my Lord's enemies turned to retreat from this second barrage of flying steel, only to be met at the forest's edge by Lord Suzuki's mighty army. The battle raged but a few short hours.

Before the sun had reached the noon zenith, the battle had ended. Nearly three thousand enemy soldiers lay dead along the roads and battlefield. Hundreds of wounded were huddled in groups, awaiting their fate.

My Lord, upon his mount, rode through the devastation, seeking the leaders of this anarchy. When he found that just one survived, he delivered a one-handed slashing blow with *katana*, slicing the man downward from the left side of his neck with the cut known as *o-kesa*, or "priest's robe". With this one move my Lord cut the man's body in two.

Lord Suzuki was satisfied with *katana's* performance, and slowly sheathed the sword.

He had won this first battle; *katana* had killed its first warrior.

Unable to see what he had been writing, Alexander Akira sat motionless in awe: The battle scene about which he had written was the very battle about which he had dreamt. While the description provided by the sword was more general, the battle strategy was the same, and the fighting that took place in and around the moats and in the forest was identical.

He dared not turn on the light to see if his paper was covered with legible words or unreadable scribble. Slowly he put the tablet and pencil in the drawer and suddenly realized that he had not been holding *katana* during this session! He had had a dream sequence without the sword, and had written about the first battle, again without the sword. Did this mean that the sword would communicate with him at a distance, without his having to hold it as he did before?

Stimulated as he was, he felt an incredible tiredness overcome him, and he climbed back onto the bed and pulled the covers over him. The sheets were still damp from his sweat, and he shuddered at their chill. His mind was blank, and he had no trouble falling immediately to sleep.

It was a week or so later when he next visited his grandparents' house with his parents, and this time he made a point to ask his grandmother for one of her books on Japan. Just any book, he said when she asked him if he had a preference.

He sat on the family room sofa all afternoon, absorbed in the stories and the pictures of his maternal homeland. The ladies wore the long, colorful *kimono*; the warriors had on the protective coverings of the *samurai*. His mind was filled with thoughts of the people that *katana* had described to him, and he wondered if they, too, had worn such elegant clothing or such heavy armor.

He did not have to wait long for his answer, for at the week's end he was to learn more about Lord Suzuki's life, and then about his death.

V

KATANA BEQUEATHED

At the next group meeting, young Alexander Akira paid particular attention to the discussion because it centered on the psychic experience known as "Kundalini". In this experience, the spiritual life forces center on a person's head and enter downward, instilling in the recipient the knowledge of the spirit world. This can be brought on, he learned, by intense meditation over a long period of time - monks and priests in various religions and cultures have been known to have a "Kundalini experience" during their meditation - or can come upon a person who is receptive but is not actively seeking such an experience.

Some authorities call Kundalini the "energy of consciousness". Some even believe that the Kundalini, which, he learned, is Sanskrit for "snake" or "serpent power", lies coiled at the base of the spine in every person, awaiting its arousal through spiritual discipline.

He tried to remember each and every word, because everybody in the group seemed to know something about Kundalini and there was so much to learn. From what he heard, the Kundalini experience included many other feelings, such as strange physical sensations, clairaudience, visions, brilliant lights, a feeling of bliss, ecstasy, some increased psychic powers, even pain or bizarre, uncontrollable physical movements. It was even said to make the subject transcend himself. Jean, who often acted as moderator of these deeper discussions, had brought some material to hand out that described the experience. They had read that the Kundalini is often described as liquid fire and liquid light because of its effects on people.

The yogi, believing that the Kundalini is within the individual and not an outside force that enters the person, are convinced that the Kundalini activates a person's chakras in succession, moving up the spine until it reaches the crown chakra. They report having violent trembling and shuddering all throughout their bodies as the Kundalini moves upward, and feeling intense heat and extreme coldness in various parts of their bodies during the experience. They also reported seeing the brilliant lights, all of which gave rise to the description of the Kundalini as liquid light and liquid fire.

Now, the group was discussing experiences each one had had that were similar to the Kundalini experience, and generally agreed that the Kundalini might come from within or from without.

His grandfather said, with a straight face, that he had had an experience similar to the Kundalini just the night before when he was in the back yard. He had felt something entering his scalp and immediately thought it was a spirit trying to make contact so he gave it a moment or two before putting his hand to the affected area. But it was not the Kundalini after all. It had been a mosquito.

Everyone laughed, and then agreed that things are not always what one expects them to be, nor are they always what you want them to be. The Kundalini might enter through the scalp, but so does a mosquito. "And because many of the effects of the Kundalini experience are similar to what is felt from other experiences, including stress and mental imbalances, it's up to each one of us", his grandfather said, "to exercise critical judgment to determine if the experiences are real or imagined, valid or contrived."

"How do you know if an experience is valid or contrived?" the boy asked no one in particular.

"It is certainly not clear cut", answered Edward. "For example, when you asked before about spirits talking to you, you remember we said that the voices were for real. But it is up to you to distinguish between your own thoughts and the impressions given you through ethereal voices.

And it can be confusing; you might think you are hearing voices or having an "experience" and it is only your mind thinking, or your memory working."

"This is why we have meetings like this, Akira, so we can share our experiences and let others help us determine whether what has happened to us is a valid experience, or whether it is something else. Do you have something you want to share with us?" It was his aunt Kei talking to him.

He really felt at ease with her because she and his dad were such close friends. And she lived close by so he saw her quite often. He might be a little reticent with other adults, but not with his aunt.

But should he try to tell even her about his dreams, his visions, his writings?

"I've just been listening to what everyone has been saying these past several meetings and I think I'm a little confused," he replied. "I'm too young to have any kind of experience yet. I'm just a kid."

With that he snuggled a little closer to his grandmother, feigning a shyness that was quite unnatural.

Now his father answered. "No one is too young to have real life experiences, Akira. And we believe that feeling the presence of another's spirit, whether that spirit is of this world or from beyond, is natural for those people who are receptive. It seems you are becoming receptive to these feelings and becoming attuned to the presence of others. Have you had any experience that you want to talk about?"

"Well," he said, "after I looked at the book on Japan last week I felt that I could actually see and feel the people that lived back then. I almost felt I could see how they lived. But maybe it was just my imagination." Actually, he knew it was not his imagination; it was very real, and everything he had heard over the past several meetings had confirmed it. Yet, he was not ready to reveal anything, even to his aunt, or his parents or his closest friends.

After the meeting ended, Edward hugged him tightly as he had done the last meeting, and said, "I'm getting the feeling that you have more to tell us than you have said. Remember last meeting I asked you to tell me if you heard any voices. I mean that. I can help you determine if the voices are real and what they might mean. It can be scary for you to hear voices or see images all by yourself. Don't you want to tell me what you've been experiencing?"

"It's really nothing. I'm just very curious. Everybody has been talking about seeing things and hearing things. I just want to know more for myself - just in case."

Edward knew that he would learn nothing more from the boy today, so he said simply, "Just remember that I am here to help you if you need me."

With that, Alexander Akira joined his parents on the front walkway and said his good-byes to everybody in the group. This always meant hugs and kisses and he always felt a little funny about having all the "old" women hugging and kissing him. But they seemed to enjoy it so much that he had decided to not disappoint them by refusing. So he let them hold him as closely as they wanted.

Alone in the back seat of the car as they returned home he wondered if he were having a Kundalini experience or if the sword was really talking to him. Maybe the Kundalini was really some extraterrestrial power trying to talk to us, he thought, and when we felt all hot or cold or had the shivers it was because this other "being" was trying to get our attention. He was somewhat confused by this but still firmly believed that the sword was talking to him. Whether this was a Kundalini experience or not just wouldn't matter to him right now.

He was, after all, just a little boy, exactly like he had told his aunt.

Knowing he had to get up early for school the next morning, he told his parents he was really tired and wanted to go to bed directly after dinner tonight. Of course, they wanted to know if he were ill, or if he had a stomach ache from eating too much of Ida's green Jell-O salad, or whatever. And he told them he was just tired, that's all.

But once he was in his room he took his pad and pencil from the dresser drawer. He sat in the middle of the bed, legs crossed just like he had seen the yogi do in the handouts from Jean today, closed his eyes and tried to not think of anything. Would he have a Kundalini experience, he wondered? Or could he tempt the sword to speak to him again tonight?

He sat in this position for what seemed like hours. Outside his window it had turned dark. He could hear his parents running the water as they prepared for bed themselves. Finally, with his legs numb and his back aching from sitting in this same spot for so long, he dozed off.

Much later, he popped awake and untangled his legs. They were tingly from the blood coursing through their hungry veins. He turned on the light to get into his pajamas and was shocked by what he saw on the pad. For while he had slept, *katana* had spoken to him again.

As I have told you, my Lord was not a warrior; he was a noble man of high birth who had been trained, as had all nobility of that time, in the art of combat. Yet, it troubled him to make war. He was pleased at having won this first encounter, but he was sickened at what this all must mean. For he knew that this was but the beginning. All throughout the land, battles would be fought, just like this one had been fought, between countrymen, relatives, brothers.

And he thought of his family whom he had tried to protect from this kind of strife. Had he not spent years traveling to Kamakura in an effort to keep the peace amongst all the clans? Had his parents not found for him a wife from the northwestern coast so the two families - and their relatives, their servants, their warriors - could help to build and maintain the peace? What more must he do, he angrily asked himself, to ensure that his home and his children would be safe?

It was two weeks since the fighting had taken place, and his army had buried the fallen foe, gathered up their swords, bows and arrows and lances, and readied themselves for the next battle, whenever that might take place. During this two weeks my Lord had paced the great hallways of his castle, fretting about the future, and blaming himself for perhaps not having tried hard enough to guarantee peace. Surely he knew of the dislike for the *Shogun's* policies, but he had gone along with the other nobles in supporting them, believing that to condemn the leadership of the *Shogun* would provoke conflict. Now he knew that conflict was inevitable: Neither the nobility nor the citizenry wanted the status quo, and battle was the surest way to bring change.

He thought about his eldest son, Kiichi, now only nineteen. Only nineteen? he questioned. But was I not "only nineteen" when I myself was married? At nineteen was I not a mature man, ready to take my place at the head of my own table?

But my son, my Kiichi, he is but a boy - a very tall, good-natured, somewhat clumsy, boy. He mustn't be off to war. With so many books to read, and so many poems to write, he is far too busy to fight. But perhaps fight he must.

At least, he mused, I will do his fighting, if fighting must be done, until he has read more and written more. Maybe he will never need to go to war.

Thus my master thought, and he sent his army out into the surrounding villages with orders to protect the people, and to report to him any potential disturbance. For while he knew the fighting was not over he was determined to have his family continue with their lives as normally as possible.

His younger children, now seventeen and fourteen, also were of concern. Although the oldest would assume his power and his castle, he could not forget that all three children were of noble bearing, and required proper training for their future stations in life. Their mother had seen to all of that, and he was proud of the family who now bore the wisteria family crest.

When my Lord's son, Kiichi, was twenty-two, he was married to the eldest daughter of Prince Takatsukasa. The Takatsukasa family was an ancient one of high birth and nobility; the Prince had been a trusted ally at the court in Kamakura, and owned large tracts of land near Kyoto and Gifu. Much as my Lord and Lady were introduced by their families, so were Kiichi and his eighteen year old bride Michiko. They met just three times over a two year period. And in the autumn of the year 1470 the families were joined by the marriage of their two eldest children.

Young Kiichi was given command of the citadel near the village of Fukuchiyama, some seventy miles to the northwest of the family castle near the mountains from which had come the invaders three years ago. He was charged with the security of the mountain passes and the safety of the farmers who tilled the soil daily for my Lord's well-being. And although it was not customary, he had his younger brother join him there.

My Lord's only daughter was now his only child at home, and he became the most doting of parents.

The next several years saw the marriage of his second son - for which Lord Suzuki was most pleased - and the death of his daughter from a riding accident. She had died on the eve of her betrothal to the eldest son of Arai, a wealthy family whose several homes were near Edo.

Consumed with grief, my Lord was not able to enjoy the success of his sons and in despair, retired to the family compound on the island of Shikoku. For some time he lived at the castle, still under construction, and sought solace in the wooded mountains. He remembered the times they had spent together there over the years, times that could never be repeated. And while still in apparent good health, he died in his sleep in his fifty-first year.

My Lady had a simple tombstone erected in the castle grounds and upon it she had inscribed the chrysanthemum, crest of the emperor himself, and also the symbol of her Lord's nobility. Then in black kimono, she returned to the mainland and her family.

Upon Lord Hiroshi Suzuki's death, Kiichi and his family returned to the castle near Osaka. He occupied the quarters that had belonged to his father; for his mother he provided a several room suite on the south side of the third floor for herself and her maids. She was in grieving for the year after my Lord's death, and never showed her face outside her rooms during this time.

The second son and his own family took up permanent residency in the Fukuchiyama fortress.

As for us swords, we were presented to Lord Kiichi Suzuki by his widowed mother on the thirty-ninth day after our master's death.

He had learned so much from this writing. Just as he had wanted, the sword had told him about some of his distant relatives, and he shared the pain of the loss of Hiroshi Suzuki. Does that gravestone still remain on Shikoku, he wondered? If I went to Japan, would I be able to see it there, still in the castle grounds?

He thought now about his friends and classmates; not only had they never had experiences like he was having, but they now seemed to have such dreary lives, such common family backgrounds. Could any of them say that their relatives were related to the emperor? Did they have castles and fortresses they could go to visit?

Would he ever get to see these things himself?

Again he took out that piece of paper on which he logged the family history as it had been revealed to him. He added the new information plus an arrow to show the *katana's* passage from father to son, thusly:

LADY TOSHIKO SUZUKI

Born in 1427 as Toshiko Matsudaira
Father: Marquis Matsudaira
Related to: Minamoto Chikauji

Homes: Izumo, Edo

LORD HIROSHI SUZUKI
for whom *katana* was made.
Born in 1425
Father: somebody Suzuki
Related to: Emperors Go-
    Shirakawa, Go-Daigo & Antoku
Homes: Osaka, Edo, Tojo
Died in 1476. Buried in Tojo.

Married: 1444
Family: two sons, born 1448 & 1450;
a daughter, born 1453

LADY MICHIKO SUZUKI

Born in 1452 as Michiko Takatsukasa
Father: Prince Takatsukasa
Homes: Kyoto, Gifu

LORD KIICHI SUZUKI
Second master of *katana*
Born in 1448
Father: Hiroshi Suzuki
Homes: Osaka, Edo, Tojo,
    Fukuchiyama

Married: 1470

VI

TO LIVE AND TO DIE
BY THE SWORD

Young Alexander Akira began to notice the change himself, even before anyone mentioned it to him. He noticed, for example, that he was beginning to ask more questions about everything, asking everyone to whom he spoke about anything at all. When he and his parents talked about any subject, he asked "why" and "when" and "how." And he particularly asked "How do you know this?"

At school, he was raising his hand more often, asking his teacher, Miss Haversham, to tell about something in more detail, or to tell him where he could find out more about whatever the subject was.

Of course, at the monthly meetings held at his grandparents' house, he was talking more and questioning more than he had ever done before. It was becoming noticeable to everyone who had been around him for some time that he was really curious about everything.

His questioning did not seem to doubt what he heard or from whom he heard it; he was simply eager to know more on every subject about which he heard and to which he was exposed.

Miss Haversham was delighted, at first, that this smart little boy had really opened up. "Somebody, or something, has lit a firecracker under him," she thought to herself. She was pleased to answer his many questions and even suggested that he stay a little after school, if he wanted to, so she could help him understand more about everything. She knew that most of the class got bored easily if she spent too much time going into detail for him - although it was obvious this is exactly what he eagerly wanted her to do. Gradually, though, she became a little concerned at this change in his classroom demeanor, and she decided to ask his parents to come to school for a conference with her.

"Of course," his dad had told her on the phone when she called. "We, too, have noticed some changes in him. Frankly, we are happy to see him becoming so curious about everything. But sometimes we can't answer him and then he gets a little frustrated." They agreed to a Tuesday evening meeting. Alexander was to accompany them.

When they told him they were going to meet his teacher to talk about him, he was afraid he had done something wrong. "What are we going to talk about?" he asked. "Am I getting bad grades?"

"No," his mother smiled, "it's not about your grades; they are just fine. We just want to talk to Miss Haversham about all your questions. You know, Alexander, you have been asking your dad and me to tell you everything we know about everything we talk about. We just wonder what caused your sudden interest in so many things."

"Oh, that's easy," he answered. "Now that I've started reading about the warriors in Japan I've just become curious about the whole world. Is it possible for me to learn everything? I mean, everything there is to know? Is that possible?"

His mother just shook her head. "I don't know if it's possible to learn everything there is to know, Alexander, but it is very possible to keep on learning all your life. We hope you are as eager to learn when you are a teenager, or our age, as you are right now. Then it just might be possible for you to know many things, even if you can't know absolutely everything."

He was satisfied with the answer, and did not worry about the meeting with his teacher the next week.

On Tuesday, he and his parents met Miss Haversham at five-thirty at his classroom. They all sat in the children's desks arranged in a small circle. It was funny for him to see his father squeezed into the same desk that his best friend Lauren sat in.

"I asked your parents to bring you tonight, Alexander, because I want to know if you've noticed how many questions you are asking in school lately, how curious you have become about everything. Have you noticed this yourself?"

Of course I've noticed it, he thought. I feel like I'm starved and only getting little bites to eat. I want a big hamburger but I'm having to eat sunflower seeds. He smiled as he thought of the sunflower seeds, because everybody in school was eating them. Some of his classmates stuffed them in their pants pockets and secretly put the seeds in their mouths during class, hiding their chewing by putting their hands to their cheeks. The girls usually put theirs in tissues and hid them in their desks, grabbing a couple of seeds to munch on every time they opened their desks to get a pencil or a piece of paper.

"I'm tired of eating sunflower seeds," he blurted out, still lost in his thoughts.

"You're what?" his mother asked.

"I mean, I'm not eating sunflower seeds, but I like to learn everything I can. Isn't that OK?"

Miss Haversham told him that "learning everything you can will make me a very happy teacher and will make you a very bright boy. But what we want to know is what has made you begin taking such an interest in everything lately."

"I just got curious, that's all," he said. He really didn't have any better answer than that.

Now his parents and Miss Haversham talked back and forth about his questions in school, and at home, and at the Sunday meetings. They all agreed that this was most curious, but that it was, in fact, just what they wanted him to do, so there was no real reason for them to be too concerned.

They decided they wanted him to spend an hour after school two days a week so his teacher could give him the extra attention he wanted and needed, and they asked him to tell them if there were any special thing he was interested in so they could all help him with it. He told them there was nothing special; that he just wanted to know about everything he studied in school, and everything he had read about, and everything he heard about.

That night, after they returned home from the meeting, he was very tempted to tell them about the sword, his writing, and what he had been told about his grandmother's family. But he decided that the time was not right and that they most likely would not believe him, anyhow.

Instead, he sat at his writing desk, closed his eyes and with pencil and tablet in front of him, waited to see what he would be told to write.

During this time when my Lord Kiichi Suzuki was married, the country was engaged in a series of battles known later as the *Onin Wars*. These lasted from my Lord's nineteenth year to his twenty-ninth year, and were the cause of much grief for him.

Although these battles were mostly fought in areas not near my Lord's castle in Osaka, he needed to send his warriors to fight to help protect the homes and lands he had in other areas. In 1473 they fought near Edo, siding with the local *daimyo* and his retainers and their combined armies; in 1475 he sent his men through the mountains to the northwest to fight alongside the warriors of the noble Matsudaira clan against an uprising along the coast from which had come the first insurgency some eight years ago; and finally, in 1477, while with his family at their newly completed castle in Tojo on the island of Shikoku, my Lord joined forces with the Hisamatsu family to the east and waged battle on the Plains of Dogo.

The Hisamatsu family, of old-family nobility and highly placed, were gathering their family and retainers around them when they were attacked by a party of warriors from the area around Kitakyushu on the northern tip of Kyushu Island. There had been, for several years, raiders from this area who were allegiant to the Taira clan, marauding the southern end of Honshu at Akamagaseki, which you now call Shimonoseki, and even up to Onomichi, which you now call Hiroshima, and also the western part of Shikoku. The Suzuki warriors were successful in repulsing this attack, and in gratitude, Hisamatsu-*sama* pledged his family's fealty to Lord Suzuki.

My Lord then made preparations for a continued army of warriors to be present at his southern castle to protect it, and the surrounding peoples, from future attack. His army he spread out along the northern coast of Shikoku Island, from Niihama east to the fishing village of Naruto.

All this activity was most disheartening to my Lord, who not only detested fighting but was fast becoming a patron of the art of *Takamaki-e*. This newly developed art form was the pride of *Shogun Yoshimasa* in Kamakura, and Lord Suzuki had learned of it during his many trips to the court. *Takamaki-e* was a mixing of lacquer and charcoal dust that was worked into relief on the lacquer boxes so popular amongst the noble class. They kept jewels, tobacco, writing utensils and other treasures in these ornate boxes.

My Lord had seen the most famous of these boxes, a five-box set known as *Jishoin-Yoshimasa-ko gomensuzuri*, or "Five Writing Boxes." so named for *Shogun Yoshimasa's* Silver Pavilion. He was impressed greatly by their beauty, craftsmanship, and simplicity. Soon, he began having artisans create such art for him so he could display them at each of his homes.

As this same time, my Lord was learning the art of *Renga*, wherein a person of his immense talent would create a verse to be included with a design painted on lacquer ware. *Renga* was art "by the educated, for the educated," and combined the simplest of verse with a hint of painting. It was expected that the viewer had knowledge of the myths and tales of his society so the merest reference by word or brush stroke would evoke understanding and appreciation.

His days were filled with his labors of love, writing verse and overseeing the creation of his boxes.

Consumed as he was with his art collection, he was aggravated by the need to do battle and he longed daily for the peace he had known before his father's death. He had not time for war; yet he had to make time or he would surely lose all that he owned.

But despite his travels, his artistic endeavors and his nearly constant duties with his armies, My Lord found time to be father to his two children. His wife had given birth to twins in the fall of 1471. The older, by several hours, was a daughter. The younger was a son whom they named

Seiroku. The children were his pride, and he devoted much time to their care and upbringing.

Employed in their household were nannies and tutors who traveled with My Lord and Lady wherever the family went. When the family settled at one home or another, special, local teachers were brought in to lend their skills to the training of the twins.

Gradually, their homelands came under control, and my mate and I were able to rest on the lacquered rack made especially for us. Although over the past years of strife and war we had been used in conflict many times and had felt the tear of flesh and the break of bone beneath our blades, and had tasted the blood of a score of warriors, we, too, enjoyed our master's respite from battle. He wore us during ceremonies throughout the land, at weddings and council meetings, but during this time, not as part of his battle armor.

We waited patiently for nearly twenty years as battles continued to be fought to the northeast in the area known as *Kanto*, or "east of the pass." Our own territory near Osaka, the *Kansai* or "west of the pass" region, appeared to be stable. My Lord's family again became the nobility of old, his farmers grew prosperous, his armies grew complacent - and his enemies grew brave.

In the spring of 1497, My Lord Kiichi Suzuki and a small group of his loyal retainers were traveling to the summer home of Tojo. His son, Seiroku, having now a family of his own, was planning a summer's stay at the castle of his wife's family. Married when she was but seventeen, she was the daughter of Prince Tokudaiji whose family home was near Shizuoka on the Surugo Bay. Seiroku was being taken under the tutelage of his father-in-law, and would be presented to the *Roju* as the Suzuki family's representative. The trip could be dangerous, as battles between the Taira loyalists and the *Shogun's* forces continued to be fought in that area even yet. Seiroku, his wife of six years, Masako, and their three children - two daughters and a son - were to be accompanied by a large force as they traveled the 200 or so kilometers from Osaka to her family's home. Their danger was very real, since both the Suzuki side and the Tokudaiji side of this marriage were related to and loyal to the Minamoto clan, the emperor, and the *Shogun*.

Thus, My Lord's great army was divided; yet his heart was happy, his mind at ease. He carried us at his side - we were eager to protect him and his family- but he was not prepared to wage war again on this sojourn to the south.

His foes, however, were watching the movements of the families, and were preparing to avenge their many previous losses on the battlefield.

The trip to Tojo involved a three-day trek west of Osaka along the *Osaka-wan*, or Bay of Osaka, to the village of Akashi, some 60 kilometers away. Then, by boat the short distance to Awaji on the northern tip of *Awaji-shima*. From Awaji village they again traveled by foot the 50 kilometers to the fishing village of Nandan at the southern tip of *Awaji-shima*. Finally, they took boats across the small channel that separated *Awaji-shima* from Shikoku. When they landed at Naruto, the small village on Shikoku's eastern shore, they and their samurai would mount horses for the nearly 180-kilometer journey to Tojo. The family always enjoyed this part of the trip, since they traveled along the coast of *Seto Naikai*, the Inland Sea, and thrilled at the beauty of the warm waters and the numerous small islands, which randomly protruded from the water like stubble from a samurai's unshaven chin.

In all, the journey from their castle near Osaka to their retreat in Tojo consumed the better part of three weeks.

As My Lord was preparing to embark on the several hired boats that would take the family and his retainers across the channel to Naruto, they were set upon by an army of warriors of the Taira clan. As you know, the great Taira had once been the reigning family in all of *Nihon*, and were now fighting to regain that prominence.

The Taira strategy was very simple: Separate My Lord and the family's servants from the retainers, set fire to the boats, and kill all who did not perish in the sea. Unknown to Lord Suzuki, the master of the small fleet had been paid - and threatened - by the ruthless leader of this warring party to cooperate or else. And to emphasize the "or else" part, the Taira samurai had taken hostage the wife and daughter of the captain. He had reluctantly agreed to cooperate.

Now, as My Lord embarked, the captain ordered the boats away from shore, leaving the main body of our warriors stranded ashore.

The Taira warriors and My Lord's retainers fought to the death; there was not a man alive of our valiant troop. They gave a good account of themselves, and slew their enemy three to one for every one of our group that died.

As the smaller boats burned and sank, taking to their deaths the personal maids and close family servants, My Lord drew *katana* from its scabbard and pushed the tip into the shipmaster's neck, demanding that he put out the fire and take them across the sea. The captain, realizing that he would die if he did not obey, pleaded for his life, and now, for the life of his wife and daughter.

Surely, he begged, if I comply, my family will be killed.

And just as surely, My Master told him, if you do not comply, I shall kill you. Either way, you shall be separated from your family. And what allegiance do you owe those villains? Have they not set your boat afire? Take me across or we shall all perish.

The captain ordered his crew to make way, and the boat headed out across the water. Once under way, the crew quickly doused the fire. The other smaller boats could not be saved from the fire, and My Lord's staff were lost.

My Lord, caring father, scholar, artist, poet, but not warrior, turned to pay his respects to his fallen men, and was struck in the chest by a Taira arrow.

Mortally wounded, he sheathed *katana* and grasped the hand of his dear Michiko. My mate and I were helpless, and with us still slung at his side he gasped his final breath.

The captain, fearing now that if he did not deliver his cargo safely to Naruto this noble woman's soldiers would hunt him down, took them straight to the island, begged her forgiveness and set them ashore. The loyal warriors had seen the fire across the water and were on hand to meet the ship.

Grieving, they carried My Lord's body to the castle where My Lady had him cremated. His ashes she had scattered around the perimeter of the castle walls. She then commanded that another gravestone be added to the cemetery plot on the castle grounds.

My mate and I were cleaned and given to My Lady, who knew it was her duty to give them to her son when next she saw him.

But when would that be, she wondered. Is he even still alive, or did he meet with a similar fate at the hands of these murderous anarchists?

Weary from such a long writing session the boy rubbed his eyes and re-read what *katana* had instructed him to write. How sad, he thought, that this ancient ancestor was so close to his beloved vacation home but never got to see it again. And what was to become of the pair of swords, *katana* and *wakizashi*?

What of the son's family, he wondered. They were traveling in the more dangerous section of the country. Surely they would meet with an enemy army.

Chills traversed his spine and little goose bumps covered his arms as he thought of the pain these peaceful people had endured.

Even though he was exhausted, he wanted to write all the new information on the page containing his family chronicle. When he was finished, it looked like this:

LADY TOSHIKO SUZUKI

Born in 1427 as Toshiko Matsudaira
Father: Marquis Matsudaira
Related to: Minamoto Chikauji

Homes: Izumo, Edo

LORD HIROSHI SUZUKI

for whom *katana* was made.
Born in 1425
Father: somebody Suzuki
Related to: Emperors Go-
    Shirakawa, Go-Daigo & Antoku
Homes: Osaka, Edo, Tojo
Died in 1476. Buried in Tojo.

Married: 1444
Family: two sons, born 1448 & 1450;
a daughter, born 1453

LADY MICHIKO SUZUKI

Born in 1452 as Michiko Takatsukasa
Father: Prince Takatsukasa
Homes: Kyoto, Gifu

LORD KIICHI SUZUKI

Second master of *katana*
Born in 1448
Father: Lord Hiroshi Suzuki
Homes: Osaka, Edo, Tojo,
    Fukuchiyama
Died in 1497. Cremated in Tojo.

Married: 1470
Family: twins. a daughter born 1471;
a son born 1471, hours later.

LADY MASAKO SUZUKI

Born in 1474 as Masako Tokudaiji
Father: Prince Tokudaiji
Home: Shizuoka

LORD SEIROKU SUZUKI

Born in 1471
Father: Lord Kiichi Suzuki
Homes: Osaka, Edo, Tojo,
    Fukuchiyama

Married: 1491
Family: two daughters and a son

VII

ANOTHER PIECE IN
THE PUZZLE

Saturday mornings, as usual, Alexander Akira arose early, just as on any other school day. Only on these mornings, he was going to his Japanese language class.

He always enjoyed going there, even though it took half his day, and even though when other neighborhood children were playing, he was studying. But he knew that he was studying something special and important. One day, he promised himself, he would know how to speak Japanese and he would fly across the ocean and visit all the beautiful temples and see for himself Japan's fastest train, the *Nozomi*, which travels at speeds of 170 miles per hour.

On this Saturday, he was especially eager to get to class. He had many questions to ask his teacher, a tall, lithe, young Japanese woman named Takako Hata. The students called her Hata *Sensei*. *Sensei*, he knew, meant "teacher". When his grandparents talked about their karate teachers in Japan they had always called them *Sensei*, and he knew that his grandparents considered this term most respectful.

Often, he had wondered why the children in his regular school did not say the word "teacher" with the same respect used with the word

"*Sensei*." So far as he knew, he respected Miss Haversham the same as he respected Hata *Sensei*. But then, when he said the word *Sensei* he felt just a little different. He could not explain the feeling.

His parents told him that Hata *Sensei* had graduated from Waseda University in Tokyo and had taught English to American children in Japan for several years. But then she had wanted to travel, so she got this job teaching Japanese to Japanese children whose parents were working in America. He was the only one in the class whose parents were not from Japan, and the only one who would not soon be leaving America and heading "home." The other students were very serious about their Saturday morning studies because they knew that when they returned to Japan they would be speaking, reading and writing Japanese all the time. They needed to be prepared.

Sometimes he envied them. Especially lately, now that he had started having the dreams and the writing sessions. Now, he longed to go to Japan with them.

After class began, and after the students had all stood by their desks, facing the front, and said "*O-hayo Gozaimasu* Hata *Sensei*" - Japanese for "Good Morning Teacher Hata" - and after they had all bowed low to their teacher who returned the bow, although not bowing nearly so low as did the children, and after they had all sat down, he held up his hand and waited until Hata *Sensei* recognized him. Then he asked: "Hata *Sensei*, can you please tell us the story of Asano?"

"Where have you heard about this story, Akira-*chan*?" she asked. She always used the form of address meant for children. When he talked to an older person, he had to use the word "*san*." But when she talked to the class she used the word "*chan*." Sometimes she used the more endearing form of speech, "*kun*". Either way, he always felt extra warm and snugly when he was called by "*chan*" or "*kun*". Somehow these made him feel extra special.

"I just heard that it was a nice story and that it had some special meaning. But I've never heard the story and would like to hear it. Can we hear it today?" In fact, he had read about it in one of the books he had seen at his grandmother's house. From what he read, Lord Asano was a young nobleman who had killed himself to atone for some shameful act, but his loyal retainers had believed that he was wrongly forced to commit this act, and they killed the person who forced him to do it. Then, they each took their own lives. The very thought that samurai warriors would kill themselves for their master - he could not quite understand it.

"That is a very nice idea, Akira-*chan*. We can all read the story together, and practice our reading of Japanese *Romaji*." *Romaji*, he knew, was the Roman characters in which English was written. The Japanese words were written in *Romaji* so non-Japanese could read them. But real Japanese words were written in the old Chinese type characters called *Kanji*. These were the funny-looking pictures that were very difficult to understand and even more difficult to write. Then, of course, there were two more styles of writing for him to learn: *Hiragana* and *Katakana*, which were like simplified versions of *Kanji*, and often were used to write foreign words which had no character in *Kanji*. It was all very complex, and was like having to learn four different alphabets with more than three thousand letters! So far he was just learning to read *Romaji*.

"At our next class, I will bring copies of *Chushingura*, the story of the forty-seven *ronin*, and we will read a little of the story at each class until it is finished."

With that, the class returned to its lesson. Alexander Akira sat at his desk, feeling something a little strange inside. For now he was convinced that something wonderful was happening to him. He was contacted by the *katana* and told to write the story of the sword, and the sword had said it was the sword of Asano. But who was Asano? Now, he was going to learn all about Asano, and maybe find out something more about the sword. He shivered as he thought about it. Asano was real. The sword was real. His visions and dreams were real.

Was he going crazy?

His life was becoming one of eager anticipation: He just couldn't wait for nighttime to see if the sword would speak to him; he couldn't wait to go to the Sunday meetings so he could learn more about the mysteries of his dreams and what was happening with him; and he couldn't wait for his Saturday classes so he could begin to learn the complete story about the man who had owned this beautiful sword.

The week passed so slowly. He had neither dreams nor visions and the sword did not speak to him. Even though he was preoccupied with his thoughts about the sword and its story, he was eager to get to school each day to see what new thing he would learn. Perhaps what he learned in school might help him better understand all these strange happenings. Everything seemed to be tied together, and his appetite for learning was voracious.

On the following Saturday, Hata *Sensei* told the class that she would allow the final fifteen minutes of the class period for reading of the story. She would have one person read a sentence and the class would then translate it. Everyone would have an opportunity to read, and everyone would learn to translate the Japanese into English.

When, at last, she passed out the copies of the story, he saw it was written in *Romaji*, all right. He could pick out a couple words he already knew. But this was going to be a real challenge. The story was full of words he had never seen before. Could he really learn to read and understand this?

They began the reading and she taught them the translation:

> *Shi-ju-shichi Shi no Hanashi. Genroku ju-yo nen sangatsu, Kyoto kara chokushi ga Edo-jo e kuru koto ni narimashita. Tokugawa go-dai shogun wa chokushi wo mukaeru tame ni settaiyaku wo Asano Naganori to iu wakai daimyo ni meijimashita.*

> The story of the forty-seven samurai. The third month of the fourteenth year of Genroku era, it was decided to send from Kyoto, an imperial envoy to Edo castle. Tokugawa Shogun the fifth, in order to receive the envoy, appointed the young lord Asano Naganori a reception committee.

The teacher also told them some of the meaning of the setting of this story. Genroku era was an era in Japanese history from 1688 to 1703. The third month of the thirteenth year would be March 1702. Kyoto was the location of the Imperial palace where the Emperor lived, and Edo, which is now called Tokyo, was the castle of the Japanese military rulers, called *Shogun*. In 1600, the first *Shogun* of the Tokugawa, Tokugawa Ieyasu, established the military rule called the Tokugawa *Shogunate*. This story took place during the reign of the fifth Tokugawa *Shogun*.

He sat in stunned silence as the other children were putting away their books and papers. This is exactly what he had been told by the sword when he was first contacted. Now, his teacher was repeating the very facts he had been told, verifying the story that *katana* had told him. Again, chills ran up and down his back.

Why me, he wondered. Why am I being told all of this? What am I supposed to do with all this I'm learning?

It was a very somber little boy who got into his parents' car that afternoon and headed home, a boy lost in thought and contemplation about his future.

That evening, the sword continued its tale.

When next My Lady saw her son, he related to her the tale of his journey to Shizuoka. With his large force of foot soldiers and mounted samurai, he had traveled along the Tokaido Road for some distance east, then headed north to the newly erected castle at Inuyama. They had covered the 180 kilometers in just over seven days. The foot soldiers had jogged the whole way, stopping every two hours for drink and food. At nightfall, they encamped in a sheltered area and kept guards posted throughout the night. Master Seiroku, his Lady Masako and the three children all rode horses. Yet despite this, they were exhausted upon reaching Inuyama Castle.

After resting their troops for three days, the army again set out. Now, they turned south, heading for the bridge over the *Yahagi-gawa* at the townlette of Chiryu. After sixty kilometers of mountainous terrain, they crossed this river and again turned east. Skirting *Hamana-ko* to its north, they camped beside the calm waters of this beautiful lake. Now, they were in the flatter coastal region and made much better time, traversing the remaining ninety kilometers to the castle at Shizuoka in only three days.

For three months, Seiroku and his family were guests in Lord Tokudaiji's home, where young Seiroku was groomed to take his father's place in the *Roju*. Then, a messenger brought the news of Lord Kiichi's death. Stunned, Master Seiroku left his wife and family in the good care of his father-in-law and headed west with his mounted samurai. He was determined to hunt down the Taira murderers and make them pay with their lives for their treachery.

But alas, he was too successful in finding the culprits, and in the ensuing battle on the plains near the village of Miki, he was also struck by an alien arrow.

His warriors were victorious, and hastily returned their wounded leader to his castle near Osaka.

His widowed mother, Lady Michiko, was already there, awaiting him.

She tended to his wounds, but saw her son's strength quickly fleeing his body. As her mother-in-law had done before her, she now presented *katana* and its mate, *wakizashi*, to her son.

But fate was not to look kindly on this young nobleman, for in the winter of his return, just after the celebration of the New Year, My Lord Seiroku Suzuki contracted the pneumonia virus, and died at his castle.

He never drew *katana* in battle.

He never recovered from his wound.

He never again saw his wife and children.

Alexander found himself in tears as he finished this writing. He did not know much about the life of this gallant nobleman, but he knew enough to be deeply saddened by his untimely death. How old was he when he died, the boy wondered. He mentally calculated his ancestor's age; Born in 1471; died in 1498: He was not quite twenty-seven. How unfair, he wanted to shout. What about his children? What about his wife? Who was to take care of his widowed mother? There are too many unanswered questions, *katana*, he thought.

But he was not to know the answers to these questions yet. Finally, he prepared the family genealogy, adding the new information he had received this night.

LADY TOSHIKO SUZUKI

Born in 1427 as Toshiko Matsudaira
Father: Marquis Matsudaira
Related to: Minamoto Chikauji

Homes: Izumo, Edo

LORD HIROSHI SUZUKI

for whom *katana* was made.
Born in 1425
Father: somebody Suzuki
Related to: Emperors Go-
    Shirakawa, Go-Daigo & Antoku
Homes: Osaka, Edo, Tojo
Died in 1476. Buried in Tojo.

Married: 1444
Family: two sons, born 1448 & 1450;
a daughter, born 1453

LADY MICHIKO SUZUKI

Born in 1452 as Michiko Takatsukasa
Father: Prince Takatsukasa
Homes: Kyoto, Gifu

LORD KIICHI SUZUKI

Second master of *katana*
Born in 1448
Father: Lord Hiroshi Suzuki
Homes: Osaka, Edo, Tojo,
    Fukuchiyama
Died in 1497. Cremated in Tojo.

Married: 1470
Family: twins. a daughter born 1471;
a son born 1471 hours later.

LADY MASAKO SUZUKI

Born in 1474 as Masako Tokudaiji
Father: Prince Tokudaiji
Home: Shizuoka

LORD SEIROKU SUZUKI

Third master of *katana*
Born in 1471
Father: Lord Kiichi Suzuki
Homes: Osaka, Edo, Tojo,
    Fukuchiyama
Died in 1498 in Osaka.

Married: 1491
Family: two daughters and a son

VIII

WHAT HAPPENS NOW?

Eight-year-old boys are not supposed to be forced to ponder the deeper questions of life on this planet, and most likely should not need to be questioning the mysteries of the herebefore and the hereafter.

But Alexander Akira now found himself deeply involved in all this: Involved not only from the aspect of envisioning these various events and transcribing what he was told, but feeling for these people, his kin, his ancestors.

His mind was filled with unanswered, and perhaps unanswerable, questions as a result of these most recent encounters with *katana*. If Lord Seiroku Suzuki died when he was only 27, who took over the Suzuki line? And who was given *katana* and *wakizashi*? Did his sister now become the head of the family, or did one of the orphans?

Thinking of the sister made the boy ask himself why he never heard anything about any of the daughters. Lord Hiroshi had a daughter who died early, so he understood why he knew little about her. Then Lord Kiichi had a daughter and there was no mention of her. Why not? Did something also happen to her, or was *katana* not going to tell him anything about the daughter?

How much longer, he wondered, was this fighting to go on? And what must it have been like to live in that period, when even trips to relatives

meant days of arduous journey through mountains filled with enemy soldiers who were intent on killing you? He even wondered about the things
no one wants to talk about. Like, were there public rest rooms along the
Tokaido Road, and if not, what did the travelers do? What did the wom-
en, especially, do?

He knew that his dad would have had no problem "taking care of
business" in the woods, but his mom? He could not imagine that.

Now he wondered how the ladies ever did all the wrapping and un-
wrapping of their kimonos all by themselves. Or did they always have
maids that helped them with their dressing? Even out in the woods?

All of this was very perplexing to him, and he was tempted greatly
to ask his father about it all. But then he remembered what he had been
told by *katana* on the very first day: He must not tell of this writing or
he would be scorned. He had to wait until the story was completed. But
when would that be, he wondered?

And another thing: All along the sword has been telling the story of
the Suzuki family, his family, but *katana* had said it was the Sword of
Asano. How could that be? Somehow, he reasoned, the Suzukis and the
Asanos were either the same family or were related. He hoped the story
of *Chushingura* would give him the answer to this puzzle.

He could not decide which he wanted to happen first: *katana* to tell
him more of the story or his Saturday class to take place so he could learn
more of the *Chushingura* story. The waiting frustrated him, and he pes-
tered his parents and his teacher with questions about everything under
the sun in an effort to keep his mind occupied, and to satisfy his immense
curiosity about life.

Slowly his week came to an end, and he again prepared excitedly for
his *Nihon-go,* Japanese language, class. In this special class the children
learned reading and writing, plus some crafts that would be a natural
part of their schooling in Japan. He especially liked the *sumi-e* painting
they learned, and the paper projects called *origami.* Every Saturday they
either painted or crafted something to take home and show their parents.
And every Saturday they were given stories to read and handwriting ex-
ercises to practice during the following week.

Each of the students in the Japanese class did almost as much homework weekly from this three-hour class as they did from the week of

regular school. Yet not one complained, and not one missed having the homework assignments completed by next class. How unlike his classmates in his regular school, who seemed to complain loudly about not being able to just play when they got home after school.

Who wants to just play, he asked himself? You cannot learn much from watching TV or climbing trees. With all the neat books I have at home and at my grandparents' house, I won't have time to play for years!

Finally came the last fifteen minutes of class, and they continued with the story of the 47 *ronin*:

> *Sono toji, shogun-ke no gitencho de atta Kira to iu rojin wa hijo-ni yoku ga fukaku, shokken wo riyo shite, hitobito kara wairo wo takusan totte orimashita. Chokushi-settai to iu taiyaku wo hajimete meijirareta Asano wa iro-iro muzukashii gishiki ni tsuite gitencho Kira ni shido wo tanomimashita, ga Kira wa kesshite Asano ni gi-shiki ni tsuite oshiemasen deshita. Sore wa Asano ga tadashii hito deshita kara Kira ni wairo wo tsukaimasen deshita node.*

> In those days, there was an old man by the name of Kira, who was master of ceremony of the Shogun's household, who, taking advantage of his authority, used to receive from people much bribe. Asano, who for the first time was appointed to the important duty of reception committee asked master of ceremonies Kira about the various difficult formalities that had to be complied with, however, Kira would by no means instruct Asano about the prescribed ceremonial. That was in consequence of the fact that Asano, being an upright man, would not give any bribe.

The words were very difficult for the class to learn, and they were not the sort of words young children would be required to know and say. But they were all caught up in the story, and after they finished the class, many of the youngsters gathered around Hata *Sensei* to ask her more questions about the story. One of the older boys, whose father was a department head for one of the large Japanese trading companies in town, came over to him as he packed his school bag.

"I'm very happy you asked Hata *Sensei* to get this story for us," he said. "I asked my father about it after the last class, and he said this is the best known story in all Japan!"

"I heard a little about it and it sounded very exciting," replied Akira-*chan*. "I'm glad you like it. I was a little afraid that I would be the only one in class who wanted to know the story."

As he traveled home with his parents, he asked if they knew the *Chushingura* story. They both said they had heard about it from his grandparents, and they believed it to be an incredible story of loyalty and faithfulness. He told them he had asked Hata *Sensei* to tell them the story and now they were reading and translating it in class.

His parents were very happy that he was learning the story and that he was enjoying his Japanese language lessons.

The next Sunday was meeting day at the grandparents', and he was up and dressed early. He did not want to be late, and kept hurrying his parents.

"We don't have to eat breakfast, do we?" he asked.

"Would '*ba-san* mind if we got there a little early today?" he whined. Sometimes when he talked about his grandmother, he used the Japanese word *Oba-san*, or the child's version of just '*ba-san*. When he had been just a toddler, he had called her *ba-ba*. His grandmother had taught him that, and also the words for grandfather: *ji-ji* in baby talk, *Oji-san* in regular talk, and '*ji-san* in more familiar terms. The "O" in front of the title meant a higher form of respect, and was generally used by younger people when talking to or about older people. But with the family it was always '*ba-san* and '*ji-san*.

"Do you want me to wipe the car windows?"

"May I start the car and get it warmed up?"

"Did you get gas?"

After a while, his parents decided he should straighten up his room while they finished getting ready. His incessant questions and hurry-up attitude were getting to them. After he left them in the kitchen, they exchanged glances and shared the same thought: We're really glad he enjoys going with us. He could be whining about having to go and being grumpy about not getting to play with his friends when we go to the meeting.

At this day's meeting, the group had a visitor. She was a friend of Bonnie's who owned a rock shop. She had brought a collection of different rocks and they discussed the actual and spiritual properties of the different stones. On the dining table she had laid out a number of smaller stones; you could pick up each one and hold it tightly to see if it felt "right" to you. If so, you could keep it.

He asked how he would know what "right" would feel like, and she told him that he would know; No one else could tell him. He found a shiny black hematite stone that fit his hand and felt warm. "If it feels warm, is it right?" he asked.

"That is usually a sign the stone is for you," the visitor had replied. "If you like it, put it in your pocket. And always keep it with you. The hematite is good for your blood and your constitution. You have made a good choice."

He felt good about picking out the stone. Then he remembered that his grandfather also carried a hematite with him always. When he had asked *'ji-san* about it, he had been told that this stone was much older than was Alexander. And grandfather would be lost, now, without it on him.

After he picked out his stone, he lost interest in the rest of the discussion, and wandered into the family room to find a good book to read. This was his favorite room in his grandparents' house, and he never tired of looking at all the books on the shelves and picking a new one to look at.

This time he chose a book on Ireland, and spent the rest of the afternoon engrossed in the story and pictures of yet another culture.

The following week he made sure he kept his hematite stone with him at school, secretly feeling it in his pocket throughout the day, making sure it was OK. At night, he rinsed and towel dried it as Bonnie had told him to do - so its healing properties would not be scattered by the grease and dirt of his hands.

As patiently as possible, he waited for the sword to speak to him again, but he was most impatient by Friday night when, as he had done each evening during the week after his bath, he sat alone in his bedroom, pencil and paper at the ready, awaiting the return of *katana*. His wait was not in vain, for as he nearly dozed, he sensed the mysterious presence, and his hand began to move.

Turmoil reigned at the castle of Suzuki. The Lord was dead; the Lady was two hundred kilometers away with the heir; in between them, armies were still battling each other and laying siege to one another's castles.

Obasan, as Lady Michiko was now called, was concerned about what she should do. As the maternal head of the family, she could decree her mother-in-law's second son as titular head of the clan. But this, she knew, might cause a split between her brother-in-law and her grandson; a split that would affect their families and their armies. Her decision now, she was sure, would determine whether this great family stayed together or came apart.

She sent for her husband's younger brother, Jiro, meaning second son, to join her at the castle. He arrived in a week's time and strode like a nobleman into the formal reception hall of the main floor. His sister-in-law, still in her black grieving *kimono* from the death of his brother Lord Kiichi, sat facing the door, *katana* and *wakizashi* laid out in front of her. As a woman, she was not allowed to touch the swords. Yet as the head of the family, she handled them with a firmness respected by family and servants alike.

Jiro, seeing her in black and all alone in the large room, softened perceptibly.

Are you well, Honorable Big Sister? he had asked.

I am well, Younger Brother, she had replied.

She then told him that, as the eldest surviving male member of the family, he must decide what action should be taken by the family with respect to the son of Seiroku. And she warned him to consider carefully his answer, for the future of the whole family rested on his reply.

If he should choose to become Lord Jiro Suzuki, she would hand the swords to him today, and he would move into this castle from Fukuchiyama. Thereupon, he would travel to Kamakura to make known to the *Shogun* his position as leader of the Suzuki family.

But he should be prepared for battle from the maternal grandparents of his great nephew. For they would surely fight for his right to become the family head. And his grandfather was, after all, Prince Tokudaiji.

She further reminded him that the country was at war; his father, his brother and now his nephew, had fought for the restoration of peace.

Two of them had died recently in this conflict. If the family were to fight amongst itself, she feared all the women would be wearing black, and the Suzukis would be no more.

In fairness, she told him, he must also consider the sacrifice he would be making by giving up his chance to lead the clan. Certainly if he makes that choice, he will be well remembered for it.

But despite what she had told him, he must make up his own mind, today. For he would either leave this room, she said, as Lord Jiro Suzuki, or as the great uncle to Lord Michio Suzuki.

Jiro had not expected to hear what he had just heard. Knowing of his brother's death, and then learning of his nephew's death, he had expected that he was being summoned to the great castle to be given control of the family fortune and destiny.

Now, he was being called upon to make the most important decision of his life: To forego power, fame and nobility in return for personal sacrifice and honor.

He knelt in front of his sister-in-law, bowing low and grasping *katana* as it lay before him. I pledge my life and my fealty to Master Michio, he intoned gravely, Lord of the Suzuki family, and I charge this noble's sword to be the guardian of my promise; for if I should betray my word and my family's honor then by *katana* should I perish.

Lady Michiko was moved to tears, yet she dared not show any emotion. Already, she chastised herself, she had prattled on like a kitchen maid about the consequences of her brother-in-law's decision. Surely he knew the immensity of his actions here today.

Arigato, Oniisan, she murmured. Thank you, Younger Brother.

Then she asked his assistance. The heir was but six years old. Would Jiro take him to Fukuchiyama Castle and train him in the ways of a nobleman, preparing him for the day when he would assume the real responsibility for the family?

Again she was moved to tears by his answer.

Obasan, he replied, I shall raise him as my own, ever mindful that into his hands shall *katana* and *wakizashi* pass, and onto his shoulders shall the burden of authority be placed.

After they had supped, she sent a courier to the castle of her grandson, now to be Lord Michio Suzuki. The message he carried calmed the concerns felt by Lord Tokudaiji, who immediately recalled his general and the army of samurai that were already making preparations for an assault, if necessary, on the Suzuki family compound near Osaka.

Instead, he readied a small force as guardians for the boy as he traveled first to Osaka to receive the matriarch's blessing and the pair of family swords, then to Fukuchiyama. These warriors he charged thusly: Protect the Lord with your lives from this day forward until he dismisses you from his service.

Having a grandson not much older than she, Lord Tokudaiji adopted his granddaughter into his own family. Then, he betrothed the girl to the boy, planning for their marriage in fifteen years. It would be a worthy union, he knew, just as had been his daughter's marriage to Lord Seiroku seven years ago.

The boy could not believe what he had just written. He could not believe that a little girl, younger than he himself was this very evening, had already been pledged to a boy just about his own age. This was certainly something new to him, and he vowed to ask about it when he next saw his grandmother.

He was learning much about the society as well as the sword and its history, and he tried to not worry too much about what happened to the young Lord. The sword had been filling in all the detail, albeit not exactly when Alexander wanted it.

So before retiring for the night, he added all that he could from this session.

LADY TOSHIKO SUZUKI

Born in 1427 as Toshiko Matsudaira
Father: Marquis Matsudaira
Related to: Minamoto Chikauji

Homes: Izumo, Edo

LORD HIROSHI SUZUKI
for whom *katana* was made.
Born in 1425
Father: somebody Suzuki
Related to: Emperors Go-
    Shirakawa, Go-Daigo & Antoku
Homes: Osaka, Edo, Tojo
Died in 1476. Buried in Tojo.

Married: 1444
Family: two sons, born 1448 & 1450;
a daughter, born 1453

\|/

LADY MICHIKO SUZUKI

Born in 1452 as Michiko Takatsukasa
Father: Prince Takatsukasa
Home: Edo

LORD KIICHI SUZUKI
Second master of *katana*
Born in 1448
Father: Lord Hiroshi Suzuki
Homes: Osaka, Edo, Tojo,
    Fukuchiyama
Died in 1497. Cremated in Tojo

Married: 1470
Family: twins. a daughter born 1471;
a son born 1471, hours later.

\|/

LADY MASAKO SUZUKI

Born in 1474 as Masako Tokudaiji
Father: Prince Tokudaiji
Home: Shizuoka

LORD SEIROKU SUZUKI
Third master of *katana*
Born in 1471
Father: Lord Kiichi Suzuki
Homes: Osaka, Edo, Tojo,
    Fukuchiyama
Died in 1498. Buried in Osaka.

Married: 1491
Family: two daughters and a son,
born 1492

LORD MICHIO SUZUKI
Fourth master of *katana*
Born in 1492
Father: Lord Seiroku Suzuki
Homes: Osaka, Edo, Tojo
    Fukuchiyama

IX

THE RISING SON

It was several weeks before the boy again took up his pencil and tablet. He had not felt the sword talking to him nor had he been able to enter into the trance-like state which had seemed to induce the sword's visitations.

Now, he sat at his table and wrote feverishly, as though chased by the spirits of all the ancestors of whom he had yet to write.

Life for the young Lord was not easy. The castle at Fukuchiyama was little more than a military outpost. Warring factions continued to maraud throughout the territory, and his days were filled with simulated battles and actual ones, too. For the Suzukis and all the inland residents of Honshu, the castle was strategically situated.

The village of Fukuchiyama is built on the river *Yura-gawa* which flows north to the Sea of Japan. It is through the pass created by the river that the insurgents had first traveled inland from the coast in 1467. They labored along the side of *Oe-yama*, the predominant mountain of that range at over 800 meters high. Then, they had followed the southern flowing river *Kako-gawa* south to the fertile plains of Himeji. Only the castle at Fukuchiyama could stand in the way of their further intrusions.

Unlike the comfortable life he had experienced with his parents and sister while living at the family castle in Osaka, his routine now was harsh, strenuous, and highly regimented. His great uncle rarely was home to see him, and his upbringing was dutifully handled by his great aunt. His education was the province of select nannies who performed their labors with skill and great deference. And although no one ever once said to him that his uncle should have been the Lord and not he, they created for him a cold and distant atmosphere.

Thus, it was a surprise to no one that Lord Michio developed into a fiercely independent warrior, with a strong spirit and a hard, sinewy body. By his 12th birthday he was a highly skilled fighter, able to defend himself with swords, his hands, and his mind.

But it definitely was a surprise to everyone when, on his 12th birthday, he petitioned his great uncle Jiro for *katana* and *wakizashi*, so he might carry us himself and take his rightful, hereditary position as leader of the Suzuki family.

During these past six years, we swords had been stored and unused. We were awaiting the day that our master was old enough to slide us beneath his waist sash and make use of us on the fields of battle.

Now Uncle Jiro, as he was called, resisted My Lord's request.

"You are yet too young," he insisted. "Your education is not yet completed. You cannot lead an army because no one will follow you."

But My Lord was as insistent.

"I am as capable a warrior as any man in your army," he inveighed. "And I have the name Suzuki. If one should dare resist my orders his neck shall surely regret such insolence."

After much discussion - discussion that pitted Jiro's desire to remain as family head against Lord Michio's rights - My Lord was successful.

Gathering his most senior and trusted samurai in the main chamber, Jiro presented the youth with the two swords. He then backed several steps away from Lord Michio and bowed deeply. As he did so, all the assembled warriors also silently bowed. Then, they all shouted "Banzai! Banzai! Banzai!"

Jiro addressed the group in a loud voice, telling them that from this day forward Lord Michio would be the head of the Suzuki family, and all those gathered there and all the men under their command would show him their total obeisance and fealty.

Next, My Lord spoke to the assemblage. "You who are of Honored Uncle's army shall continue here. His commands shall be obeyed as though spoken by me. You who are of my grandfather's castle shall remain my personal guard, and when I depart here for my home castle near Osaka, you too shall depart with me."

"Let no man," he continued, "be misled. I am a warrior amongst warriors and a leader of warriors. The Suzuki name will be respected and honored, and we shall strive, fight and, if necessary, die to bring peace to our land. Wear your crest with pride, for no shame shall come to you for following this man."

It was not many weeks later that we swords accompanied Lord Michio and his samurai to Osaka.

Upon his arrival, Lady Michiko, his widowed grandmother and matriarch to the clan, met him in the Great Hall where six years earlier she had presented the swords to her brother-in-law.

Now, the boy noble strode upon those polished floors with the same confidence that had been his great uncle's. Short in stature but great in resolve, he now bowed slightly to the kneeling woman.

"I have come home, *O-obasan*," he said. "Together, we shall do honor to the memory of my father."

Not long thereafter Lady Masako, My Lord's mother, returned to the castle near Osaka. She had been summoned by Lord Michio and with heavy heart at having to leave behind her daughter and her own parents, she obeyed his command.

With his family now reassembled, the young Lord devoted his days to the constant training of his warriors. He was determined to make the army as prepared as possible for any attack from the ever present bands of renegade warriors. And when they were not training, he had them working about the castle, strengthening its walls and shoring up its fortifications.

Periodically he sent smaller companies of men into the villages and farms that dotted the family-owned territory. They traveled twenty miles in all directions, ensuring peace for the peasants who tilled and toiled on behalf of their master. Only to the southwest did they cut short their journeys, for it was only five or six miles in this direction until they reached the land controlled by the mighty Sakai family whose domicile included the land on which Hideyoshi later built Osaka castle.

In this time of instability, it was unwise to venture onto the lands of even a friendly Lord for fear of instigating conflict and unnecessary bloodshed.

When Lord Michio was seventeen he decided to take to himself a wife. During the five years in which he had governed the Suzuki interests from their Higashi-Osaka castle, he had become well known to the several other noble families in the region. One family in particular that he had impressed with his brash, imperious ways was the Rokkaku branch of the Sasaki clan. This wealthy and wide spread family had holdings primarily in Omi province on the western shore of *Biwa-ko*, the large lake at which the later battle of *Sekigahara* took place. Those Sasakis traced their ancestry to the Omi *Genji*, descendants of *Minamoto Yoritomo* who had defeated the Taira clan some 300 years earlier.

Amongst the various retainers of the Sasakis was a family called Mitsui. This samurai class clan, being small in build, owed their very existence to the Sasaki power and influence. Having once even lived near by the Sasaki castle at Kannonji, the Mitsui clan had eventually built their own castle at Namazue, east of Lake Biwa. There, they lived as a petty *daimyo* clan under the aegis of the Sasaki warlords. In fact, so closely tied were the Mitsui and Sasaki clans that a younger son of Lord Sasaki, known as Takahisa, married the eldest daughter of Mitsui. Young Takahisa Sasaki, who was but four years older than My Lord, became head and protector of the Mitsui house, having become an adopted heir, or *yoshi*, after his marriage into the Mitsui family. As I have said before, such adoptions were common amongst the nobility as a means of keeping the family name intact in the event there were no natural male heir.

My Lord Michio and his entourage attended the marriage of his noble friend and counterpart Takahisa, at which time Lady Masako's marriage broker inquired of the elder Sasaki who might be an appropriate mate for his young charge. Having no daughter himself, Lord Sasaki proposed to his vassal, Mitsui-*sama*, the possibility of his youngest daughter, sixteen-year-old Tomiko, becoming betrothed to Lord Michio. The plan was quickly agreed to, as the Mitsuis knew the value of another daughter's marriage into the noble class.

In the autumn of My Lord's seventeenth year, he and young Tomiko Mitsui were wed. Through this marriage into a family so closely tied to Sasaki and ultimately to *Genji*, Lady Masako hoped the Suzuki family's reputation would be restored. She knew well that the family had had to take a lesser position in the politics of Kamakura as a result of the Suzuki's earlier mistake of fighting on the *Heike* side in the *Gempei* war in the twelfth century.

The young couple had a fruitful union, and soon produced, in 1512, an heir whom they named Tomishiki. They used the three *Kanji* that represented the syllables of his name thusly: 'Tomi' from Tomiko, his mother; 'shi' from Lord Hiroshi, for whom *katana* was made; and 'ki' from his great-grandfather Kiichi. It was an appropriate tying together of the family, and showed their great hope in having their son carry on the proud tradition of the noble Suzuki family name.

Altogether they raised four children; after Tomishiki they had three daughters, all of whom were eventually married well in their own class.

But My Lord's life was not always to be joyous, for although he had no trouble with anarchists that he could not easily quell - his army was well trained and extremely loyal - in his eighteenth year he had been told that a meeting was being arranged with the leader of the renegade faction from Maizuru, a seaport on the northern coast at the head of *Maizuru-wan*, the Bay of Maizuru. He was to meet at the castle of his great uncle, Jiro, in Fukuchiyama.

He had not returned there since leaving six years earlier, and although he had heard rumors of his great uncle's ravings about the "child leader" of the clan, he had had no reason to become personally concerned. His uncle's army had done its duty on many occasions, repelling all attacks that had come through the mountain pass, and Lord Michio did not question his great uncle's loyalty. In fact, his counselors had advised him that his esteemed relative was in very poor health, due mainly to his advanced age of sixty years.

Thus, My Lord took my mate and me as he traveled with a small contingent of samurai to the northern outpost. He was certain he did not need to take a large company of men to his great uncle's garrison. And he was just as certain that he would have to listen to his enemy's complaints that no one from the interior of the country could understand their miserable living conditions, and hence their reasons for revolt. Theirs was a climate of cold winds blowing in from *Nihon Kai* - the Sea of Japan - and long winters filled with heavy, wet snow. Living in such a rugged environment, they contented themselves by believing that they were *Ura Nihon*: The Backbone of Japan.

But My Lord was in no mood to listen to their complaints. Did not all of Japan use the *kotatsu*, a sunken heating pit, for warmth on the coldest days? And did they not all warm their wrists over the *hibachi*, thus giving the body heated blood for circulation?

He arrived in Fukuchiyama ready for a fight.

But he did not expect the fight to be with his great uncle. For the "meeting" was but a ruse used by Jiro to get the youngster alone in that great chamber where years ago he had pledged his life to Lord Michio. Now, alone, he challenged his great nephew to a duel "so the real leader of the clan would be known to all." In a moment, the young noble drew *katana* and fought skillfully against the man who had been as his own father.

This was a struggle between youth and experience, insolence and arrogance, purity and deceit. And very quickly my blade again tasted an opponent's blood, for Lord Michio was both strong and fast. He had learned well his *kendo* lessons while a boy in his great uncle's care. Now as Jiro lay gasping his final breaths, young Michio railed against him in anger and despair. Seeking atonement, Jiro begged My Lord to use *katana* to deliver the coup d'grace, the final blow across his neck.

My Lord was to carry with him the shame of his uncle's actions until he, too, drew his last breaths.

This was all very alarming to the boy, and he found himself railing, along with his ancestor, against the stupid actions of the great uncle. How could one relative turn against another, he wondered aloud. He thought about his own family, and believed that he could never do anything to harm any one of them. There was just so much he did not understand about life - perhaps when he got older he would be able to figure out why the uncle had been so jealous of the nephew that he wanted to kill him. But for now, it just did not make any sense.

He was still troubled and perplexed when he arrived the next Saturday morning at his *Nihon-go* class. During these past weeks since the sword had spoken through him, they had continued their reading of the Chushingura incident. While he waited for class to start, he opened his notebook and reviewed the past weeks' work.

Aru hi, denchu de, Kira ga Asano wo hijo-ni bujoku shimashita kara, Asano wa katto nari, denchu ni mo kakawarazu, Kira ni kiri-tsukemashita. Shikashi, ta no daimyo ni tomerarete Kira wo korosu koto ga dekimasen deshita.Toji, Edo-jo-chu de wa katana wo nuku koto wa genkin sarete ori, moshi, sono ho wo okaseba gembatsu ni shoserareru no deshita kara Asano wa sono hi no yoru ni seppuku wo saseraremashita.Sono ue, Asano-ke wa danzetsu, kare no shiro wa tori-agerare, keraitachi wa zembu ronin ni narimashita.

One day, in the (Shogun's) palace, Kira having greatly insulted Asano, Asano, bursting into a passion and in spite of the fact that he was in the (Shogun's) palace, slashed at Kira (with his sword). However, having been held by another daimyo he could not kill Kira. (As) in those days unsheathing one's sword inside the Yedo palace was strictly prohibited (and) if (someone) broke that law one would be condemned to severe punishment, on the night of that (very) day Asano was obliged to commit harakiri (seppuku). Moreover, the Asano family became extinct, his castle was confiscated and all his retainers became masterless.

Sonogo, Asano no moto karo Oishi to sono chonan oyobi chugi-na ke-rai awasete shi-ju-shichi mei wa hijo-na kuro wo shite tsui-ni Asano seppuku-go ichi-nen shichi-ka-getsu-me no aro o-yuki no yonaka ni, Kira no yashiki ni uchi-itte, Kira no samuraitachi to tatakai, toto, Kira no kubi wo uchi-torimashita. Sono yoake ni, Oishi wo sento ni ikko wa, Asano no haka no aru Sengakuji e yuki, Kira no kubi wo shujin no bozen ni suemashitaKoshite, karera wa shikara wo awa-sete shujin no ada wo rippa-ni uchimashita.

After sometime, Asano's former chief retainer Oishi, his eldest son as well as (some) loyal retainers, joining together, (formed a combination of) forty-seven persons (who, after) undergoing great hardships, on a snowy night, one year and seven months after Asano's harakiri (seppuku) broke into Kira's mansion, fought against his (Kira's) retainers (and) at last (they caught) Kira and cut off his head. At daybreak, with Oishi in the lead, the party (of the 47 retainers) went to Sengakuji temple where there is Asano's grave (and) placed Kira's head in front of their (former) master's tomb. Thus, they, combining their efforts, took a brilliant revenge upon their master's enemy.

Class seemed to drag for him as he awaited the final fifteen minutes so they could finish the story. Although he usually enjoyed the different stories they read, or script they practiced writing, or the arts and crafts on which they worked, today all he could think about was the story of Asano. At last, Hata *Sensei* had them set aside their other study materials and take out their copies of the story.

Shibaraku nochi ni, shi-ju-shichi shi wa shizuka-ni seppuku shi-mashita node, shujin no haka no aru Sengakuji ni homuraremashita. Sono toki kara, konnichi made, mainichi tasu no hitobito ga karera no haka ni mairi, bozen no senko no kemuri ga taeta hi ga arimasen.

Sometime later, the forty-seven samurai, having calmly performed harakiri, were laid to rest at Sengakuji temple, in which there is the grave where their master is buried. Since then, every day, a large number of people have been visiting their graves and no day passes by without (seeing) the smoke of incense (burning) before them.

Hata *Sensei* then told them what every Japanese boy and girl learns about these brave men. The great vendetta, or revenge, by the ronin, took place on December 15, 1703. On the next February 4th the 47 ronin were ordered to end their life, also by harakiri. According to the law of the land, vendettas were prohibited, and having rightly avenged their master's death, they had wrongly done so in the eyes of the law.

Each man had left his family so there would be no shame brought on them by his actions that night, and in each one's will he asked to be laid to rest in Sengakuji temple, next to his master.

This story, she said, typified fidelity to one's lord and master. And even *Shogun* Tsunayoshi, the actual ruler of Japan at that time, was anxious to save them from death. But he too had to abide by the law. And the law had been designed to help stop the fighting that had gone on between families and clans. But now, it had inadvertently been used to protect the guilty.

Every year, on February 4th, the anniversary of the death of the 47 ronin is observed at Sengakuji temple in Tokyo, even to this day. And in December every year, plays are given and movies are shown depicting Chushingura. These are always very well attended, as this is now perhaps the most memorable event in Japanese history.

For young Alexander, this story was doubly impressive, for he now believed that the very *katana* he secretly held was the very sword which Asano had drawn in the castle that day. What if it really were the same sword, he excitedly asked himself. I can't just go on with life every day as though none of this had happened, can I?

Caught up in the intrigue of the story and eager for *katana* to continue its tale, he could hardly pay attention to his parents' questions and conversation as they drove home. Finally it was bedtime and after giving his parents their nightly hug and kiss, he went to his bedroom and closed the door behind him. Then, sitting at his desk, he closed his eyes and waited for any new revelation. It was not long in coming to him, and the writing began without his even noticing.

Just as he had been schooled in all the combative and intellectual arts, so did Lord Michio provide for the intense education of his son Tomishiki. As the boy matured, his father took great pleasure in the strength and discipline he exhibited. Certainly their forebears could be proud of his progeny, thought my master. As his years advanced My Lord increasingly allowed his son's management of the family affairs, and eventually moved to the castle in Tojo permanently, leaving the young man, and the army, in Higashi Osaka.

Perhaps it was the fact that he had had to mature so quickly, or that he had borne such emotional pain over the killing of his great uncle, that My Lord was unable to enjoy his leisure years in Tojo, for in his thirty-eighth year he suffered a heart attack while riding with Lady Tomiko near the River of the Fountain - *Izumi-gawa* - on their estate. Unable to leave his body there alone, My Lady remained for her final years at the Shikoku castle.

When young Tomishiki learned of his father's death, he visited his mother at Tojo where she presented my mate and me to him, thus passing us again from father to son.

Alexander awoke with a start. His paper was covered with this final episode in the life of the young man to whom he had grown so close. Tired and ready for bed, he nonetheless completed the sheet upon which he was recording the chronology of his family.

LADY TOSHIKO SUZUKI

Born in 1427 as Toshiko Matsudaira
Father: Marquis Matsudaira
Related to: Minamoto Chikauji

Homes: Izumo, Edo

LORD HIROSHI SUZUKI

For whom *katana* was made.
Born in 1425
Father: somebody Suzuki
Related to: Emperors Go-
    Shirakawa, Go-Daigo & Antoku
Homes: Osaka, Edo, Tojo
Died in 1476. Buried in Tojo.

Married: 1444
Family: two sons, born 1448 & 1450;
a daughter, born 1453

\|/

LADY MICHIKO SUZUKI

Born in 1452 as Michiko Takatsukasa
Father: Prince Takatsukasa
Home: Edo

LORD KIICHI SUZUKI

Second master of *katana*
Born in 1448
Father: Lord Hiroshi Suzuki
Homes: Osaka, Edo, Tojo,
    Fukuchiyama
Died in 1497. Cremated in Tojo

Married: 1470
Family: twins. a daughter born 1471;
a son born 1471, hours later.

\|/

83

LADY MASAKO SUZUKI

Born in 1474 as Masako Tokudaiji
Father: Prince Tokudaiji
Home: Shizuoka

LORD SEIROKU SUZUKI

Third master of *katana*
Born in 1471
Father: Lord Kiichi Suzuki
Homes: Osaka, Edo, Tojo,
    Fukuchiyama
Died in 1498. Buried in Osaka.

Married: 1491
Family: two daughters and a son,
born 1492

\|/

LADY TOMIKO SUZUKI

Born in 1493 as Tomiko Mitsui
Father: Mitsui-*sama*
Home: Namazue

LORD MICHIO SUZUKI

Fourth master of *katana*
Born in 1492
Father: Lord Seiroku Suzuki
Homes: Osaka, Edo, Tojo
    Fukuchiyama
Died in 1530. Buried in Tojo.

Married: 1509
Family: a son, born 1512;
3 daughters

\|/

LORD TOMISHIKI SUZUKI

Fifth master of *katana*
Born in 1512
Father: Lord Michio Suzuki
Homes: Osaka, Edo, Tojo
    Fukuchiyama

X

CAN THERE BE PEACE?

Life for young Alexander Akira seemed to be settling into a very satisfying pattern: His weekly after school sessions with Miss Haversham did much to appease his continuing questions about everything and anything, and she expressed to his parents her increasing satisfaction with his progress, attitude and maturity; the Saturday morning *Nihon-go* classes filled him with delight and excitement, and even Hata *Sensei* commented to his parents about his apparent thirst for learning; and the monthly meetings held at his grandparents' home increasingly became a forum in which he was a comfortable and active participant.

The change had been dramatic - from the innocent little boy of several months ago to the inquisitive, confident and knowledgeable young man of today. All who knew him throughout this period were aware of the transformation that was taking place in him. Even his playmates noticed that he was changing. They were not entirely sure what the change was, but he appeared more serious, more confident, more mature. And to them, he seemed less interested in playing their games with them, or talking about the things that interested them. It was as though he had moved into a different generation from them.

At home, he spent more of his free time reading books; books about any subject. It did not seem to matter to him what he read so long as he was reading something. This made his parents very happy, yet they worried, as parents do, about his not getting enough physical exercise, or about his straining his eyes too much.

Yet to Akira himself, the days did not contain enough hours for him to do all that he wanted to do. So fascinated was he by his expanding world that he felt constrained by the need to eat or sleep or do any of the other things that kept him away from the activities he really enjoyed. The only change he noticed about himself was that his parents did not seem quite so much older now as they had seemed before, and his friends seemed just a little sillier now than they had before. But otherwise, he thought of himself today just as he always had.

His special delight was the unfolding saga of the Suzukis, and he eagerly awaited the sword's continuing telling of this story.

So he was prepared when, again, he felt compelled to take pencil in hand and write the words being dictated to him by his psychic mentor.

Lord Tomishiki, at age eighteen, had become the head of one of Japan's most powerful and influential families. To him fell the obligation to join the other nobles in Kamakura sitting on the *Roju*, determining what actions need be taken in the running of his great country. With that high privilege came also the duty to financially support the *Shogun*, and he both collected taxes and paid taxes. His own staff gathered the bushels of rice that were each village's tax payment, and after keeping for their master the amount he was credited for his noble position, they transported the remainder under heavy guard to the *shogun's* warehouses in Osaka, Kyoto, Kamakura and Edo.

With My Lord's armies ensuring peace and tranquility in the many villages on his lands, the farmers were able to harvest abundant crops of rice, cabbages, soy beans and all the variety of marketable vegetables and fruits that grew so well in this region. Consequently, before Lord Tomishiki entered his second decade he was already well established as a man of wealth, and immersed himself in the many functions that befit a young noble.

His own personal pleasures were served by periodic travels to his favorite temples; several of these were nearby and could be visited frequently, and others were found only on Shikoku and whose visits were a part of his annual winter respite at the family compound in Tojo.

One of his most preferred local temples was *Kinkaku-ji*, the Temple of the Golden Pavilion. This three storied, pagoda-shaped, building is situated on *Kyoko-chi*, the Mirror Pond. The Pond is named thusly because its waters are so calm and still they reflect images as though from a polished glass. From nearly any spot on the shore of *Kyoko-chi* one can observe the temple and gain from it a different perspective of both the structure, and of life itself. The more pedestrian visitors could only marvel at its simple beauty, while a learned man of My Lord's stature drew from it the inspiration for *haiku* or the *Renga*, much as his great-grandfather Lord Kiichi Suzuki had done nearly one hundred years before.

This Temple had been constructed by *Shogun* Ashikaga Yoshimitsu, the third *Shogun*. It dates to the late fourteenth century and, during *Shogun* Ashikaga's lifetime, was a part of his estate. Later, it became a Zen temple, and is used as such to this day.

My Lord often visited, and found much solace in its many facets.

Then, when ensconced in the estate at Tojo, the young Lord took it upon himself to visit many of the temples established six hundred years earlier by Kobo Daishi in honor of the great Buddha Dainichi and the many other deities. These eighty-eight temples encircle the island of Shikoku, and many are the pilgrims who trek the well-worn paths that connect them. Some number of the temples are nearby the Tojo castle, and My Lord made his offerings there frequently. During his youth, the family had made the complete circuit, visiting all eighty-eight temples one summer. Now, his busy life allowed no such time, and he contented himself with attendance at only the nearer ones in the mountains near Saijo.

These temples, numbers sixty-one through sixty-four, honor several deities, and pilgrims pray to them for different blessings. His favorite, though, had been *Koon-ji*, number sixty-one, whose patron was the Buddha Dainichi himself. It was said that couples coming to this temple were in particular need of fertility enhancement, and My Lord, though not married yet himself, sought the Buddha's blessing in advance.

As also befits a young nobleman, Lord Tomishiki found it incumbent upon his position to take a wife, and the husband of his aunt, she the daughter of his grandfather Lord Seiroku Suzuki, acted as his matchmaker.

His aunt had married well, becoming wife to the eldest son of an old family whose ranking as *Danshaku*, or Baron, would be considered below her, but nobility nonetheless. Baron Yamashita had vast land holdings near Nara, the birthplace of the Imperial family. His grounds touched on the land on which Japan's first emperor was crowned some two thousand years before. The Baron's castle grounds even housed one of the original, sacred Buddhist temples, and for this, his family was well received by devotees throughout the country.

The Baron found for My Lord a most acceptable mate in the young daughter of a politically well-placed Edo family named Ikeda. While not of nobility or wealth themselves they had managed to gain the respect and support of the *Shogun*, and were making a name for themselves as trusted counselors, emissaries and political hacks. They knew how to get a job done, and were valued for their contacts.

Thirty-three days after his twenty-first birthday, Lord Tomishiki married Lady Miki, then but eighteen. His visits to *Koon-ji* were rewarded, as they produced an heir in 1534, and had three more children in the next five years.

Their eldest son they named Shin. The two youngest boys were named Sadao and Hirohisa. Of the four children, all but the youngest were born at the summer castle.

We swords were sheathed and again placed in an honorable position within the family's Great Room. At least between the main castle in Higashi-Osaka and the *Shogun's* citadel in Kamakura, peace had settled upon the land and its peoples, and our master had no need to use us in battle throughout his lifetime.

My Lord and Lady enjoyed the peace, and devoted their lives to the upbringing of their family. The boys were schooled, as were all the Suzuki men before them, in the intellectual arts of painting and poetry as well as the arts of war. Their daughter was well trained in the traditional dance, tea ceremony and music.

Life was good for them, and in his forty-eighth year Lord Tomishiki honored his son Shin with the presentation of us, *katana* and *wakizashi*, in the ceremonial transfer of family power from father to son.

When the son was twenty-eight, My Lord passed peacefully at the Osaka castle, and my mate and I became the symbols of power for Lord Shin Suzuki, now our sixth master.

Fascinated by the telling of family life as well as the history of his ancestral homeland, the boy sat reading what he had just written. The mood of *katana* was much more peaceful during this writing than when it spoke of war and killing, and Alexander Akira was happy that his family had, at last, found peace.

He asked Hata *Sensei* about the eighty-eight temples on Shikoku when he was at the next Saturday morning class. She knew he was curious about all aspects of life in Japan, so she was no longer surprised by his questions, and no longer wondered where he came up with all the different bits of information about historical events - some of which she was even unsure.

This morning he asked particularly about Kobo Daishi, who he was and why he built all the temples. This sparked a discussion in class about the two main religions in Japan, Buddhism and Shinto. He found it very satisfying that the Japanese are very religious but it is an internal religion, a way of life to them, rather than being something "worn on their sleeves" as he had found with the Christian friends he had. Those people, he reflected, said a lot about their religion but it did not seem to really affect them or their life style. Their religion seemed to be a convenience or an obligation, but not really part of their life.

Hata *Sensei* told the class that it was common for the Japanese to make frequent visits to their favorite temples where they would pray and make donations - but where no "services" were held as in the churches here in America. Everyone else in the class, he found out, participated in Buddhist or Shinto religious ceremonies at temples in his own city, and he decided he would ask his parents if they, too, could visit a temple.

Religion, he was learning, was pervasive. It played a part in the lives of his ancestors, and was the basis for many discussions held at the monthly meetings at his grandparents' home. He was confused by much of the talk, and wondered how there could be just one God but so many different religions.

So, at the next Sunday meeting he asked, "Why are there so many religions? And why are they all so different?"

His grandfather, once a ministerial student and now an atheist, answered him.

"Frankly, Alexander, the real reason is because religion is what is in people's minds. It has very little to do with God. So there are really as many religions as there are people. When many people think alike, they form a religion and call it by a certain name. But even then, many of those people have different ideas about their religion and sometimes the religions split up when the people cannot agree on everything."

Alex always liked it when his grandfather talked to him because his grandfather explained everything in words he could understand.

"There is most likely not one religion in the world that has not split at least once. And we, all of us in this group, all have different ideas about what religion really is. But because we all share a desire to learn and are willing to ask questions, we believe that we are closer to finding the real answers than those people who believe their religion has all the answers so they don't bother to ask any questions."

"Do you think those other people don't believe in ghosts or spirits, either," he asked.

His father answered him. "People who don't ask questions, who have very closed minds, will usually only believe what is accepted. They won't make the effort to consider the possibility of other answers. So you are right: Generally speaking, most religious people will not believe in real ghosts or real spirits. And although we all know it to be true, they also do not believe in the ability of spirits to communicate with us."

"I have always found it curious," said Edward, "that religious people will believe in prayer, and will say that they believe their God is listening to them. Yet they will refuse to believe that their God, or any other spirit, can talk back to them. Their idea of God is a lot smaller, a lot more constrained, than my idea of God. To me, nothing is impossible if God wants it to be so. And this includes having ghosts and spirits all around us and having them communicate with us."

The boy found this all very satisfying, for he knew they were saying exactly what he already knew to be true. There were real spirits, and they did talk to us. At least to him!

How he wished he could tell them about his experiences with the sword, and with the writing. Certainly they would understand and not scorn him as the sword had warned him. But he said nothing about it.

Next time, he told himself, I will ask if they think the spirits can make you do things, like write. Maybe Edward knows something about this, he thought.

That evening he made sure he had written all the new information on his chronology. He was now on the second page and he wondered how many generations he would finally end up with.

LADY TOSHIKO SUZUKI

Born in 1427 as Toshiko Matsudaira
Father: Marquis Matsudaira
Related to: Minamoto Chikauji

Homes: Izumo, Edo

LORD HIROSHI SUZUKI

for whom *katana* was made.
Born in 1425
Father: somebody Suzuki
Related to: Emperors Go-
  Shirakawa, Go-Daigo & Antoku
Homes: Osaka, Edo, Tojo
Died in 1476. Buried in Tojo.
                              |
Married: 1444 |
Family: two sons, born 1448 & 1450; |
a daughter, born 1453 |
                              |
                              \|/

LADY MICHIKO SUZUKI

Born in 1452 as Michiko Takatsukasa
Father: Prince Takatsukasa
Home: Edo

LORD KIICHI SUZUKI

Second master of *katana*
Born in 1448
Father: Lord Hiroshi Suzuki
Homes: Osaka, Edo, Tojo,
  Fukuchiyama
Died in 1497. Cremated in Tojo.
                              |
Married: 1470 |
Family: twins. a daughter born 1471; |
a son born 1471, hours later. |
                              |
                              \|/

LADY MASAKO SUZUKI

Born in 1474 as Masako Tokudaiji
Father: Prince Tokudaiji
Home: Shizuoka

LORD SEIROKU SUZUKI
Third master of *katana*
Born in 1471
Father: Lord Kiichi Suzuki
Homes: Osaka, Edo, Tojo,
    Fukuchiyama
Died in 1498. Buried in Osaka.

Married: 1491
Family: two daughters and a son,
born 1492

LADY TOMIKO SUZUKI

Born in 1493 as Tomiko Mitsui
Father: Mitsui-*sama*
Home: Namazue

LORD MICHIO SUZUKI
Fourth master of *katana*
Born in 1492
Father: Lord Seiroku Suzuki
Homes: Osaka, Edo, Tojo
    Fukuchiyama
Died in 1530. Buried in Tojo.

Married: 1509
Family: a son, born 1512;
3 daughters

LADY MIKI SUZUKI

Born in 1515 as Miki Ikeda
Father: Ikeda-San
Home: Edo

LORD TOMISHIKI SUZUKI
Fifth master of *katana*
Born in 1512
Father: Lord Michio Suzuki
Homes: Osaka, Edo, Tojo
    Fukuchiyama
Died in 1562. Buried in Osaka.

Married: 1533
Family: a son, born 1534; a daughter
and sons Sadao & Hirohisa

LORD SHIN SUZUKI
Sixth master of *katana*
Born in 1534
Father: Lord Tomishiki Suzuki
Homes: Osaka, Edo, Tojo
    Fukuchiyama

XI

THE STRIFE CONTINUES

I have told you how my blade, and the blade of my mate *wakizashi*, was made of virgin steel. You must know that the blood of numerous of my masters' foes was wiped from my blade and it was always bright and shiny, as it is even now. But my hilt and my blade guard, the *tsuba*, were not so easily cleaned. Even to this day, my hilt is stained with the enemy's blood. And the *tsuba*, itself made of porous iron and inlaid with fine jewels, is now pitted and discolored from years of gory accumulation.

Katana had awoken him early on Sunday morning, compelling him to sit at his desk and write for hours. Whereas the last contact by the sword had been peaceful, this early morning episode was tense, urgent, and forceful.

Daily, each of my masters would take the *uchiko* pouch and daub it along our blades, then with a soft cloth, wipe us until the fine limestone powder had removed all traces of blood. They would apply the oil of cloves, coating our blades against the corrosive effects of moisture. Our sheaths are made of wormwood, as I have told you, so they absorb moisture from the air and keep us softly protected.

I tell you of all this because the cleaning was more than physical; it was symbolic for both master and sword. The cleansing of the blade was accompanied by the ritual cleansing of the spirit. While I have tasted much blood, I am free from the spirits of the deceased.

But for the hilt, the *tsuba*, it is not so. For imbedded in its very pores is the blood of dozens, perhaps many gross, of the slain enemy. And now, tonight, their spirits cry out to me, and I must tell you of the nightmare that was life in *Nihon* during this period.

Fortunately for my masters and each of their progeny, it was the Suzuki family custom to school the sons in the arts of battle as well as literature and music. As I have told you, the boys underwent strictly disciplined training from a very early age, often being sent to a special place for such training. Today you would call this place a military academy; but during these times it might be the home of a great warrior, or the castle of a relative, or the lower floors of the Suzuki castle itself. Here, the boys would study and practice, living with the other warriors, eating as they eat, sleeping on *tatami* as they slept. The teachers, *Sensei* as I have said, took care to ensure that the mind and spirit was as tough and disciplined as the body. When the boys returned home at age thirteen, they were men, warriors, leaders. They were worthy of the Suzuki name.

Fortunately, I say, because in the late sixteenth century, the final battles were fought to determine the perpetual rulers of our homeland, and the Suzuki families were caught up, involved, and nearly destroyed, in these battles.

I have told you of the times which led to the establishment of the Tokugawa *Shogunate*. Our master, Lord Shin Suzuki, had for some time been a member of the *Roju*. He had traveled the Tokaido Road from Higashi-Osaka to Kamakura several times each year, leaving his family at the main castle or sometimes at the southern retreat in Tojo. The meetings of his peers did not go well, and he feared for his family's safety: There was continuing talk of overthrow of the Emperor, and this talk always troubled him deeply. He was, after all, kin to the Emperor's family, and revolt against the throne could mean revolt against his position as well.

My Lord Shin Suzuki had married at age twenty-one the daughter of another noble, the Viscount Itakura. Lady Kuniko had borne My Lord three children, and by the time Lord Tomishiki presented my mate and me to Lord Shin, the older two children were already beginning their own schooling. They sometimes traveled with my master to Kamakura as Lady Kuniko's family resided in Edo, where she and the children would stay while my master was dealing with the intrigue of the court. The Viscount was a prominent *Shogunate* cabinet minister, and was a most influential nobleman.

The children, two daughters born in 1555 and 1558 and a son, Masatoshi, were bright and energetic, and it did not take much effort for them to become dedicated to the family's station in life. The boy, born in 1556, was a natural fighter, and excelled in the many arts of the warrior.

The family traveled to their retreat at Tojo as often as they could, and Lord Shin reveled in taking them to the nearby temples, just as his father Lord Tomishiki had taken him. The wooded hills, the view of *Seto Naikai* - the beautiful Inland Sea - and the sweet smelling air all contributed to their sense of peace and tranquility.

But peace and tranquility were not to be theirs for long, for tensions were mounting between the warrior leaders in Kamakura and the Emperor in Kyoto. At the ancient palace, guards had been posted in fear of an assassination attempt on the Emperor's life. His clothes and bedding were checked for the presence of *mamushi*, the poisonous snake of the mountains. His food was tasted, his water sipped, even his concubines searched for weapons. They took all precautions.

The Emperor, realizing that he could not control the situation, pacted with several of the Council members that they should fight to gain control, he would help them secretly, and they would then support him as Emperor after they were in command.

Thus was the genesis of the last great war upon our lands.

In My Lord's thirty-fourth year, a Kamakura general named Oda Nobunaga laid siege upon the palace in Kyoto. He was party to the pact, but decided that if the Emperor's position was so weak as to bargain, then he must be too weak to resist attack. Oda's vast army moved across the plains of Kanagawa and Yamanashi, across the *Akaishi-sanmyaku* Mountains of Shizuoka and along the Tokaido road towards *Biwa-ko*, Lake Biwa. It is at the southern end of *Biwa-ko*, in the majestic city of Kyoto overlooking the cascading waters of the river *Yodo-gawa*, that the Imperial Castle of the Emperor stood, well-guarded by the castles and towns of his loyal subjects.

Oda's army easily overcame all resistance in the plains and mountains and at Inuyama Castle, just 60 kilometers from the lake itself, he added yet more troops to his juggernaut. He felt invincible as he swept along the lakeshore. The Emperor's scouts feared there was no way to resist his onslaught. But Oda's troops were stopped temporarily when they reached the Omi region on the southeastern shore of *Biwa-ko*. There they waged battle against the families of the Suzukis.

At Omi, the Rokkaku House of Sasaki and their vassals, the family Mitsui, struggled brilliantly against Oda's greater force. So ferocious was the fighting and so incensed was Oda Nobunaga at the fierceness and audacity of his enemy that Oda razed the Sasaki castle in Omi and eliminated the Rokkaku House of Sasaki forever. Every man, woman, child, maid and servant was killed. To this day, there is nothing that remains of their once mighty fortress, and the town of Kannonji itself was destroyed totally. Then, the castle of Mitsui at Namazue was similarly razed. But because they were but vassals of Sasaki their lives were spared, although they were forced to depart this area close to the Emperor's castle and move towards the coast.

My Lord, fearing that so great an army as Oda Nobunaga's would devastate the entire area, sent emissaries to meet with the general. Lord Shin proposed that, in return for Oda's sparing our family castle, our towns and their inhabitants, the Suzukis would not enter into the battle on the side of the Emperor. This was quickly agreed to, as even Oda-*san* did not want to incur the wrath of the Suzuki family and its wealthy and widespread relatives. General Oda had wanted our armies to join his, but his cunning told him that the political value of having the Suzuki family abstain from opposing his battles was of more value than the addition of our armies to his campaign. For cunning as he was, he also feared the cunning of others, and feared greatly that our warriors, once privy to his battle plans, would side with nobility and fight against him.

Secretly, though, My Lord sent a small contingent of his most trusted samurai to the Emperor's castle. Disguising the Emperor as a Shinto priest, and dressing themselves as pilgrims, they quietly departed Kyoto for the temple at *Kinkaku-ji*. As you know, this temple had long been a favorite retreat of My Lord's family, and the Emperor remained in seclusion there for some time.

It was not at all unusual for an emperor to travel in disguise, and My Lord, being a patron of the arts, had read of a similar trick played by his ancestor, Emperor Go-Shirakawa, some four centuries before. While it was true that Oda had amassed a great army about him, it was equally true that he was not of the same class as my master, and was not a literate man as was my master. Perhaps a more intellectual leader would have suspected such a ruse, but not Oda. Thus, My Lord's plan worked to perfection and the forces of Oda were able to level the castle, but could not kill the emperor.

Young Akira was in awe as much by this intrigue as he had earlier been of the descriptions of the battles themselves. Surely, he reasoned, one had to be strong of body and quick of mind to stay in power in those times. He wondered how he and his family would have fared then. Could they have been strong enough to run the miles or fight the battles or climb the castle walls; could they have outwitted their enemies?

But he had no time to dwell on this, for the sword soon had his hand again moving across the page in its desperate need to tell of the impending ravage of the land the boy had come to think of as home.

General Oda's forces then took control of the central area of *Nihon* as bounded to the northeast by Edo and Kamakura, and to the southwest by Kyoto and Osaka. Over the next several years, they fought battles to the north of Edo and to the south of Osaka, extending their dominion over the mainland island of Honshu.

Five years after seizing Kyoto, Oda's control was completed as the rule of the *Ashikaga Shogunate* was ended. He was now firmly in control of the main areas of wealth and commerce. Only the outlying areas - Hokkaido Island to the far north and Shikoku Island to the southwest - were not under his direct control. However, he spent little effort on conquering these two areas since Hokkaido offered him little but the denigrated *Ainu* peoples and Shikoku was overseen by the forces of the Suzukis whom he believed to be loyal to his cause.

The one remaining island, Kyushu, to the far southwest, was home to numerous rival bands of warriors. Many were the castles of his enemies there. He was not prepared to travel that far south to do battle, and they had many hundreds of miles to traverse if they wanted to dislodge his armies from their entrenched holdings. There was time, he knew, to wage battle against the anarchists in Nagasaki, or Fukuoka, or Kitakyushu, or Miyazaki. There was much time. But first he had to deal with one last rebel.

In 1575 Oda's army met the army of Takeda Katsuyori on the plains of *Nagashino*. In a bloody battle lasting ten straight days the tide of battle swung back and forth; General Oda's army was vast and well equipped, but Katsuyori's force was determined to take control and make him the new *Shogun*. Then, when it almost seemed Katsuyori might prevail, they were surprised and overwhelmed by fusiliers using secretly imported muskets. For the first time in the history of the country, a battle was fought and won using weapons not of Japanese origin. Thousands of Katsuyori's valiant samurai were slain by the musket shots. Neither their armor nor their tactics were prepared for the deadly fusillade.

My Lord, upon hearing of the defeat of the Katsuyori army, knew that the supremacy of the samurai bearing the traditional *katana* and *wakizashi* was coming to an end quickly.

Now, he feared for the life of his only son Masatoshi, just nineteen, and his grandson Satoru. He could not prepare them for the changes they would experience, for he had not lived his life fearing the unseen lead ball that could pierce his breastplate or pass through his charge's chain coating. Surely Satoru, still just an infant, would learn the new techniques and would have a chance of surviving a battle in which the arquebus was used. But what of Masatoshi? Was he already too set in his ways to adapt? Was this new instrument of death to be the end of his family line?

It was with a heavy heart that My Lord Shin visited with General Oda Nobunaga at his new castle in Azuchi on the southeastern shore of *Biwa-ko*. He knew that he must pledge his family's support of the revolution that was taking place in order to ensure the longevity of his son and grandson. The General proudly showed him the great fortress, just completed in 1576. Its parapets had not only the usual racks for his archer's arrows but also bins for black powder and musket balls. It had the best equipped armaments that My Lord had seen. Even the emperor's castle itself or the other castles near Kyoto, owned by various lords, barons, counts and viscounts, were not so well designed for today's type of warfare.

With my mate and me strapped to his side, Lord Shin Suzuki now went a step further than he had just eight short years ago: Then, he had merely agreed to not oppose Oda; now, he agreed to fight alongside him.

They discussed at length the menace from Kyushu. Lord Shin reminded General Oda that some time before our family had fought against marauders from the southern island of Kyushu, and since then we had posted a guard at our castle in Tojo. Our samurai maintained watch along the coast of *Seto Naikai* from Naruto to the east to Misaki to the far west. We were prepared, he said, to control our territory.

"In fact," he elaborated, "the Suzuki patrols not only watch for invaders from the neighboring island but from across the sea, as well. We must remember that it has not been too long since the barbarians encroached our shores, and there are signs that they will do so again, and soon."

"I have commissioned my son, Masatoshi, to captain the guard in Tojo. He and his family already make their home in our summer castle there. Should there be trouble for us or for our great cause, our samurai are prepared to do battle."

The General knew that this was so, for the stories of the Suzuki warriors and their dedication to the family name were well known amongst the nobility of Japan. And while General Oda was not nobility himself he had been associated with the ruling class for long enough that he often felt himself to be one of them.

So we formalized our pact with the anarchists - those whose mission it was to overturn the emperor's control of our country, whose mission, it seemed, was to keep our land in constant war and upheaval. And now, we were a willing part of it all.

With his heart still heavy, Lord Shin traveled the short distance from Azuchi to Higashi-Osaka. Saddened as he was with the peace he had made with General Oda, he took his wife and youngest daughter to the new retreat he was having built in Karuizawa in the mountains of Nagano prefecture. Here, the emperor and many other nobles had built a peaceful village. In spring the mountainsides were covered with blossoms; in fall, the leaves turned color and dazzled one's eyes with a palette of orange and brown. But in winter, the deep snow and crisp, clean air had a calming effect on all the inhabitants; no one wanted to venture outside to sully the smooth, white surface nor make a sound that would shatter the quiet.

It took them several weeks to make the trek, first along the Tokaido road to Edo, then north to Takasaki, then westerly up into the mountains. Within a short distance of the village were three peaks ranging from just under three thousand feet to nearly eight thousand. Karuizawa sat nestled in a valley amongst the three, shielded, secluded and safe.

They arrived in fall and planned to spend just the winter there. Once the snow fell, they knew, few travelers would be making their way up the mountains and they would be virtually cut off from the strife that would surely continue in the lower lands. But this is just what My Lord and Lady wanted: Peace, quiet, solitude.

Their eighteen-year-old daughter Goto was not inclined to complain about spending the winter in deep snow and frigid air, hoping her parents would think better of their plan after several weeks there. But this did not happen. Instead, the family stayed in the village for two years, leaving just in time to arrive back at the family compound in early January for the celebration of Goto's coming of age.

The *Seijin-Shiki* festival, celebrated in mid-January for centuries, announces to the country that a young woman or young man is now an adult, and at this time, many families announce the betrothal of their offspring. Marriages long in the planning are now made public. For those youths for whom no plans have already been made, parents and *nakodo*, the matchmakers, alike begin the active search for an appropriate mate.

Lord Shin's oldest daughter had married before reaching her twentieth year, as had the boy Masatoshi. His marriage had been arranged by his grandmother, Makoto Suzuki-*sama*. Knowing that the royal classes were in danger of losing their power and respect, Makoto-*sama* had wanted to ensure that the Suzuki family name would be forever associated with another *Shogun*-class family. Through the services of a *nakodo*, they wed Masatoshi in his nineteenth year to the twenty-two year old daughter of Lord Nagata, Haruko-*san*.

The Nagata family was one of three, along with the Suzukis, that were recognized as ruling class, often referred to as *Kishu no gosanke*. This means "The Three Noble Families of Kishu." Kishu is the general area around Nara and Ise wherein lies the fount of Japanese civilization, as I have said before. These three families were believed to be descended from earliest times and were revered above all others, excepting only the emperor's family. You can readily see how this noble designation helped our family again and again.

Before the death of Makoto-*sama* at age sixty-one, Masatoshi and Haruko had had a son, born in 1575, and a daughter, whom they named Satoru and Nanami, respectively. After the death of the elder Suzuki, the couple had another two sons.

The family and all its possessions were in grave danger, for the political climate in our country was deteriorating fast. As had happened in the prior centuries, the country was again on the brink of civil war. Shin Suzuki, now the leader of our clan, was in failing health. His had been a life of stress and conflict. He had drawn his weapons, *wakizashi* and myself, on many occasions, in defense of his class and his country. Though still in his middle years, he knew his time was limited, and he made preparations for the transfer of the family mantle of power to his son, Masatoshi.

The boy had been writing now for several hours. *Katana* had not taken a break in relating this story, seemingly compelled to tell all. Now, in exhaustion, young Alexander Akira dropped his head down on the desk and slept fitfully. Visions of battles and palace intrigue played tag in his mind.

He was awakened by the pulsating in his arm. Apparently he had been sleeping with his one arm curled up on the desk and his head resting on that arm; now, the arm was asleep and the blood was throbbing. He decided to reread what he had just written before making his notes on the family genealogy. And he pledged to ask Hata *Sensei* if there ever was a General Oda Nobunaga. For while he believed every word *katana* had told him, he was enough of a skeptic to always want to get verification of all he was told.

Many questions and thoughts bounced through his head as he read through this amazing tale: Who lived in the other homes when the family was not in them? Were there servants at all the castles and houses all the time? Did they have locks on the doors? Are all the houses and castles still there, and if I went there could I still see them?

He thought about the one house his own family lived in. It had furniture and clothing. Now, if they had a second house, it would need furniture and clothing, he was certain, because they would not want to move everything they owned from house to house every time they went from one to another. But the Suzukis had at least five homes that he knew of: the three castles in Osaka, Tojo and Fukuchiyama; and the two homes in Edo and Karuizawa. How much it must have cost to have clothing and furniture in all these places at the same time!

Finally, tired and sleepy, he took out the pages on which he was keeping track of the family's history, and made all the necessary entries based on what had been revealed to him during this session.

When he was finished, he now had three sheets that looked like this:

LADY TOSHIKO SUZUKI

Born in 1427 as Toshiko Matsudaira
Father: Marquis Matsudaira
Related to: Minamoto Chikauji

Homes: Izumo, Edo

LORD HIROSHI SUZUKI

for whom *katana* was made.
Born in 1425
Father: somebody Suzuki
Related to: Emperors Go-
 Shirakawa, Go-Daigo & Antoku
Homes: Osaka, Edo, Tojo
Died in 1476. Buried in Tojo.

Married: 1444
Family: two sons, born 1448 & 1450;
a daughter, born 1453

LADY MICHIKO SUZUKI

Born in 1452 as Michiko Takatsukasa
Father: Prince Takatsukasa
Home: Edo

LORD KIICHI SUZUKI

Second master of *katana*
Born in 1448
Father: Lord Hiroshi Suzuki
Homes: Osaka, Edo, Tojo,
 Fukuchiyama
Died in 1497. Cremated in Tojo.

Married: 1470
Family: twins. a daughter born 1471;
a son born 1471, hours later.

LADY MASAKO SUZUKI

Born in 1474 as Masako Tokudaiji
Father: Prince Tokudaiji
Home: Shizuoka

LORD SEIROKU SUZUKI

Third master of *katana*
Born in 1471
Father: Lord Kiichi Suzuki
Homes: Osaka, Edo, Tojo,
    Fukuchiyama
Died in 1498. Buried in Osaka.

Married: 1491
Family: two daughters and a son, born 1492

LADY TOMIKO SUZUKI

Born in 1493 as Tomiko Mitsui
Father: Mitsui-*sama*
Home: Namazue

LORD MICHIO SUZUKI

Fourth master of *katana*
Born in 1492
Father: Lord Seiroku Suzuki
Homes: Osaka, Edo, Tojo
    Fukuchiyama
Died in 1530. Buried in Tojo.

Married: 1509
Family: a son, born 1512; 3 daughters

LADY MIKI SUZUKI

Born in 1515 as Miki Ikeda
Father: Ikeda-San
Home: Edo

LORD TOMISHIKI SUZUKI

Fifth master of *katana*
Born in 1512
Father: Lord Michio Suzuki
Homes: Osaka, Edo, Tojo
    Fukuchiyama
Died in 1562. Buried in Osaka.

Married: 1533
Family: a son, born 1534; a daughter
and sons Sadao & Hirohisa

\|/

LADY KUNIKO SUZUKI

Born as Kuniko Itakura
Father: Viscount Itakura
Home: Edo

LORD SHIN SUZUKI

Sixth master of *katana*
Born in 1534
Father: Lord Tomishiki Suzuki
Homes: Osaka, Edo, Tojo
    Fukuchiyama, Karuizawa Died ?

Married: 1555
Family: daughter born 1555 & daughter
Goto in 1558 a son Masatoshi born 1556

\|/

HARUKO SUZUKI

Born in 1553 as Haruko Nagata
Father: Lord Nagata
Home: Kishu area

MASATOSHI SUZUKI

Born in 1556
Father: Lord Shin Suzuki
Homes: Osaka, Edo, Tojo
    Fukuchiyama, Karuizawa

Married: 1575
Family: son Satoru born 1575, daughter
Nanami born 1576, two more sons

XII

CROSSED LINES:
A WEB, OR A NET?

It had been a fitful night of unrest for young Alexander Akira. Bloody visions of ancient battles had filled his dreams, and voices, seemingly coming from outside his bedroom, mixed in his dream-state with these terrible scenes to produce in him a panicky, apprehensive state as he struggled to awaken. This was the worst night of sleep he had ever had, he thought, as he slowly opened first one eye, then another. Carefully moving only his eyes, but not his head, he looked around to get his bearings. To make sure that all that he had dreamt and all that he had heard were, in fact, just dreams and nothing more, he tried to slow down his racing heart.

But slowly, as he began to actually hear the voices coming from outside his room, he realized that all was not right, that something terrible had happened, and that there was violence and death and suffering not just in the story he was learning from *katana*, but right here in his own home.

The voices he heard were that of his grandparents and his parents; crying voices, quiet sobbing voices; questioning voices that never received a reply. Quickly his mind jumped gears and reminded him that questions like this were called rhetorical and did not expect a reply. "How silly," he thought, "for me to be analyzing the type of question I hear. Am I turning into an English teacher?"

As he slowly padded down the hallway, his pajama bottoms swishing in tempo with his slippers, the voices became more distinct, and his stomach quickly turned to knots as he heard the words: "she was only twenty-seven;" "how could this happen to our daughter?" "she was over for her birthday dinner just two weeks ago;" "how will we live through this?"

He knew they were talking about his aunt Kristina. She was his favorite aunt and they had spent a lot of time together, doing crossword puzzles, playing games. Their favorite game together was Scrabble. He loved learning new words and she was such a good player because she did the crossword puzzles. It helped her in her work, she had told him, to expand her vocabulary and he had tried hard to emulate her. "An expanding vocabulary," she had said, "is like the door to the universe; it just keeps growing, feeding on itself. You will never regret the time you take to learn your language."

But what could have happened? Was she dead? He had never seen a dead person; well, not in real life. He'd seen plenty of corpses - the dying wounded, the amputees and gorily disfigured - in the stories shown to him by *katana*. But a real person, his aunt, dead? The thought turned his skin ashen, his breathing shallow, his heart racing.

At the living room entry he paused, unsure if he should enter, afraid that if he spoke to them he'd learn the awful truth: that his aunt was, in fact, dead.

"I heard voices," he said to no one in particular. He saw his grandparents and his parents, all sitting together, sadness etched on their faces, and he knew, without asking, that his fear was true. "She's dead?" he asked, again to no one in particular. "What happened?"

At that, his grandfather – *ji-san* – motioned for Alex to come over to him, where he held Alex close and said softly, "She was riding a motorcycle and had an accident and was killed. Others who saw the accident said they think she did not suffer. Now, *ba-san* and I have to put our baby to rest."

Alex was suddenly overwhelmed with an incredible sadness, and without knowing what to call the feeling, he felt very empty inside, as though his body had been turned inside out and all the insides had evaporated. "I'm very sad," he said, again to nobody in particular.

His grandmother – 'ba-san – told him that they had to go make arrangements for her funeral and that he should try to remember the special times he had with his aunt, for she had loved him very much.

That night, as he again slept fitfully, he felt compelled to awaken, hold the *katana*, and write on his tablet.

The sadness you feel, the emptiness that permeates your heart, has been felt by all who have preceded you. The families of every soldier who has died in battle have experienced these feelings; the parents of every child who died an early death have gone through this. One cannot truly live and appreciate life until one has suffered a loss such as yours. The deeper your pain, the more you have room in your heart for love, and joy, and thanks for your life, for of such travail is the glory of your life made.

Now I will tell you of a strange coincidence so you can learn that all you do in your life and all you experience in your heart has gone before you. Remember your ancient ancestor who, when he was but fifty-one years, lost his daughter in a riding accident, and he grieved so greatly that he himself soon expired? His daughter was but twenty-seven when she fell from her horse and left her family in tears. Your 'ji-san is but fifty-one and your aunt had just turned twenty-seven when she fell from her mount and expired. Such is the ongoing evolution and revolution in life, and you may see this again and again as you grow older. But you will be stronger for it. You will be braver for it. You will be more compassionate and empathetic for it. And that is the measure of a man.

These were strange words to young Alex, and he tried to make sense of them. He well knew that *katana* had always taught him well and he wanted to understand this lesson, as painful as it was to him. He wished he could learn this lesson about pain and emptiness without having to lose his aunt.

The following morning Alex resolved to be as strong as he could possibly be, and to try to be the best kind of man he could ever become. He knew that he would miss his aunt, yet he felt some comfort that *katana* was going to be with him, helping him and guiding him.

When young Alexander Akira asked Hata *Sensei* about Oda Nobunaga after the next Saturday morning class, he was delighted - and maybe just a tiny bit smugly satisfied - that she told him all about the fierce battles of the sixteenth century in Japan. General Oda Nobunaga was a major figure in the country's history all during that time, she affirmed.

"What have you been reading, Akira-*kun*, to have learned the name of Oda-*san*," she asked him. While no longer at all surprised by his questioning she was ever curious about his sources of information and still incredulous that this youngster was becoming a walking encyclopedia of Japanese history.

"Oh," he tried to avoid a direct answer, "my grandma tells me things and I just wanted to know more about him." Now, he thought, he had to ask about the sword of Asano, too. The story they had read did not say anything about the sword, the family, what happened to Asano's wife and children, or anything else. Did anyone know about these things?

"Hata, *Sensei*, do you have any more stories about Lord Asano and what happened to his family after his death?" His curiosity and impatience was getting the best of him, and although he knew that he must be very careful about asking questions so no one would get suspicious, he nonetheless pressed forward. "I've been wondering: Did he leave his castle to his wife? Did he have any children? What happened to them? And where did the sword go? I mean, did the *Shogun* take it for himself or did someone give it to his wife, like they give a folded flag to the wife of one of the soldiers today?"

"Those are all very good questions, Akira-*kun*. I can only tell you that I know no more about what happened than you do, for I have only read the same story that you and the class have read. Perhaps you should ask your grandmother if she has any other information about this. In the meantime, I will try to find out anything more that I can. Does that sound all right?" She was always very understanding and helpful, and never once had she made fun of his curiosity nor had she taken offense at his incessant questioning.

Perhaps *katana* felt his urgency, for that very evening it spoke to him again.

Much time has elapsed, and much has happened to my Lord Shin and his family since I last communicated. Now in failing health, My Lord and his family returned to the Higashi-Osaka castle from Karuizawa in the year 1578. His eldest son Masatoshi had lived with his wife and children in the compound in Tojo since three years prior, leaving the main castle in the care of junior members of the family and their retainers.

My Lord Shin thereupon traveled with his wife Kuniko to the castle in Tojo, overlooking the beautiful *Seto Naikai,* to see for the final time the temples of Shikoku. They completed but half of the eighty-eight temples when he expired, a man filled with happiness and peace at the life he had led. But he had a foreknowledge that this was to be his final pilgrimage, and in a ceremony at the Tojo compound, Lord Shin handed me and my mate to his son, Masatoshi.

Lady Kuniko had him cremated and his ashes spread about the castle's grounds, in keeping with his wishes. His happiness was heightened by having his grandson Satoru – the boy was but nine - on this pilgrimage, introducing him to the many mysteries of these sacred places. The boy, who adored and respected his *Ojisan,* was comforted by the knowledge that he had been with his grandfather during his final days.

The boy's father, Masatoshi, had no time for such travels, as raiders from the southern island of Kyushu were encroaching onto Shikoku, and, along with warriors from the Hisamatsu family of the West Castle of Matsuyama, he and his army were in a constant state of war. These battles with insurgents were to continue for a total of twenty-one long, difficult, years, during which time Lord Masatoshi had little time for family matters.

The country, wracked by ongoing battles, saw great armies fighting back and forth for control. It was during these long years of war that Masatoshi and his armies also joined forces with those of Naganao Asano and Tadaoki Hosokawa in the Battle of Sekigahara, fought on the plains near *Biwa-ko* in the year 1600. This battle saw the great warlord

Tokugawa Ieyasu, successor to the preeminent daimyo, warrior, general and politician Toyotomi Hideyoshi who expired in 1598, attain a final victory, for which he had given the title *Tozama*, "Outer Daimyo," to the Lord of the Asano clan.

To the head of another great warrior clan, the Hosokawas of Kyushu, Ieyasu, as he was known, bestowed the title of *Daimyo*, for helping to secure the island of Kyushu. It was this great Lord, Hosokawa, who had begun, along with Kiyomasa, the building of the Kumamoto castle on the western shore of the island.

But Ieyasu, remembering that we Suzukis had fought on the "wrong" side during the Gempei war some 300 years early, decreed that our illustrious family name should not bear the title Daimyo.

Our family connection, though, to the Hosokawas had been cemented by the marriage, in 1596, of Masatoshi's daughter Nanami, at age twenty, to young Tsutomo Hosokawa who was two years her senior. Masatoshi, before he had become my Lord, had therefore tied our family's future to the Hosokawa clan as part of the effort to bring them into the Hideyoshi side of this ongoing battle. And it was to be that, during that great battle of Sekigahara, in 1600, Lord Masatoshi carried us in battle alongside the leader of the Hosokawas, Tadaoki, who was now his daughter Nanami's father-in-law.

The Hosokawa clan, you should know, were fierce warriors and had married into some of the best-known families of the country. The marriage of Nanami and Tsutomo, then, was very much a strategic marriage for both families. During the construction of the great castle at Kumamoto, the Hosokawas lived in their smaller castle at Ogura. Tadaoki also entreated Tsutomo and Nanami to live in the new castle at Kumamoto, and upon his death, no Hosokawas were to ever reside again in Ogura Castle

So great was this Battle of Sekigahara, that Japan's most famous swordsman, Minamoto Musashi, was a warrior on the opposing Ashikaga side from my Lord Masatoshi, and, although they did not engage each other during this battle, all of Japan had family members who were involved in this bloodiest of conflicts.

It was the general Tokugawa Ieyasu, who years earlier had fought alongside the great leader Oda Nobunaga, and who attained the victory at Sekigahara, thereupon established the Tokugawa Shogunate, which was to rule all of Japan for two more centuries. Lord Masatoshi had aligned our family on the winning side, and due to that fact, we continued to prosper.

So it was that many years later, after this most famous battle, Satoru, himself a pacifist, entertained Musashi and discussed his well-known feats during that three-day conflict, where Musashi, though just a young man of sixteen, had made such a name for himself. Satoru was interested since his younger brother, Shuji, had died at age 23 while fighting alongside his father, Masatoshi, in that battle. Of particular interest to Satoru was Musashi's most famous swordfight against Tadaoki Hosokawa's retainer Kojiro Sasaki at the Hosokawa castle at Ogura in 1612, wherein Musashi engaged the swordsman with an oar and used it to kill his completely befuddled opponent. The Musashi name is now the most famous of all Japanese swordsmen.

During Lord Masatoshi's lifetime, he saw not only his daughter Nanami's marriage, but also that of his oldest son Satoru's marriage to the eighteen-year-old Takako Arai, the scion of another of Japan's noble families, in 1595. My Lord Masatoshi was the father of yet another child, a son born in 1579 who died as a youngster.

As you can imagine, Lord Masatoshi did not pass along his family *katana* and *wakizashi* to his first son, Satoru, due to the pacifism of the younger man. When he died in 1604, my mate and I were in the hands of his widow, Lady Haruko.

Our Lord's second born, the boy Shuji, died on the field of battle at Sekigahara in 1600, fighting alongside the Ako clan leader, Naganao Asano, who carried the lifeless body of the twenty-three year old Suzuki to where our Lord's men were encamped, and helped lay him to rest on that bloody plain.

The Suzuki lineage was hurt severely by the death of Shuji, as our Lord's third son had died as an infant in 1579.

It was a nearly lifeless young Alexander Akira who read over all that he had written and tried to make sense of the great battle, as *katana* had called it. So many men had died, he thought, but for what? Was anything gained by all of those deaths? He silently wept for his ancestors who had suffered for so many years of conflict.

And then he had yet another thought, for he knew that countries were still at war – he heard the news on television. Battles and wars and blood and death, he thought, and it never seems to end.

But he did not have much time for reflection, for *katana* urged him to continue the story of this remarkable era.

In the year 1616, Tokugawa Ieyasu expired and due to his efforts, the country had been experiencing relative peace at long last. My Lord, Masatoshi, had been gone for a dozen years and my mate and I had been kept in a place of quiet reverence by Lady Haruko. We were thankful for the peace and tranquility that had descended upon the house of Suzuki, yet what was to become of us now? Satoru had had just one child, a son, Masaharu, who was born in 1599.

So it was that the end of May, 1616, saw the Suzuki family – matron Haruko, father Satoru and mother Takako and the young man Masaharu - embark on a journey to the castle in Osaka for the marriage of Masaharu to the young Lady Noriko Matsudaira of the Osaka Matsudaira clan. She was at the time three years the junior of Masaharu. The Matsudaira family had intermarried with the Suzukis previously – all on this journey recalled that Lord Hiroshi Suzuki had married Toshiko Matsudaira back in the middle of the fifteenth century.

After the wedding and the grandiose socializing between these two families, and in high spirits, then, Lord Satoru and his family departed on June 1, 1616, across the Seto Naikai for their home castle in Tojo. Lord Satoru was dressed in his finest ornamental armor and stood proud-ly at the bow of the ship taking the family home, when a sudden storm swamped the ship.

The crew was able to save all the Suzuki family members but Satoru who, weighted by his armor, sank quickly and was lost. Another boat was nearby and retrieved the grieving family from the waters. Upon concluding their journey and arriving home, they learned of the death of Tokugawa Ieyasu on the same day that had claimed Satoru, and pondered the irony: That a peaceful man such as Satoru should die in a violent storm, but a man who had waged war for most of his seventy-three years should die peacefully in his sleep.

Young Alexander was simply too tired to continue; his fingers hurt from holding the pencil in hand; his eyes hurt from looking at all the words he had written on his tablet pages; and his head hurt from thinking about all the devastation that *katana* had described to him. As much as he enjoyed hearing about all that *katana* had told him, he was sleepy and ready for bed. Yet, once again, *katana* was not yet finished.

This chapter of the story of my mate and me cannot be completed without a final word about the family that Satoru left behind. His son, Masaharu, was expected to carry on the family traditions and the family honor, even without having my mate and me at his side.

Keeping the Suzuki family tradition of incorporating ancestor's names in the name of a child, Satoru and Takako used the kanji of "Masa" from Masaharu's grandfather Masatoshi's name, and used the "haru" kanji from his grandmother Haruko's name. Thus were the families of Suzuki and Nagata honored in the naming of young Masaharu at his birth in 1599.

After his marriage to Lady Noriko, Masaharu moved into the family's castle in Osaka. That castle, you should know, had been lived in by various family members for some time, beginning with Sadao, who was the son of Lord Tomishiki Suzuki and younger brother to Lord Shin Suzuki. When Sadao died in 1594 at age 58 leaving no sons, his younger brother Hirohisa occupied the great family castle in Osaka, from 1594 until 1602, when he too expired. But Hirohisa had a son, Chonan, who then lived in the castle until 1616, when young Masaharu and his new bride became the rightful residents of that family estate. Their son, Masanobu, was born the fourth year after Lord Satoru's untimely death.

With the blessing the Matron Haruko, my mate and I were present-ed to the young Masaharu when the family next gathered at the estate in Tojo, where we had been kept for the years since the death of Lord Masatoshi.

Young Alexander was nodding off as he wrote this intriguing story that *katana* had just related to him.

Before closing his eyes, though, he completed the information he had learned about these families and their complex relationship.

LADY TOSHIKO SUZUKI

Born in 1427 as Toshiko Matsudaira
Father: Marquis Matsudaira
Related to: Minamoto Chikauji

Homes: Izumo, Edo

LORD HIROSHI SUZUKI
for whom *katana* was made.
Born in 1425
Father: somebody Suzuki
Related to: Emperors Go-
    Shirakawa, Go-Daigo & Antoku
Homes: Osaka, Edo, Tojo
Died in 1476. Buried in Tojo.

Married: 1444
Family: two sons, born 1448 & 1450;
a daughter, born 1453

\|/

LADY MICHIKO SUZUKI

Born in 1452 as Michiko Takatsukasa
Father: Prince Takatsukasa
Home: Edo

LORD KIICHI SUZUKI
Second master of *katana*
Born in 1448
Father: Lord Hiroshi Suzuki
Homes: Osaka, Edo, Tojo,
    Fukuchiyama
Died in 1497. Cremated in Tojo.

Married: 1470
Family: twins. a daughter born 1471;
a son born 1471, hours later.

\|/

LADY MASAKO SUZUKI

Born in 1474 as Masako Tokudaiji
Father: Prince Tokudaiji
Home: Shizuoka

LORD SEIROKU SUZUKI
Third master of *katana*
Born in 1471
Father: Lord Kiichi Suzuki
Homes: Osaka, Edo, Tojo,
    Fukuchiyama
Died in 1498. Buried in Osaka.

Married: 1491
Family: two daughters and a son, born 1492

LADY TOMIKO SUZUKI

Born in 1493 as Tomiko Mitsui
Father: Mitsui-*sama*
Home: Namazue

LORD MICHIO SUZUKI
Fourth master of *katana*
Born in 1492
Father: Lord Seiroku Suzuki
Homes: Osaka, Edo, Tojo
    Fukuchiyama
Died in 1530. Buried in Tojo.

Married: 1509
Family: a son, born 1512;
3 daughters

LADY MIKI SUZUKI

Born in 1515 as Miki Ikeda
Father: Ikeda-San
Home: Edo

LORD TOMISHIKI SUZUKI
Fifth master of *katana*
Born in 1512
Father: Lord Michio Suzuki
Homes: Osaka, Edo, Tojo
    Fukuchiyama
Died in 1562. Buried in Osaka.

Married: 1533
Family: a son, born 1534; a daughter
and sons Sadao & Hirohisa

\|/

LADY KUNIKO SUZUKI

Born as Kuniko Itakura
Father: Viscount Itakura
Home: Edo

LORD SHIN SUZUKI

Sixth master of *katana*
Born in 1534
Father: Lord Tomishiki Suzuki
Homes: Osaka, Edo, Tojo
Fukuchiyama, Karuizawa Died ?

Married: 1555
Family: daughter born 1555 & Goto in 1558
a son Masatoshi born 1556

\|/

HARUKO SUZUKI

Born in 1553 as Haruko Nagata
Father: Lord Nagata
Home: Kishu area

LORD MASATOSHI SUZUKI

Seventh master of *katana*
Born in 1556
Father: Lord Shin Suzuki
Homes: Osaka, Edo, Tojo
Fukuchiyama, Karuizawa

Married: 1575
Family: son Satoru born 1575, daughter
Nanami born 1576, son Shuji born 1577
Died 1600 at Sekigahara, son born
1579 died as a child

TAKAKO SUZUKI   **SATORU SUZUKI**
                                           Born as Takako Arai
Born in 1577   Born in 1575
                                           Died 1616

Family: son Masaharu born 1599

NORIKO SUZUKI   **LORD MASAHARU SUZUKI**
Born as Noriko Matsudaira   Eighth master of *katana*
Born in 1602   Born in 1599

Married: in Osaka, 1616; son Masanobu born 1620

XIII

MOVING ON

During the week following his aunt's death, young Alexander Akira was an active participant in the memorial service and the last of meeting of the Sunday discussion group. His *'ba-san* – he had decided to try to use the more grown-up term for his grandmother and grandfather as consistently as possible - and *'ji-san* had invited to the memorial all of aunt Kristina's coworkers, her school friends, and of course, all the folks in the discussion group.

He was happy to see all these people, some of whom he had never met before, but was, of course, heartbroken at the necessity for the service.

His grandparents, in keeping with his aunt's wishes, had had her cremated and his father had made a lovely container in which to keep her urn. They planned to place that container on a shelf in their family room alongside the urn containing the ashes of their family friend from India, Srini Srinivasan.

And then, on the Sunday following the memorial, the group of friends gathered once again in his grandparents' living room for the last time until ... well, no one knew just when. His *'ba-san* had called it a 'hiatus', and said that that means they are taking a break for a while. He knew he would miss the wonderful conversations he had heard and the wise and helpful counsel of this group of people, but he also felt that a break might do them all some good.

His sessions with *katana* had taken a brief hiatus during this busy and emotional week, as well, and Alex was happy to feel the need to secretly hold the sword, take up his pencil and paper and prepare for more of the story from *katana*.

As you have been told previously, the great leader, Tokugawa Ieyasu, had gained an important victory in the Battle of Sekigahara. By defeating the combined forces of his enemies, he now had the opportunity to unify Japan for the first time in its history. This was a victory for the people of Japan, and in particular, for the family of Matsudaira.

At the time of the battle, there were over fifty branches of this old and noble family. General Ieyasu decreed that, should he become *Shogun* – the military leader of the nation – he would consolidate these disparate families into just twenty-seven major clans. And, why was he so concerned about this particular family? Because he was, himself, of the Matsudaira clan.

Once he took upon himself and his lineage the mantle of *Shogun*, he moved his headquarters to Edo, and began construction of his new castle there. The Matsudaira family had owned for some generations a large park not far from where the castle was being built, and he had a temple built in that park to honor his victory.

The temple he named *Sengaku-ji*, and in the year 1612 it was completed.

Shortly after the completion of *Sengaku-ji*, in 1614, the *Shogun* Ieyasu summoned our Lord Satoru to meet with him. Although, as you have been told, Satoru was a peaceful man, and had not carried my mate and me into battle, he was the leader of the powerful Suzuki clan, and the *Shogun* had an important message to deliver.

When they met at the smaller retreat in Kamakura, on the water's edge of Edo-*wan*, the Great Lord bowed low to Satoru, and in a loud voice for all the assemblage to hear, complimented the Suzuki family for standing with him during this long and difficult period.

"We have again had to meet our enemies on the battlefield, Suzuki Satoru-*sama*," the *Shogun* said, "and we have again prevailed, this time overcoming what we can all hope will be the last samurai conflict, the

"*Osaka natsu no Jin*" – the Osaka Summer Campaign. "I did not tell you before now that I was injured by the lance of an opposing warrior in this conflict and fear that I may not have long to live. So it is important that I thank you and honor you for all you have done."

The aging *Shogun* had to pause to catch his breath before continuing. "Your father Masatoshi and his army were decisive in securing my southern flanks over the years by keeping in check the raiders from Kyushu. And on the battlefield of Sekigahara, he himself fought bravely alongside his valiant samurai. Yet I could not honor your family's participation with the title of *Daimyo*, as the Suzuki clan had been enemies to our great cause so many generations ago."

Of course, the Tokugawa *Shogun* was referring to the Suzukis fighting on the side of the Gempei some three hundred years prior.

"Since I could not honor your family in the same way I honored the other great houses which fought on my side in this recent conflict, I must tell you personally of my deepest respect for you, a peaceful man in a turbulent world, and your support of our unification effort."

"Your armies did well in holding off the samurai of Goto Mototsugu, from Kyushu, as I put down the rebellion at Osaka. And while the title of *Daimyo* would be a respectable thing for Suzukis, I tell you this: The Suzuki family is of true nobility. In the future, under the rule of the *Shogunate*, such nobility will have little meaning. So I tell you now, in person, that Japan honors you, your family and its *kamon*, and will continue to do so, even without a title."

The boy was startled at this admission by the ruler of Japan; startled that he would call the Suzuki family true nobility. Wasn't this what he had heard his father say before? That 'ba-san had come from the nobility of Japan? Now he was hearing this very same thing from *katana*!

Here was more confirmation, he thought, of the story being told by *katana*. For he had already known of his 'ba-san's family background, but none of that had meant anything to him before. He thought that he should spend more time talking with his grandmother so he could learn all he could about his "family" in Japan.

The sword was impatient to continue, and so it did.

As the *Osaka natsu no Jin* campaign would indicate, peace during this time was not at all peaceful. The Tokugawa *Shoguns* had to contend with uprisings small and large, and on different occasions, my mate and I were useful to Lord Masaharu Suzuki in his service to the *Shogun*.

A particular problem were the Christian missionaries who saw our country as heathen and backward, and flooded our shores in an attempt to convert our peoples to their way of belief. Did they not understand that our religions were of far longer duration than theirs? Did they not understand that we revered our ancestors, honored our women, and lived the life that was best suited to ourselves? The *Shoguns* tried on several occasions to impress on these Westerners – Spanish, Dutch, Portuguese and some English – that they were welcome in our country only so long as they abided by our rules and customs.

But they were not willing to try to understand us and our ways, and our second *Shogun*, Tokugawa Hidetada, son of Ieyasu, in 1616 found it necessary to close all seaports to foreign shipping, excepting only Nagasaki to the west of Kumamoto on Kyushu Island, and Hirado, a small port at the far west of that island. Due to their continued unruliness, the Portuguese and Spanish, missionaries and seamen alike, were confined to the city of Nagasaki; and likewise, the Dutch and English were confined to the smaller port of Hirado.

Did this impress on these foreign people the need to obey our laws and customs? No, it did not, and just eight years later, our third *Shogun*, the Great General Ieyasu's grandson Tokugawa Iemitsu, deemed it necessary to expel all the Spanish from our shores, as they were unable to control their Franciscan monks. Those hooded monsters were creating much unrest amongst the common people and the samurai – the latter being men who were accustomed to daily fighting but were now restless and unoccupied.

Their continued intransigence led the *Shogun* Iemitsu to enact *Sakoku* in 1635; this foreign relations policy decreed that no foreigner could enter or depart our country under penalty of death. Likewise, our own peoples could not leave our country under the same penalty. We had become a "chained country", as the name *Sakoku* implies, and were tightly bound to ourselves for our future.

But the unrest fomented by the priests and missionaries still did not cease, and on the snowy, cold seventeenth of December, in the year 1637, some number of Christian samurai in the city of Shimabara rebelled against the rule of the army of the *Shogun* – the "bakufu army" – and that battle raged well into the next year. The *daimyo* of that region, Shigeharu Matsukura, was most effective in quelling that uprising, and took many heads before it was over.

When control was finally attained, the Portuguese were expelled from their domicile in Nagasaki, just as the Spanish had been forced to leave our shores some fourteen years prior. Finally, in 1641 our *Shogun* moved the Dutch and their trading post, the Dutch East India Company, to a small compound on an island built just for the purpose in the middle of the great harbor of Nagasaki. That island, Deshima, was the only foreign settlement allowed in Japan for many years thereafter.

You are told these things so you can understand that, although the major battles in our country had been concluded, our Lord Masaharu Suzuki was nonetheless busy with supplying men and their daily keep to the other *daimyo* on whose lands these continuing conflicts occurred.

My Lord Masanobu was not only about being the leader of his warriors, though. He was married in 1640 to the daughter of the head of the Kikuchi clan of northern Kyushu. These two families hoped the union of the young man and the woman, Akemi, two years junior to my Lord Masanobu, would help to control the Kyushu tribes and ensure peaceful times both in Kyushu and in Shikoku.

Their union soon produced the girl Sachiko, who joined their household in 1641. As my Lord was often away with the various duties helping quell the sporadic uprisings, the Lady Akemi was left to run the estate, take care of her child, and ensure the crops were bountiful. There was still the annual taxes to pay to the *Shogunate*, and the *Jito* made their regular rounds to collect rice and other forms of payment to the government.

Sitting motionless for what seemed like hours, the boy pondered what *katana* had told him. The major battle, he recalled, had been at a place called Sekigahara, near where the Asano castle now stood. But there had been other, ongoing battles in which *katana* had been involved. He wondered how many more men had died under the sharp blade of this majestic sword. And, who made the swords carried by the other samurai? Surely, he reasoned, Seki no Magoroku could not have made all the thousands of swords used during these many battles and other conflicts. Were there other sword makers who were famous in Japan? He thought to ask his teacher at the next Japanese language class he was to attend this coming Saturday morning.

Just as he had decided to do, he raised his hand near the end of class and said, "Hata *Sensei*, can you tell us about the maker of the sword used by Lord Asano in the story we've read? And are there other sword makers we could learn about?"

His teacher, now accustomed to his keen questions, replied that she did not know off-hand about such craftsmen, but why didn't he do some research and tell his classmates at the next class session what he finds out. "Is there anyone else who is interested in Japanese sword makers?" she asked. Nearly all the class raised their hands.

"Well, Akira-*kun*, can you do that for your homework assignment? We would all like to know more about this interesting subject."

When he next saw his '*ba-san*, he told her about his question and his assignment, and asked if she had any books about sword making that he could look at. He knew, of course, that she did, as he had seen several on her bookshelf. Naturally, she was delighted in his interest in this very ancient Japanese art, and said she would help him any way he wanted.

That made him very happy and contented, and when he returned to his room, he looked at the page on which he had written all that he had learned from *katana*:

LADY TOSHIKO SUZUKI

Born in 1427 as Toshiko Matsudaira
Father: Marquis Matsudaira
Related to: Minamoto Chikauji

Homes: Izumo, Edo

LORD HIROSHI SUZUKI

for whom *katana* was made.
Born in 1425
Father: somebody Suzuki
Related to: Emperors Go-
    Shirakawa, Go-Daigo & Antoku
Homes: Osaka, Edo, Tojo
Died in 1476. Buried in Tojo.

Married: 1444
Family: two sons, born 1448 & 1450;
    a daughter, born 1453

\|/

LADY MICHIKO SUZUKI

Born in 1452 as Michiko Takatsukasa
Father: Prince Takatsukasa
Home: Edo

LORD KIICHI SUZUKI

Second master of *katana*
Born in 1448
Father: Lord Hiroshi Suzuki
Homes: Osaka, Edo, Tojo,
    Fukuchiyama
Died in 1497. Cremated in Tojo.

Married: 1470
Family: twins. a daughter born 1471;
    a son born 1471, hours later.

\|/

LADY MASAKO SUZUKI

Born in 1474 as Masako Tokudaiji
Father: Prince Tokudaiji
Home: Shizuoka

LORD SEIROKU SUZUKI
Third master of *katana*
Born in 1471
Father: Lord Kiichi Suzuki
Homes: Osaka, Edo, Tojo,
    Fukuchiyama
Died in 1498. Buried in Osaka.

Married: 1491
Family: two daughters and a son,
born 1492

\|/

LADY TOMIKO SUZUKI

Born in 1493 as Tomiko Mitsui
Father: Mitsui-*sama*
Home: Namazue

LORD MICHIO SUZUKI
Fourth master of *katana*
Born in 1492
Father: Lord Seiroku Suzuki
Homes: Osaka, Edo, Tojo
    Fukuchiyama
Died in 1530. Buried in Tojo.

Married: 1509
Family: a son, born 1512; 3 daughters

\|/

LADY MIKI SUZUKI

Born in 1515 as Miki Ikeda
Father: Ikeda-San
Home: Edo

LORD TOMISHIKI SUZUKI
Fifth master of *katana*
Born in 1512
Father: Lord Michio Suzuki
Homes: Osaka, Edo, Tojo
  Fukuchiyama
Died in 1562. Buried in Osaka.

Married: 1533
Family: a son, born 1534; a daughter
and sons Sadao & Hirohisa

LADY KUNIKO SUZUKI

Born as Kuniko Itakura
Father: Viscount Itakura
Home: Edo

LORD SHIN SUZUKI
Sixth master of *katana*
Born in 1534
Father: Lord Tomishiki Suzuki
Homes: Osaka, Edo, Tojo
  Fukuchiyama, Karuizawa
Died ?

Married: 1555
Family: daughter born 1555 & Goto in 1558
a son Masatoshi born 1556

HARUKO SUZUKI

Born in 1553 as Haruko Nagata
Father: Lord Nagata
Home: Kishu area

LORD MASATOSHI SUZUKI
Seventh master of *katana*
Born in 1556
Father: Lord Shin Suzuki
Homes: Osaka, Edo, Tojo
  Fukuchiyama, Karuizawa

Married: 1575
Family: son Satoru born 1575, daughter
Nanami born 1576, son Shuji born 1577
Died 1600 at Sekigahara, son born
1579 died as a child

TAKAKO SUZUKI   **SATORU SUZUKI**
Born as Takako Arai
Born in 1577   Born in 1575
                                Died 1616

Family: son Masaharu born 1599

NORIKO SUZUKI   **LORD MASAHARU SUZUKI**
Born as Noriko Matsudaira   Eighth master of *katana*
Born in 1602   Born in 1599

Married: in Osaka, 1616; son Masanobu born 1620

AKEMI SUZUKI   **MASANOBU SUZUKI**
Born as Akemi Kikuchi
Born in 1622   Born in 1620
Home: Northern Kyushu

Married: 1640. Dau. Sachiko born 1641

XIV

A CHANGE IN DIRECTION

The youngster was hardly prepared when, late one night, after he and his parents were sound asleep, *katana* awoke him and insisted on relating more of the story of the wonderful family heirloom.

You know the ongoing history of the Suzuki family, from the one who commissioned my blade into being in the middle of the fifteenth century during the era of Emperor Go-Hanazono, and up to the great bloodshed we called Sekigahara, nearly two hundred years later.

My mate and I had been the mark of the Suzuki family lineage and control, passed from father to son or grandson, but always within the Suzuki family.

Now I must relate how that all changed.

Katana certainly knows how to get my attention, even when I'm sleepy! thought young Alexander. What could have changed? Does this have something to do with the Asano crest on *katana's* hilt? He was so nervous and excited that he could hardly write the words that *katana* said to him.

It was in the year 1658 that my Lord Masanobu sought the assistance of a *nakodo*, a marriage broker as I have explained before, to find a suitable mate for his daughter, Sachiko. This was fourteen years after the death of his father, my Lord Masaharu, who had passed without trauma at the family compound in Tojo, on the island of Shikoku. Gravely ill with chills and a fever, Lord Masaharu had called his only child to his bedside and passed to him my mate and myself. Just days after that, Lord Masaharu succumbed and Lord Masanobu was now the family head.

Concerned that his own son was but a small boy, he decided to offer his family's *katana* and *wakizashi* to the man who would wed his lovely daughter. This was a fateful decision and one he did not take lightly, but he was concerned that his son, the boy Korekiyo, was too young and too anemic to carry on the proud battle traditions for which my mate and I were well regarded. And he knew also that, although he was a hale and hearty thirty-eight years, the concern that he might die unexpectedly and put the burden of responsibility on the boy was more than he was comfortable with.

Lord Masanobu and Lady Akemi used the services of longtime family friends from the *daimyo* family of Hino, in the person of the grandson of Gamo Ujisato, Lord of Hino Castle in Omi Province, to the west of Hiroshima. This fiefdom faces the Japan Sea and is known for its fierce warriors. After a short time, the parties all agreed on a union of young Sachiko and Nagatomo Asano, he the son of the Asano clan leader who had fought at Sekigahara alongside Masanobu's grandfather, Masatoshi. These three families – the noble Suzukis, the *tozama* Asano and the *daimyo* Hino – had been close for many years, having fought alongside each other in many battles for the unification of our country.

When the wedding was arranged, the Asano family needed to travel from their alternate residence in Edo to the family compound on Lake Biwa. As I have mentioned, but will elaborate on, families of the *tozama* and *daimyo* were required by the edict of *Shogun* Tokugawa Iemitsu, called *"sankin-kotai"*, or the Alternate Attendance System, to keep their immediate families year round in Edo. Each of these families was obliged to build mansions in Edo to house themselves, and the various lords could reside with their families during their mandatory visits to the *Shogun's* castle in Edo. But when they returned along the Tokaido Road, or along other main thoroughfares throughout the countryside, to their ancestral homes, they traveled without their wives and children.

This policy was put in effect in order to maintain the peace amongst all the two hundred seventy *daimyo* throughout the land, as any uprising against the *Shogun* would imperil the families still residing in Edo. By this method, the *Shogun* controlled all the factions who might try to rise against him, and peace was maintained.

The Asano castle was in the town of Otsu on *Biwa-ko*. It was on land originally ceded to the Ikeda clan and their fiefdom was valued at 35,000 *Koku*. But, as you have been told, the *Shogun* Ieyasu gave the fief to the Asano clan in 1645 with a value of 53,000 *Koku*. Three years after taking over this area, Naganao Asano began the construction of Ako Castle, and it was completed in 1661.

My Lord Masanobu, Lady Akemi, daughter Sachiko and the young boy Korekiyo, then only two years old, traveled there in 1659, where Sachiko was wed to Nagatomo Asano at the not yet completed castle. My Lord presented my mate and me to the eldest son of the Asano clan, my newest master, Lord Nagatomo Asano. In preparation for this giving of us to one who was not a Suzuki, my Lord Masanobu had the *menuki* ornaments under the handle wraps of our hilts changed from the Suzuki wisteria design to the Asano crossed feathers design.

And thus, for the first time since we were made by the master sword smith Seki no Magoroku we would be held in hands other than Suzuki. It was considered a great honor for the Asano clan to be presented with Suzuki swords of this high caliber by such a noble family as ours, and there was much rejoicing by the two families at this union.

As you have perhaps noted in all you have been told, our family had not married into other families of Shikoku Island, and for very good reason: At this time there were few who were of the class and caliber of the noble Suzuki family, and we had always preferred to join in marriage with others of similar class.

Though tired and barely able to stay awake, young Alexander sat bolt up-right at what he had just written. Is this the reason the sword he held now wore the crest of the Asano clan? Was this really the sword that had been used by the Lord Asano in the Chushingura story they had all read together in class? In stunned silence, he sat and read over this information again, and then again.

There was no mistake: He had been instructed to write that the Suzuki *katana* had been given by Lord Masanobu to the husband of his daughter, the young Nagatomo Asano, as a wedding gift. Now he understood how the Asano *kamon* came to be on the Suzuki family sword.

But one more thing puzzled him: How did the sword return to the Suzuki family?

He tried to be patient, as he was certain *katana* would reveal all to him in time. And, although it was his nature to question all that he had been told, he knew deep inside him that he would find out that all he had been told by *katana* was the absolute truth. Of this, he was very, very certain.

In preparation for his next Saturday morning *Nihon-go* class, Alex asked his 'ba-san about swordsmiths – *Kajiya* – and they sat together on the couch in her family room to look at the several books she had on her bookshelf about that subject. They read through "Nippon-To, The Japanese Sword" by Inami Hakusui first, as this was a good overview of smithies. Then they looked at "The Arts of the Japanese Sword" by B.W. Robinson, considered by some as the best of the genre. In particular, his 'ba-san went over Robinson's coverage of Kanemoto II, another name for Seki no Magoroku. The last book they reviewed was "The Samurai Sword: A Handbook" by John M. Yumoto. Young Alex asked many questions and was delighted to learn that all the things he had been told by *katana* were verified in these several heavily researched and highly respected books about Japanese swordsmiths.

But before he even returned to his classmates with all he had learned, *katana* urged him to again take up pencil and paper, and continue the story.

The period after the Battle of Sekigahara was filled with castle building. Throughout the land, wealthy *daimyo* and *tozama* alike raised their structures upon flat plains and high hills. While they all wanted to believe that the wars and battles were a trademark of past times, they were all also leery of their neighbors and friends, having seen neighbors and friends fighting each other for control in years past.

The grand castle of the Ii clan was raised in Hikone, in the Omi province on *Biwa-ko*. Then the lovely but dark and brooding castle of the Kyogoku clan was built on a hilltop overlooking the Sea of Japan; the Matsue castle is somewhat unique in not having white plaster at the roofline of its outer walls. The *Shogun* built the huge Nijo castle in Edo, and that castle stands to this day as the palace of the Emperor. As I have said, Matsuyama castle was built to the west of Shikoku Island at this time and offset the Suzuki castle in Tojo, called East Castle. Another castle about which I have told you was Kumamoto castle in western Kyushu.

These and many more were built in the event of another countrywide bloodbath, but most were consumed by fire, not from battle, but from candles and cooking apparatus.

The Aso fiefdom, as I have said, had been awarded to Naganao Asano in 1615 by the *Shogun*, Tokugawa Ieyasu, just a short time before his death in 1616. At that time, the value of the fief was 53,000 *koku*. One *koku* equals one bale, the amount of rice necessary to feed one person for a year. So, by this calculation, one can easily see the size of the estate under Asano control. The Asanos, you will recall, were but *tozama*, and their estate was small compared to some of the *daimyo* at that time. The Matsudaira, for example, had multiple fiefdoms, each worth over two hundred thousand *koku*. They were amongst the wealthiest of all families in the land.

This valuation meant that these wealthy landowners could employ many samurai, hundreds of families of field workers growing crops and herding animals, blacksmiths, swordsmiths, brick layers and carpenters – all the talent necessary to maintain a complete city unto themselves, as the castles were, in fact, the centerpieces of the towns and cities that grew around them.

The Suzukis, by contrast, were not awarded their fiefdom, and their armies, their farm workers, their smithies, their masons and carpenters, were all paid by the Suzuki family from its vast land holdings in the areas which I have told you previously. Their name was respected for its nobility and high ranking, and not so much for its wealth.

Amazed at all he was learning about Japan and Japanese history, and not just the family of his 'ba-san, the boy reflected on the life of his ancient ancestors. On his grandmother's bookshelf, he also found books on castles around the world, and he noted how different were the Japanese castles from the ones in England, or France, or Germany. Their construction helped make them impervious to assault, and perfectly suited the environment in which they were constructed.

Feeling just a slight bit smug, he arrived at his *Nihon-go* class the following Saturday morning.

"Have you learned anything about Japanese samurai swords, Akkun?" his teacher asked near the end of the class period. "Can you share with us the answer to your question from last week?"

He confidently went to her desk at the front of the classroom and, showing the several books that his 'ba-san had allowed him to bring to class, told his friends and classmates about the various styles of swords, and the kind of sword, the *katana*, that had been used by Lord Asano on that fateful day back in 1702.

They were all as excited at his short talk as he had been when writing the dictation by *katana*, and amongst themselves discussed swords and the act of *seppuku*, ritual disembowelment, that the *tozama* had committed so many years before. Now they, as well as he, knew that the story of Chushingura was true. As temped as he was at that moment to share with them what he also knew from *katana's* story to him about the maker of Asano's sword, Seki no Magoroku, he knew that he dare not mention that at all.

So, when Hata *Sensei* asked if he had found out who made Asano's sword that they had all read about in the Chushingura story, he simply said he didn't have an answer to that yet.

The fiefdom of the Asano clan, around the time of Lord Nagatomo's marriage to Lady Sachiko, had been reduced to a valuation of 50,000 *koku*, following the trend amongst other landowners of having their wealth somewhat curtailed by the *Shogun* due to the peaceful times that they were all enjoying; there was less need for large, standing armies of highly trained samurai.

But, they were still wealthy *tozama*, and were pleased to welcome a son, born in Edo during a trip there by Lord Asano in September, 1667. They named the boy Naganori.

LADY TOSHIKO SUZUKI

Born in 1427 as Toshiko Matsudaira
Father: Marquis Matsudaira
Related to: Minamoto Chikauji

Homes: Izumo, Edo

LORD HIROSHI SUZUKI

for whom *katana* was made.
Born in 1425
Father: somebody Suzuki
Related to: Emperors Go-
    Shirakawa, Go-Daigo & Antoku
Homes: Osaka, Edo, Tojo
Died in 1476. Buried in Tojo.

Married: 1444
Family: two sons, born 1448 & 1450;
    a daughter, born 1453

\|/

LADY MICHIKO SUZUKI

Born in 1452 as Michiko Takatsukasa
Father: Prince Takatsukasa
Home: Edo

LORD KIICHI SUZUKI

Second master of *katana*
Born in 1448
Father: Lord Hiroshi Suzuki
Homes: Osaka, Edo, Tojo,
    Fukuchiyama
Died in 1497. Cremated in Tojo.

Married: 1470
Family: twins. a daughter born 1471;
    a son born 1471, hours later.

\|/

LADY MASAKO SUZUKI

Born in 1474 as Masako Tokudaiji
Father: Prince Tokudaiji
Home: Shizuoka

LORD SEIROKU SUZUKI
Third master of *katana*
Born in 1471
Father: Lord Kiichi Suzuki
Homes: Osaka, Edo, Tojo,
    Fukuchiyama
Died in 1498. Buried in Osaka.

Married: 1491
Family: two daughters and a son, born 1492

\|/

LADY TOMIKO SUZUKI

Born in 1493 as Tomiko Mitsui
Father: Mitsui-*sama*
Home: Namazue

LORD MICHIO SUZUKI
Fourth master of *katana*
Born in 1492
Father: Lord Seiroku Suzuki
Homes: Osaka, Edo, Tojo
    Fukuchiyama
Died in 1530. Buried in Tojo.

Married: 1509
Family: a son, born 1512;
    3 daughters

\|/

LADY MIKI SUZUKI

Born in 1515 as Miki Ikeda
Father: Ikeda-San
Home: Edo

LORD TOMISHIKI SUZUKI
Fifth master of *katana*
Born in 1512
Father: Lord Michio Suzuki
Homes: Osaka, Edo, Tojo
    Fukuchiyama
Died in 1562. Buried in Osaka.

Married: 1533
Family: a son, born 1534; a daughter
and sons Sadao & Hirohisa

LADY KUNIKO SUZUKI

Born as Kuniko Itakura
Father: Viscount Itakura
Home: Edo

LORD SHIN SUZUKI
Sixth master of *katana*
Born in 1534
Father: Lord Tomishiki Suzuki
Homes: Osaka, Edo, Tojo
    Fukuchiyama, Karuizawa
Died ?

Married: 1555
Family: daughter born 1555 & Goto in 1558
a son Masatoshi born 1556

HARUKO SUZUKI

Born in 1553 as Haruko Nagata
Father: Lord Nagata
Home: Kishu area

LORD MASATOSHI SUZUKI
Seventh master of *katana*
Born in 1556
Father: Lord Shin Suzuki
Homes: Osaka, Edo, Tojo
    Fukuchiyama, Karuizawa

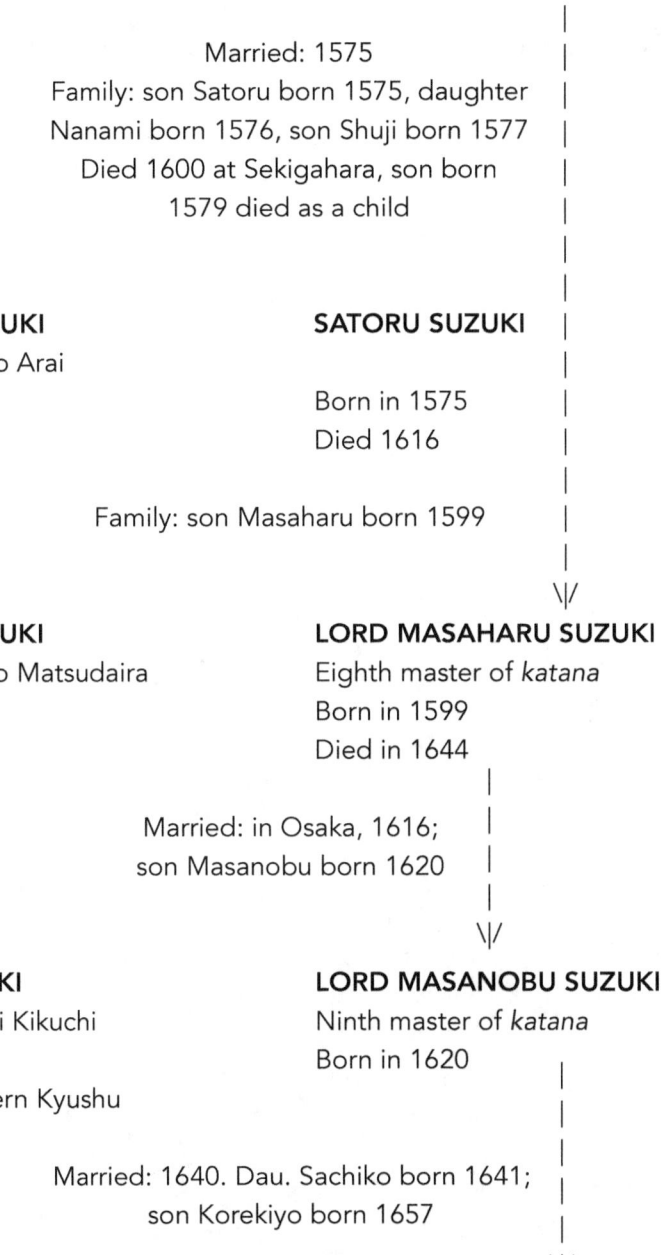

Married: 1575
Family: son Satoru born 1575, daughter
Nanami born 1576, son Shuji born 1577
Died 1600 at Sekigahara, son born
1579 died as a child

TAKAKO SUZUKI
Born as Takako Arai
Born in 1577

SATORU SUZUKI

Born in 1575
Died 1616

Family: son Masaharu born 1599

NORIKO SUZUKI
Born as Noriko Matsudaira
Born in 1602

LORD MASAHARU SUZUKI
Eighth master of *katana*
Born in 1599
Died in 1644

Married: in Osaka, 1616;
son Masanobu born 1620

AKEMI SUZUKI
Born as Akemi Kikuchi
Born in 1622
Home: Northern Kyushu

LORD MASANOBU SUZUKI
Ninth master of *katana*
Born in 1620

Married: 1640. Dau. Sachiko born 1641;
son Korekiyo born 1657

SACHIKO ASANO
Born as Sachiko Suzuki
Born in 1641
Home: Tojo

LORD NAGATOMO ASANO
Tenth master of *katana*
Born in 1643
Home: Ako Castle, on Biwa-ko

Married 1659. Son Naganori, born Edo 1667.

XV

ASANO'S FATEFUL DEMISE

Naganori.

The name stuck in young Alexander's head and he reflected on it. He had seen that name before.

Naganori. He looked back over his papers from his Saturday morning *Nihon-go* class and, yes, there was the name. This was the Lord Asano who, as the Asano clan leader, drew his sword in the *Shogun's* palace in Edo and was condemned to commit *seppuku*. He pondered this for some time. Would *katana* now tell him what he already knew? That the son of Nagatomo Asano, about whom the sword had already told him, actually lived and actually died as the Chushingura story had said?

He was beside himself with excitement and expectation, awaiting that magic moment when the sword would again speak to, and through, him.

The wait did not last long, as *katana* soon urged him to record the words the sword would relate.

It was in the year 1675 when my master, Lord Nagatomo Asano died at such a young age, leaving his oldest son, Naganori, to lead his clan at age nine. My Lord had fathered two children, with the second son, Daigaku Nagahiro, being but four years old at the time of my master's death.

As the clan leader, young Naganori underwent extensive training in the arts, in the use of his armaments, and in the economics of managing his estate.

And, as a young Lord, now carrying my mate and me at his side, he was appointed in 1680 to the office of "Takumi-no Kami," which was the Head of Carpentry at the Imperial Court. As the Emperor had little power during the era of the *Shoguns*, this was, at most, a ceremonial position. But in those days, young clan leaders still garnered the respect of others and he was, after all, the Third Master of the Banshu-Ako clan.

Several years into these duties the Fifth *Shogun*, by the name of Tokugawa Tsunayoshi, in 1683 made Asano's appointment in the Office of Imperial Protocol. In this capacity, my Lord Naganori, along with one other high-ranking lord, hosted emissaries of the Imperial Court when they were on official business at the *Shogunate*. The man in charge of this office was of the Highest *Koke* – you would say 'Highest Honor' – Head of Ceremonies, Lord Yoshinaka Kira, whose full Japanese-style name was Kira Kozuki-no-Suke Yoshinaka.

That man had been in the *Shoguns'* employ for some decades, and had a reputation for surliness towards his younger appointees, forcing them to give him continuous bribes in return for his training necessary in their duties. Many young men, including Lord Kamei of the Tsuwano Domain who worked alongside Lord Asano, acquiesced, under duress, to the bribery demands of Lord Kira.

But not so my master. He resisted verbally these demands, and their angry voices echoed in the halls of the *Shogun's* Palace in Edo.

You must know also that my Lord had been stricken with a terrible disease in 1694 which left him childless, so he adopted his younger brother, Daigaku Nagahiro Asano, as his legal heir, as was the privilege of such men of rank in those days.

However, as was also the privilege of such men, my master took to himself in 1694 a mistress, the young Satomi Hino, who had been born in 1679 of Lady Ryoko Hino – she of the Suzuki clan – and the *daimyo* Lord Hino of Nara. As you can see, Satomi Hino was the young Lord Asano's second cousin, as his own grandmother was Sachiko Suzuki whose daughter Ryoko had married Lord Hino in 1678, when she was aged seventeen and Lord Hino was twenty-four.

My Lord's wife, Akuri Miyoshi, was also a distant relative, being the daughter of Nagaharu Asano of the Hiroshima Asano clan. She was seven years his junior and all who knew them believed their lack of family to be the result of my Lord's illness.

But, the mistress Satomi gave birth in 1695 to a girl baby who was to become known as Asano no Kinume, meaning 'Golden Plum.' As she matured, her gracefulness and expertise in weaponry earned her the appellation *Koneko*, meaning Little Cat. Can we imagine that the lack of fertility was my Lord's wife's problem, and not really his, as he had successfully fathered an illegitimate daughter by his mistress?

As is so well known now, Lord Asano could bear no longer the insults and disrespect shown him daily by Lord Kira, and in the *Matsu no Oroka* – the Great Corridor of Pines – in Edo Castle on March 14, 1702, which you know as the Ides of March, my Lord drew me from my scabbard and slashed at Lord Kira's face, intending to deal him a mortal blow. However, Kira avoided death and suffered but a cut along his cheek. In terror for his life, Kira turned and ran along the corridor, yelling for the palace guards to protect him. Lord Asano lunged yet again but missed, and buried my blade deep into a stanchion. As he struggled to extract me – my keen edge had cut well into the wood – guards of the palace apprehended him, taking my mate and me from him, and binding him securely.

Eyes wide in disbelief, the boy stared at his writing tablet. There, by his own hand, he had written the gist of the story that he and his classmates had read some time back at his Saturday *Nihon-go* class.

Quickly the enormity of these words began to sink in: This very sword had been used nearly three hundred years earlier in the most famous incident in all of Japanese history. He imagined Lord Asano's fingerprints still on the hilt. Deep in his subconscious, he wondered if there might be Lord Kira's blood on the iron hilt, under the wrapped wooden handle.

The thought of these possibilities caused him to tremble and shake; sweat beaded itself on his young brow.

The *Shogun*, torn between leniency to the young man who was justified in defending his honor and his *tozama* station, and the edict against drawing weaponry of any kind in the palace, was compelled to pronounce a sentence of sacrifice by *seppuku*.

That very evening my Lord was taken to the grounds of the temple *Sengaku-ji* and, with the *Shogun* himself holding me in his hands while acting as his *kaishakunin* – that is, his second – my Lord used my mate to open his bowels and kill himself for his impertinence in the *Shogun's* castle.

Before being taken to the temple grounds, Lord Asano wrote his death poem, which he laid on the cloth beside him as he knelt to do his final deed. The poem read thusly:

> *"Kaze sasofu*
> *Hana yori mo najo*
> *Ware wa mata*
> *Haru no nagori o*
> *Ika ni toyasen."*

> "More than the Cherry Blossoms,
> Inviting a wind to blow them away,
> I am wondering what to do,
> With the remaining springtime."

As that day drew to a close, the *Shogun* ordered the fiefdom of the Banshu-Ako clan to be forever forfeited to the *Shogunate*, and all of the samurai of the Asano household to become *ronin* – masterless samurai.

I've been told of battles in which hundreds, or thousands, have died, thought Alexander, but this must be the most senseless and heartbreaking death I know of. If the *Shogun* really was torn about what to do, why couldn't he just have Lord Asano leave Edo and return home? Get him out of the palace and away from that nasty Lord Kira? Even though I know this is what happened, it's not fair!

But as upset as he was, he knew that *katana* was not finished telling its tale, for he again took up his writing implement and prepared for more of the story.

Lord Hino, being the respected *daimyo* closest to my departed master, was given us two swords by the *Shogun* himself for safe transport back to his home castle.

We never arrived at the home of this great *daimyo*, however, as he had arranged to meet with his illegitimate granddaughter, the Lady Asano no Kinume, who was still a child and would not be suspected of having us in her possession. Lady Asano no Kinume was under the guardian-ship of a trusted samurai from the Suzuki family's own province, Tosa, on Shikoku Island. That warrior, who had pledged his life in defense of the child and the weapons of her father, was called Hanshiro from Tosa: Tosa no Hanshiro.

When the sword had finished relating what it had to say about this tragic event, the boy added to his chronology all that he had been told, thusly:

LADY TOSHIKO SUZUKI

Born in 1427 as Toshiko Matsudaira
Father: Marquis Matsudaira
Related to: Minamoto Chikauji

Homes: Izumo, Edo

LORD HIROSHI SUZUKI

for whom *katana* was made.
Born in 1425
Father: somebody Suzuki
Related to: Emperors Go-
    Shirakawa, Go-Daigo & Antoku
Homes: Osaka, Edo, Tojo
Died in 1476. Buried in Tojo.

Married: 1444
Family: two sons, born 1448 & 1450;
    a daughter, born 1453

LADY MICHIKO SUZUKI

Born in 1452 as Michiko Takatsukasa
Father: Prince Takatsukasa
Home: Edo

LORD KIICHI SUZUKI

Second master of *katana*
Born in 1448
Father: Lord Hiroshi Suzuki
Homes: Osaka, Edo, Tojo,
    Fukuchiyama
Died in 1497. Cremated in Tojo.

Married: 1470
Family: twins. a daughter born 1471;
    a son born 1471, hours later.

LADY MASAKO SUZUKI

Born in 1474 as Masako Tokudaiji
Father: Prince Tokudaiji
Home: Shizuoka

LORD SEIROKU SUZUKI

Third master of *katana*
Born in 1471
Father: Lord Kiichi Suzuki
Homes: Osaka, Edo, Tojo,
    Fukuchiyama
Died in 1498. Buried in Osaka.

Married: 1491
Family: two daughters and a son, born 1492

\|/

LADY TOMIKO SUZUKI

Born in 1493 as Tomiko Mitsui
Father: Mitsui-*sama*
Home: Namazue

LORD MICHIO SUZUKI
Fourth master of *katana*
Born in 1492
Father: Lord Seiroku Suzuki
Homes: Osaka, Edo, Tojo
  Fukuchiyama
Died in 1530. Buried in Tojo.

Married: 1509
Family: a son, born 1512; 3 daughters

\|/

LADY MIKI SUZUKI

Born in 1515 as Miki Ikeda
Father: Ikeda-San
Home: Edo

LORD TOMISHIKI SUZUKI
Fifth master of *katana*
Born in 1512
Father: Lord Michio Suzuki
Homes: Osaka, Edo, Tojo
  Fukuchiyama
Died in 1562. Buried in Osaka.

Married: 1533
Family: a son, born 1534; a daughter
  and sons Sadao & Hirohisa

\|/

LADY KUNIKO SUZUKI

Born as Kuniko Itakura
Father: Viscount Itakura
Home: Edo

LORD SHIN SUZUKI
Sixth master of *katana*
Born in 1534
Father: Lord Tomishiki Suzuki
Homes: Osaka, Edo, Tojo
  Fukuchiyama, Karuizawa
Died ?

Married: 1555
Family: daughter born 1555 & Goto in 1558
a son Masatoshi born 1556

\|/

HARUKO SUZUKI

Born in 1553 as Haruko Nagata
Father: Lord Nagata
Home: Kishu area

LORD MASATOSHI SUZUKI

Seventh master of *katana*
Born in 1556
Father: Lord Shin Suzuki
Homes: Osaka, Edo, Tojo
        Fukuchiyama, Karuizawa

Married: 1575
Family: son Satoru born 1575, daughter
Nanami born 1576, son Shuji born 1577
Died 1600 at Sekigahara, son born
1579 died as a child

TAKAKO SUZUKI
Born as Takako Arai
Born in 1577

SATORU SUZUKI

Born in 1575
Died 1616

Family: son Masaharu born 1599

\|/

NORIKO SUZUKI
Born as Noriko Matsudaira
Born in 1602

LORD MASAHARU SUZUKI
Eighth master of *katana*
Born in 1599
Died in 1644

Married: in Osaka, 1616;
son Masanobu born 1620   \|/

AKEMI SUZUKI
Born as Akemi Kikuchi
Born in 1622
Home: Northern Kyushu

LORD MASANOBU SUZUKI
Ninth master of *katana*
Born in 1620

|
|
Married: 1640. Dau. Sachiko born 1641; |
son Korekiyo born 1657 |
|
\|/

SACHIKO ASANO
Born as Sachiko Suzuki
Born in 1641

Home: Tojo

LORD NAGATOMO ASANO
Tenth master of *katana*
Born in 1643
Died 1675
Home: Ako Castle, on Biwa-ko

|
Married 1659. Son Naganori, born Edo 1667. |
|
\|/

AKURI MIYOSHI
Born 1674
Born as Akuri Miyoshi
Father: Nagaharu Asano of Hiroshima

LORD NAGANORI ASANO
known as Takumi-no Kami
Born in Edo, Sept. 28, 1667
Eleventh master of Katana
Died: *Seppuku* March 14, 1702
Mistress: Satomi Hino
Dau: Lady Asano no Kinume
Born 1695

Ryoko Suzuki b.1661, married:
Married 1678 at age 17
Daughter Satomi Hino b. 1679. Became mistress to Lord Asano Takumi-no
Kami in 1694.

Lord Hino b. 1654
He the Daimyo of Nara

XVI

KATANA HIDES OUT

After considering all that *katana* had last told him, young Alexander Akira pondered the motive for Lord Hino to pass along the sword to the young illegitimate daughter of the deceased Lord Asano. Could the purpose have been to hide the swords from any who might want to take them? *Katana* had said that no one would expect her to have them. But why? His eight-year-old mind did not have the experience necessary to understand the reasoning of Asano no Kimune's benefactor.

As he struggled with this, he suddenly remembered that the *Shogun* had confiscated Lord Asano's fiefdom and sent the Asano retainers away from their castle. Well, if that's the case, he thought, what became of them? And their families? And Lord Asano's wife? Were they just out on the street? Did they have to resort to begging on the corners as he had seen some people having to do?

Then he thought about the man with no name. All the people *katana* had told him about had names, but not this man, the one to whom Lord Hino had entrusted young Lady Asano no Kimune. Did he not have a family name? Only Hanshiro from Tosa? But then, he recalled something *katana* had said long ago, that in those days in Japan the common people, and even some samurai, had no family names. That they often used their village name as their family name.

So, Hanshiro was using his province name as a family name. He remembered something his father had told him about some of his friends' family names: That the name Smith had once meant that the family had been blacksmiths. Likewise, the name Johnson meant that the family was from the son of John. And so on.

Well, at least that makes a little sense to me, he mumbled. But *still!*

There are so many questions, he realized, that *katana* needed to answer, but would that happen? Soon? His youthful impatience was getting the better of him.

At his *Nihon-go* class, he asked some of these questions to Hata *Sensei*, even though she had told him that she knew nothing more than the story of Chushingura that they had all read together.

"Akira-*kun*, I'm afraid that we cannot spend any more time on the lovely story of Chushingura. You will have to find out the answers to these questions on your own." That was what Hata *Sensei* had told him, and his face flushed at the mild rebuke.

Determined to know more, and know it right NOW, he asked these same questions of his *'ba-san*. But she was no more helpful than had been Hata *Sensei*.

"Ak-*kun*," she gently told him, "there may be more answers available, but I don't have any more books on the subject and it might not be possible to find answers here in the United States. Remember that this story took place several hundred years ago in Japan, and we might need to actually look for our answers there, and not here."

Disappointed at reaching these two dead ends, he decided that all he could do was wait until *katana* spoke to him again.

And once again, he did not have to wait too long.

Sadly, the *Shogun's* edict meant that Lord Asano's wife, Lady Akuri, was banished from the Banshu-Ako clan, which was no more. The more than three hundred samurai were all let go, and some small number of them, forty-seven to be exact, plotted revenge against Lord Kira on behalf of their Lord Asano's good name and reputation.

In preparation for this, the married men divorced their wives, and many of them took to public intoxication and open displays of wantonness, convincing the *Shogunate* and especially Lord Kira that they had taken their master's death very badly, and had become but noisy rabble in the streets.

Secretly, these forty-seven masterless samurai, *Ronin*, as they were called, planned how and when to carry out their *Akoroshi*: Their revenge for the house of Ako.

There are some *ronin* names you can know, and what they did as their part of the plot.

The leader was the Chief Counselor to Lord Asano, Oishi Kuranosuke, who was forty-five when his master died. His youngest son, Chikara, who was but fifteen, joined this group.

Then there was Otaka Gengo, a retainer who cleverly disguised himself as a draper and applied to Lord Kira's tea master as an apprentice, a position he held to learn all that went on inside Kira's Edo mansion.

Another was Gihei, who became the owner of the *"Amagawa-ya"*, the "Celestial River" in Sakai in Edo. This was a geisha house that had amongst its many clients some of the Kira retainers.

One ingenious retainer, named Kanzaki Yogoro, posed as a rich Kyoto rice merchant and used this cover to gain entrance to Kira's Edo mansion, on the pretext of purveying rice.

Oishi's Chief of Staff, the sixty-one year old Onodera Junai, was also amongst this band of determined men and he, too, had divorced his wife so she would be spared any consequence of their actions.

Lesser known *ronin* were Junai and Chuza, who were just foot soldiers. Hara Soyemon and Mase Kyudayo were older lieutenants and trusted aides.

The retainer Kinemon Kanehide Okano married the daughter of the builder of Kira's mansion, solely to learn the design of the house and the layout of its many rooms and hallways.

Of this group, the oldest was seventy-seven; the youngest fifteen. Five were men in their sixties; four were in their forties. None of these men expected to do anything less than what their master, Lord Asano, had done: Protect the Ako honor.

So it was that on a cold, snowy Tuesday, the 15th of December, 1703, the *ronin*, led by Oishi, attacked Lord Kira's mansion from different directions. They forced open the front gate while also having archers on the roofs of nearby homes – archers who could immediately cut down any of Kira's men who escaped the melee inside and tried to summon assistance.

It did not take these determined warriors very long to find Kira cowering in a laundry room with his wife and some female servants. When Oishi arrived, he held a lantern so all could see the face of the man who had caused the death of their master; that face had a long scar on it from *katana's* blade. Bowing and giving Kira a dagger, Oishi told him that it was his duty to commit *seppuku*, just as Lord Asano had done. However, to honor Lord Kira's elevated status, he, Oishi, would act as Kira's *kaishakunin*, his "second."

Kira was a man broken; he trembled and cried, clawing at the walls as though he wanted to pull them over him. But he could not take responsibility for his actions and they cut off his head with the dagger that Oishi had offered him, put the head upon a spike, and left the house.

As their final act as a group, they carried Kira's head to the grave of Lord Asano in *Sengaku-ji* temple, walking some six miles through the snow. The townspeople praised them for their courage and for the revenge they had exacted on the house of Kira.

By now, of course, the *Shogun* had heard of their exploits, and assigned four daimyo to guard the men.

Again, the *Shogun* was in doubt as to how to handle this episode; representatives of the people pleaded their case for the release of these brave *ronin* who had done no more than uphold the honor of their deceased master. Nonetheless, the *Shogun* sentenced them all to death by *seppuku*.

They each one – including young Chikara who turned sixteen on that day – committed *seppuku* in the temple grounds of *Sengaku-ji* on the cold and snowy morning of February 4, 1704.

All that they wore, and all that they carried with them on that fateful day, was collected and has become a national treasure to this day.

This was much more than the boy had expected to know, and he sat in stunned silence at these revelations. Knowing that it was the style of *katana* to take short breaks in the story before continuing, Alex did not worry about learning the rest of the story, and knowing what happened to the Lady Akuri Asano. He was confident that he would find out soon enough.

As for Lady Akuri Asano, the Lord's ex-wife, she first resided with her clan until her Lord's death had been avenged. Then, taking his tonsure as a remembrance, she committed her life as a nun, using the name Yosen-in.

The Ako Domain was transferred to Nagai Naohiro and on to other owners thereafter, never again to be known as the fiefdom of the Asano clan.

When Kinume was fifteen, in 1710, she married Hanshiro of Tosa and, to keep her identity a secret, took no last name either. We swords, symbols of the noble status of the Suzuki family and instrumental in the spellbinding story of Chushingura, remained hidden in the humble home of Hanshiro and Kinume, wrapped in burlap and buried beneath their floor.

Many strange events had happened just before Hanshiro took Kinume as his wife, and prompted him to do so, despite his being fifteen years her senior. In 1706, a devastating typhoon had struck Edo and destroyed many homes and even some mansions that were still under construction. Temple coffers were filled to overflowing from the donations by nervous townsfolk who feared the wrath of nature was upon them for the handling of the Asano affair by the *Shogunate*.

Then, following quickly on the heels of the typhoon was a large earthquake in 1707 that set our Mount Fujiyama afire, spewing burning rock and ash for miles around. In the small town of Subasiri, famous for its *Onsen* – hot springs – more than seventy homes were destroyed and three Buddhist temples fell to the ground from the quake and the fires. It was as though the gods were angry, and were letting the frightened people know it.

Most troubling to him was the news that the *Shogun's* wife – she the daughter of the Emperor Reigen – killed her husband and then herself on February 19, 1709. There had been some talk that the *Shogun* was keeping young boys for his pleasure, and no one, not even Hanshiro, knew for certain if this is what caused the *Shogun's* demise. Hanshiro had good cause to fear that the empire itself was falling apart.

Due to all this, Hanshiro expressed his concern for his charge by marrying her – out of love for her, and out of fear for her life. She did not resist his affections, and their union produced a son, whom they named Tsuyoshi, in 1712. Upon his father's death in 1754, Tsuyoshi took his father's name of Hanshiro as his family name, becoming Tsuyoshi Hanshiro. Prior to that, when Lady Asano no Kinume, now living quietly with her husband Tosa no Hanshiro, passed quietly from earth in 1752, Hanshiro passed along my mate and me to his son.

This was all that young Akira could have hoped for. The complete story of Chushingura as told by the sword that participated in Lord Asano's demise and was then hidden away as the Ako estate was no more.

As was his wont, the boy completed all that he had learned from this long session with the beloved *katana*. He decided to use Xs instead of dashes to denote the passing of the sword for safekeeping when the recipient did not become the master of *katana*.

LADY TOSHIKO SUZUKI

Born in 1427 as Toshiko Matsudaira
Father: Marquis Matsudaira
Related to: Minamoto Chikauji

Homes: Izumo, Edo

LORD HIROSHI SUZUKI

for whom *katana* was made.
Born in 1425
Father: somebody Suzuki
Related to: Emperors Go-
    Shirakawa, Go-Daigo & Antoku
Homes: Osaka, Edo, Tojo
Died in 1476. Buried in Tojo.

Married: 1444
Family: two sons, born 1448 & 1450;
a daughter, born 1453

\|/

LADY MICHIKO SUZUKI

Born in 1452 as Michiko Takatsukasa
Father: Prince Takatsukasa
Home: Edo

LORD KIICHI SUZUKI

Second master of *katana*
Born in 1448
Father: Lord Hiroshi Suzuki
Homes: Osaka, Edo, Tojo,
    Fukuchiyama
Died in 1497. Cremated in Tojo.

Married: 1470
Family: twins. a daughter born 1471;
a son born 1471, hours later.

\|/

LADY MASAKO SUZUKI

Born in 1474 as Masako Tokudaiji
Father: Prince Tokudaiji
Home: Shizuoka

LORD SEIROKU SUZUKI
Third master of *katana*
Born in 1471
Father: Lord Kiichi Suzuki
Homes: Osaka, Edo, Tojo,
     Fukuchiyama
Died in 1498. Buried in Osaka.

Married: 1491
Family: two daughters and a son, born 1492

LADY TOMIKO SUZUKI

Born in 1493 as Tomiko Mitsui
Father: Mitsui-*sama*
Home: Namazue

LORD MICHIO SUZUKI
Fourth master of *katana*
Born in 1492
Father: Lord Seiroku Suzuki
Homes: Osaka, Edo, Tojo
     Fukuchiyama
Died in 1530. Buried in Tojo.

Married: 1509
Family: a son, born 1512; 3 daughters

LADY MIKI SUZUKI

Born in 1515 as Miki Ikeda
Father: Ikeda-San
Home: Edo

LORD TOMISHIKI SUZUKI
Fifth master of *katana*
Born in 1512
Father: Lord Michio Suzuki
Homes: Osaka, Edo, Tojo
     Fukuchiyama
Died in 1562. Buried in Osaka.

Married: 1533
Family: a son, born 1534; a daughter
    and sons Sadao & Hirohisa

LADY KUNIKO SUZUKI

Born as Kuniko Itakura
Father: Viscount Itakura
Home: Edo

LORD SHIN SUZUKI

Sixth master of *katana*
Born in 1534
Father: Lord Tomishiki Suzuki
Homes: Osaka, Edo, Tojo
     Fukuchiyama, Karuizawa
Died ?

|
|
Married: 1555 |
Family: daughter born 1555 & Goto in 1558 |
a son Masatoshi born 1556 |
|
\|/

HARUKO SUZUKI

Born in 1553 as Haruko Nagata
Father: Lord Nagata
Home: Kishu area

LORD MASATOSHI SUZUKI

Seventh master of *katana*
Born in 1556
Father: Lord Shin Suzuki
Homes: Osaka, Edo, Tojo
     Fukuchiyama, Karuizawa

|
Married: 1575 |
Family: son Satoru born 1575, daughter |
Nanami born 1576, son Shuji born 1577 |
Died 1600 at Sekigahara, son born |
1579 died as a child |
|
|

TAKAKO SUZUKI
Born as Takako Arai
Born in 1577

SATORU SUZUKI

Born in 1575
Died 1616

|
|
|
|
Family: son Masaharu born 1599 |
|
\|/

NORIKO SUZUKI

Born as Noriko Matsudaira

Born in 1602

LORD MASAHARU SUZUKI

Eighth master of *katana*

Born in 1599

Died in 1644

Married: in Osaka, 1616;
son Masanobu born 1620

\|/

AKEMI SUZUKI

Born as Akemi Kikuchi

Born in 1622

Home: Northern Kyushu

LORD MASANOBU SUZUKI

Ninth master of *katana*

Born in 1620

Married: 1640. Dau. Sachiko born 1641;
son Korekiyo born 1657

\|/

SACHIKO ASANO

Born as Sachiko Suzuki

Born in 1641

Home: Tojo

LORD NAGATOMO ASANO

Tenth master of *katana*

Born in 1643

Died 1675

Home: Ako Castle, on Biwa-ko

Married 1659. Son Naganori, born Edo 1667.

\|/

AKURI MIYOSHI

Born 1674

Born as Akuri Miyoshi

Father: Nagaharu Asano of Hiroshima

Became Yosen-in

Died 1714

LORD NAGANORI ASANO

known as Takumi-no Kami

Born in Edo, Sept. 28, 1667

Eleventh master of *katana*

Died: Seppuku March 14, 1702

Mistress: Satomi Hino

Dau: Lady Asano no Kinume

Born 1695

X

X

\|/

Ryoko Suzuki b.1661, married: Lord Hino b. 1654
Married 1678 at age 17   He the Daimyo of Nara
       Daughter Satomi Hino b. 1679. Became mistress to
       Lord Asano Takumi-no Kami in 1694.   X
                                   \|/

Tosa no Hanshiro < - - - - - - - - - - - - - - Lady Asano no Kinume
Born 1680; died 1754   Born 1695; died 1752
Twelfth master of *katana*
   |
   | Married 1710; son Tsuyoshi born 1712
   |
  \|/

TSUYOSHI HANSHIRO
Home: Tosa province, Shikoku
Born 1712
Thirteenth master of *katana*

XVII

A DIFFERENT KIND OF LIFE

Would the Hanshiros really hide *katana* and its mate under the floor of their house? The boy resolved to ask his *'ba-san* about this when he next saw her.

Realizing that he just might need to go to Japan when he was older and try to find answers to some of his questions, he knew that each Saturday's classwork at the *Nihon-go* school was becoming increasingly important. No longer questioning the veracity of the story that he was learning from *katana*, he knew it was not necessary to question Hata *Sensei* about what he had written. There was ample proof, now, to convince him that all that he was writing was actual fact.

"*'Ba-san,*" he began, "do you think that in the olden days, in Japan, people hid their valuables? Like, underground, or in their basement?"

"Why do you ask such a strange question, Akkun?"

"Oh, I don't know," he shrugged, "the thought just kind of popped into my head."

His grandmother knew him better than that, and was sure that he had been reading something or thinking about something for quite some time before he asked his question.

"Well, Alexander, I can tell you this. My family's sword was hidden in the ground during World War Two. My grandparents had several family swords, and when my uncle was in the Navy, he took a long sword from one set and the short sword that is the mate to the sword I now have. Then, my grandparents wrapped up the remaining swords and buried them. They did this because the government was confiscating swords in order to melt them for bullets, planes and ships.

Does this help answer your question?" She looked at him kindly; the intensity of his returning gaze was nearly overpowering.

"I thought something like that might have happened," he replied casually. "Sometimes I just get a feeling about things and I need to see if I'm right."

With that, he went to her bookshelf and picked out a book on medieval art, feigning an interest in that subject so his 'ba-san would not question him about his interest in hidden swords.

While flipping the pages, he thought smugly how much he was learning, and how right *katana* had been to instruct him to not reveal any of this story just yet. But when? I'm bursting with information, he thought. If I don't tell someone soon, I might just explode!

He giggled at the thought.

"Do you find that artwork to be funny, Ak-*kun*?" his 'ba-san asked him.

"No, I'm just having silly thoughts!"

When he was alone again in his room, his thoughts turned from silly to the incredulous: The *Shogun's* wife was the daughter of the Emperor? And she killed him? Why would the Emperor be so close to the people who were keeping him from being the Emperor? Again, his young mind could not comprehend the complexities of life in Japan during that time.

There were changes inside the nation, brought about slowly by the *Shogunate*, as each new *Shogun* tried to make the country conform to his ideas. After the death of *Shogun* Tsunayoshi, as you have been told, his nephew Ienobu took control. But that lasted only a short time and had little impact on life for the Hanshiro family and the boy Tsuyoshi.

His family lived a quiet life in Niihama, and when he was seventeen he was united with the youngest daughter of the Sasaki family, they of the Rokkaku Sasaki clan from Oruga, Kyushu. Although Sumiko Sasaki was four years his senior, she was lovely and graceful and he felt she was far above his humble status. Unbeknownst to young Tsuyoshi, his parents had asked their *nakodo* – the matchmaker - to seek a family of some repute, as the boy would be the master of the Suzuki / Asano *katana* one day. For this reason, the Sasaki family was encouraged to have their daughter marry beneath their rank.

Hence, in the year 1729, when Tsuyoshi was seventeen and the lovely Sumiko was but 21, they were married and lived, initially, with her family on Kyushu.

His parents by now were the owners of an orchard of *nashi* pears, and were becoming well known and somewhat affluent. But since they were not of the Sasaki class, they encouraged their only son to study the arts of calligraphy and *haiku*, and the sword fighting art of *kendo* while living with the Sasakis. When he and his wife returned to his family home, he was more self-assured and confident, carrying his head with pride. His father, Tosa, and his mother, Kinume, were proud of the fine young man he was becoming.

By this time, a new *Shogun* was ruling our country. Tokugawa Yoshimune had little use for the trappings of his office, and often wore cotton rather than silk as was expected of one with his status. Just before the marriage of Tsuyoshi and Sumiko, the *Shogun* allowed for the importation of foreign books, and this young couple began learning the foreign language of English.

So busy were they with their work at the family fruit farm that they put off having a family until nearly five years into their marriage. Their daughter arrived first, followed in 1734 by their son Michio.

This fine young man was eighteen when his grandmother died and his father became heir to the Asano *katana*.

But being the sword of a noble Suzuki was without compare, and I secretly longed to be returned to the family of my origin.

Katana's seeming despair was evident to the boy as he dutifully wrote all that he had been told. There was less excitement in the story now, and he wondered just how and when the sword was returned to the family of his grandmother. Certainly she was a Suzuki and not of the Hanshiro family.

I guess I'll know the answer to all of this when *katana* is ready to tell me, he thought. The additional information he had been given was added to the outline he was keeping.

LADY TOSHIKO SUZUKI

Born in 1427 as Toshiko Matsudaira
Father: Marquis Matsudaira
Related to: Minamoto Chikauji

Homes: Izumo, Edo

LORD HIROSHI SUZUKI

for whom *katana* was made.
Born in 1425
Father: somebody Suzuki
Related to: Emperors Go-
    Shirakawa, Go-Daigo & Antoku
Homes: Osaka, Edo, Tojo
Died in 1476. Buried in Tojo.

Married: 1444
Family: two sons, born 1448 & 1450;
    a daughter, born 1453

LADY MICHIKO SUZUKI

Born in 1452 as Michiko Takatsukasa
Father: Prince Takatsukasa
Home: Edo

LORD KIICHI SUZUKI

Second master of *katana*
Born in 1448
Father: Lord Hiroshi Suzuki
Homes: Osaka, Edo, Tojo,
    Fukuchiyama
Died in 1497. Cremated in Tojo.

Married: 1470
Family: twins. a daughter born 1471;
    a son born 1471, hours later.

LADY MASAKO SUZUKI

Born in 1474 as Masako Tokudaiji
Father: Prince Tokudaiji
Home: Shizuoka

LORD SEIROKU SUZUKI

Third master of *katana*
Born in 1471
Father: Lord Kiichi Suzuki
Homes: Osaka, Edo, Tojo,
    Fukuchiyama
Died in 1498. Buried in Osaka.

Married: 1491
Family: two daughters and a son, born 1492

LADY TOMIKO SUZUKI

Born in 1493 as Tomiko Mitsui
Father: Mitsui-*sama*
Home: Namazue

LORD MICHIO SUZUKI

Fourth master of *katana*
Born in 1492
Father: Lord Seiroku Suzuki
Homes: Osaka, Edo, Tojo
    Fukuchiyama
Died in 1530. Buried in Tojo.

Married: 1509
Family: a son, born 1512; 3 daughters

LADY MIKI SUZUKI

Born in 1515 as Miki Ikeda
Father: Ikeda-San
Home: Edo

LORD TOMISHIKI SUZUKI

Fifth master of *katana*
Born in 1512
Father: Lord Michio Suzuki
Homes: Osaka, Edo, Tojo
    Fukuchiyama
Died in 1562. Buried in Osaka.

Married: 1533
Family: a son, born 1534; a daughter
and sons Sadao & Hirohisa

LADY KUNIKO SUZUKI

Born as Kuniko Itakura
Father: Viscount Itakura
Home: Edo

LORD SHIN SUZUKI
Sixth master of *katana*
Born in 1534
Father: Lord Tomishiki Suzuki
Homes: Osaka, Edo, Tojo
    Fukuchiyama, Karuizawa
Died ?

Married: 1555
Family: daughter born 1555 & Goto in 1558
a son Masatoshi born 1556

\|/

HARUKO SUZUKI

Born in 1553 as Haruko Nagata
Father: Lord Nagata
Home: Kishu area

LORD MASATOSHI SUZUKI
Seventh master of *katana*
Born in 1556
Father: Lord Shin Suzuki
Homes: Osaka, Edo, Tojo
    Fukuchiyama, Karuizawa

Married: 1575
Family: son Satoru born 1575, daughter
Nanami born 1576, son Shuji born 1577
Died 1600 at Sekigahara, son born
1579 died as a child

TAKAKO SUZUKI
Born as Takako Arai
Born in 1577

SATORU SUZUKI

Born in 1575
Died 1616

Family: son Masaharu born 1599

\|/

NORIKO SUZUKI

Born as Noriko Matsudaira

Born in 1602

LORD MASAHARU SUZUKI

Eighth master of *katana*

Born in 1599

Died in 1644

Married: in Osaka, 1616;
son Masanobu born 1620

AKEMI SUZUKI

Born as Akemi Kikuchi

Born in 1622

Home: Northern Kyushu

LORD MASANOBU SUZUKI

Ninth master of *katana*

Born in 1620

Married: 1640. Dau. Sachiko born 1641;
son Korekiyo born 1657

SACHIKO ASANO

Born as Sachiko Suzuki

Born in 1641

Home: Tojo

LORD NAGATOMO ASANO

Tenth master of *katana*

Born in 1643

Died 1675

Home: Ako Castle, on Biwa-ko

Married 1659. Son Naganori,
born Edo 1667.

AKURI MIYOSHI

Born 1674

Born as Akuri Miyoshi

Father: Nagaharu Asano of Hiroshima

LORD NAGANORI ASANO

known as Takumi-no Kami

Born in Edo, Sept. 28, 1667

Eleventh master of *katana*

Died: Seppuku March 14, 1702
Mistress: Satomi Hino
Became Yosen-in   Dau: Lady Asano no Kinume
Died   1714
Born 1695

X
X
\|/

Ryoko Suzuki b.1661, married: Lord Hino b. 1654
Married 1678 at age 17   He the Daimyo of Nara
      Daughter Satomi Hino b. 1679. Became mistress to
      Lord Asano Takumi-no Kami in 1694.   X
      \|/

Tosa no Hanshiro < - - - - - - - - - - - - - - Lady Asano no Kinume
Born 1680; died 1754   Born 1695; died 1752
Twelfth master of *katana*

   |
   | Married 1710; son Tsuyoshi born 1712
   |
   \|/

TSUYOSHI HANSHIRO   **SUMIKO SASAKI**
Home: Tosa province, Shikoku   Home: Ogura, Kyushu
Born 1712   Born: 1708
Thirteenth master of *katana*

      Married 1729. Dau. born first, then son Michio b. 1734

XVIII

KATANA CHANGES
HOUSEHOLDS - AGAIN

Akira-*chan* had been very busy with schoolwork, both from his third grade class and from his Saturday *Nihon-go* class. He was really enjoying the work that Miss Haversham had his class do, mostly in science and arithmetic. She had told his parents at their last meeting that he was beginning the study of mathematics principles, as well, and always had his reading homework completed well ahead of time.

He tried not to be too smug about this praise, because he knew that much of his enthusiasm for learning came from the stories *katana* was telling him.

His '*ba-san* helped him with his Japanese alphabets and he found the work to be fascinating. There were four styles of writing that he had to learn, and he noted that all four were used interchangeably in books, magazines and newspapers. Some words, especially all foreign words, were written in one style, called *Katakana*. But he had not begun to learn that style yet. The class was learning the basic style taught to Japanese children first; that alphabet is *Hiragana*.

He and his classmates would learn the 46 symbols in this style, then add the 46 from *Katakana*, and then add in the nearly 2,000 commonly used *Kanji* symbols. But they had already been learning the one that let them read the Chushingura story: *Romaji*. This style used the English characters that they already knew, and he could read some words phonetically in this style of writing.

His 'ba-san had told him that for her college work, she had learned more than 5,000 *Kanji* symbols. He found that number too large to grasp.

He looked at the paper on which these styles were shown: first was *hiragana*

(ひらがな); then *katakana* (カタカナ); and finally *kanji* (漢字). Someday, he promised himself, he would know them all.

After many years of toil in the fields, the Hanshiro family had expanded their orchard of *nashi*, the Japanese pear. But, as time passed, they perceived a need for more land on which to grow other crops, especially *kiwi* and *kaki*, the Japanese persimmon. These fruits were becoming increasingly popular, and their benefactors, the Suzuki family who were nearby, encouraged them to expand. The Suzukis occupied *Tojo*, East Castle, but had never seemed to be domineering or arrogant as many of the samurai and *daimyo* warriors were. For this reason, Tsuyoshi Hanshiro desired to return my mate and me to the Suzuki family at an early, appropriate time in the near future.

As the family elder, Tsuyoshi was duty bound to honor the request of his mother, the Lady Asano no Kinume, that we swords be returned to their original owners 'when the time was right.'

Recall that we had passed to Tsuyoshi before the death of his father, Tosa no Hanshiro, as his mother had requested in her final days. Thus was a tradition born in the Hanshiro family to return us to our Suzuki family at some point in time.

Michio, the third generation Hanshiro and an eager and excitable lad, eagerly studied English in a school set up near the Matsuyama Castle, known as West Castle. This school was one of many that sprang into being as a result of the *Rangaku* decree by the Shogun, allowing, and actually encouraging, the study of Western culture. While at this school, he chanced to meet the scion of the Kasai family, an intelligent young woman named Yasuko. He was delighted that her name meant Peaceful Child, as she calmed him as no other person ever had.

Her family domicile was in northern Honshu where they had been granted the monopoly by the *Shogun* to clean the sewer pits at the *Shogunate* Edo castle. So, although they were of the merchant class as was he, theirs was a well-known and very respected name.

The young lady was two years his junior and told him she had tired of life in the colder region of their country. After his parents had approved her, through the services of Matsusada Suzuki, who had agreed to act as *nakodo* for the Hanshiros, she eagerly had all her belongings moved to the temperate Shikoku area. In 1753 they were married, and joined his family at their orchard outside Niihama.

Their son, Shokei, was born the following year and they used the *kan-ji* of "sho" in his name to express their hope that he would soar into the upper reaches of their class; that he would excel and give their name even greater respect throughout all of Japan.

Just three years prior to the birth of their son, their benefactors, Matsusada Suzuki and his wife, Momo, gave birth to a son whom they named Tadoshi. Michio and Yasuko often commented on how appropriate was Momo's name, which means Peach. Her cheeks were rosy and she had a smile on her face at their every meeting; her personality was always bright and cheerful. To them, the Suzukis were more than just benefactors; they were truly friends.

The two sons, Shokei Hanshiro and Tadoshi Suzuki, were barely in their teens when the country suffered another scandal. It involved a samurai who was the student of a known Confucian teacher, and the teacher himself. The country's Imperial Family was headed by Empress Go-Sakuramachi and, as you have been told, the Imperial Family had little to no power in the governance of our country. These two, the teacher and the samurai student, petitioned loudly on the streets for the dissolution of the *Shogunate* and the restoration of the Imperial Family as the true rulers of the nation. For this act of Lese-Majeste, actually sedition, both men were condemned to death. This was an embarrassment for the Empress and, some say, brought on a huge typhoon, which devastated much of the old capital of Kyoto, bringing down the newly constructed Imperial Palace. Shortly thereafter, our country suffered its worst drought in all of our peoples' memory; the drought lasted long after the Empress stepped down.

Tadoshi's father, Matsusada, had married Momo, as I have said, the youngest daughter of the *"Goshi"* Matsukata family. *Goshi,* you should know, simply means "Rural Samurai," and denotes their family as a junior or cadet branch of the Matsukata clan. This family had their domain at the southwestern tip of Kyushu Island, with holdings near Kagoshima. Their status of *Goshi* derived after Sekigahara from an award by the *Shogun,* Tokugawa Ieyasu.

By this time, the country was under the control of the *Shogun* Tokugawa Ieshige, who was the ninth ruler from the Tokugawa family. This ruler was a man in poor health and suffered from a severe speech problem, an impediment, actually. For reasons he never shared with his countrymen, he showed little interest in the running of the nation and during that time we were as a ship adrift, without oars or sail. Few were disappointed when, in 1760, he stepped down in favor of his son, Ieharu, who was a far more capable leader.

When *katana* took a break in its story, Alexander broke into a broad smile at the name of Momo. This was not a common name for a woman, he thought, as I have not seen it before in anything I have read with 'ba-san, nor my materials at the *Nihon-go* school, nor so far in what I have learned from *katana*.

But the name is certainly not new to me, he laughed, because 'ba-san told me the children's story of Momo-Taro-San many years ago, and I remember it still!

Momo-Taro-San, he recalled, was the Peach Boy of Japanese fairy tales. The story, as he remembered it, went like this: An old woman who had no children went to the stream for water, and saw a large peach floating down the stream. She carried the peach back home and she and her husband cut it in half so they could eat it. But instead of finding a pit inside, they discovered a small boy. They called the boy "Peach Boy" – Momo-Taro-san. The boy grew older but was still quite small, and in the woods around their home, he befriended several small animals, including a talking dog, a monkey, and a pheasant. When he left his parents, years later, to fight against a band of *Oni* – he remembered that that word meant ogre or demon – the animal friends accompanied him.

Arriving at the island where these *Oni* lived, he and his animal friends beat up the gang of *Oni* and forced them to surrender.

When he left the island, he took with him all the valuables that the *Oni* had taken from their victims, and the Chief *Oni*, as well. Upon returning home to his aged parents, he gave them all the wealth and they all lived happily ever after.

His grandmother had told him that this story originated at the far end of Shikoku Island, near the town of Takamatsu, where some of the Suzuki family still lived. In that area are many caves that had been dug by earlier peoples, she had said. Later people living there, not knowing who had dug the caves, thought they were the home of the *Oni*.

On his '*ba-san's* hobby room wall hung a cloth three-dimensional picture of Momo-Taro-San returning home in his boat with his animal friends and the Chief *Oni*.

Next time I visit '*ba-san*, he said to himself, I'll take another look at that wall hanging.

Michio Hanshiro, in whose possession were my mate and me, lived up to the meaning of his name, for "Michio" means "Man on the Correct Path." Certainly all that Michio was doing with the orchard was leading his family to greater stability and respect than his forebears might have imagined possible. The close relationship that he and Yasuko had with the Suzukis was both satisfying and rewarding.

They rejoiced with their friends when, in 1753, Matsusada, though only 23 at the time, was appointed by the *Shogun* to the title of "*Roju*," or Senior Councilor. As I have told you previously, this small number of men was a select group of wealthy or well-placed men from Japan's oldest and finest families, who became advisors to the *Shogun*. In the Suzuki family from times past, this title and duty was passed on from father to son.

Likewise, they were both on hand when Tadoshi Suzuki was wed to Takako Hosokawa in the summer of 1778 when his bride was 23. She was the scion of the revered clan that owned Kumamoto Castle in Kyushu. You will recall what you were told previously about the Hosokawa clan and the Kumamoto Castle. Her family had a long and illustrious history in our nation.

Tadoshi's son, Mondo Suzuki, was born on March 14, 1792, which was the 90th anniversary of the sacrifice of Lord Asano in the gardens of *Sengaku-ji* temple in Edo. On that occasion, my master, Michio Hanshiro, presented my mate and me to Lord Tadoshi, as had been the wont of the Hanshiro line since we first fell into the hands of Lady Asano no Kimune so many years ago.

Our two families were drawn ever closer by this act of friendship and what the Japanese call *"On."* *"On"* means to the Japanese an honorable obligation, or a debt of gratitude. Such was the feeling that the Hanshiros had had over these long years while they kept my mate and me, the *katana* and *wakizashi* held by Lord Asano himself, in safekeeping; safekeeping for that special day when we would be returned to our original and rightful family.

The boy, Alexander Akira, knew that he did not need to look in any books, or talk to anyone else, to know that these events were momentous for both families. And now, he knew the circumstances behind the Suzuki family sword having its *menuki* changed to the Asano clan's *kamon*.

But, he worried aloud, why didn't *katana* say anything about the Suzuki *kamon* being put back on the two swords?

Then he bonked himself on the head and muttered, "Don't be a dummy! Of course, the *menuki* weren't changed – that's what I've known all along! The Suzuki family sword bears the Asano crest."

With so much information to add to his genealogy of the sword masters and owners, he worked long into the night to complete it so it looked like this:

LADY TOSHIKO SUZUKI

Born in 1427 as Toshiko Matsudaira
Father: Marquis Matsudaira
Related to: Minamoto Chikauji

Homes: Izumo, Edo

LORD HIROSHI SUZUKI

For whom *katana* was made.
Born in 1425
Father: somebody Suzuki
Related to: Emperors Go-
    Shirakawa, Go-Daigo & Antoku
Homes: Osaka, Edo, Tojo
Died in 1476. Buried in Tojo.

Married: 1444
Family: two sons, born 1448 & 1450;
    a daughter, born 1453

\|/

LADY MICHIKO SUZUKI

Born in 1452 as Michiko Takatsukasa
Father: Prince Takatsukasa
Home: Edo

LORD KIICHI SUZUKI

Second master of *katana*
Born in 1448
Father: Lord Hiroshi Suzuki
Homes: Osaka, Edo, Tojo,
    Fukuchiyama
Died in 1497. Cremated in Tojo.

Married: 1470
Family: twins. a daughter born 1471;
    a son born 1471, hours later.

\|/

LADY MASAKO SUZUKI

Born in 1474 as Masako Tokudaiji
Father: Prince Tokudaiji
Home: Shizuoka

LORD SEIROKU SUZUKI

Third master of *katana*
Born in 1471
Father: Lord Kiichi Suzuki
Homes: Osaka, Edo, Tojo,
　　　 Fukuchiyama
Died in 1498. Buried in Osaka.

Married: 1491
Family: two daughters and a son, born 1492

LADY TOMIKO SUZUKI

Born in 1493 as Tomiko Mitsui
Father: Mitsui-*sama*
Home: Namazue

LORD MICHIO SUZUKI

Fourth master of *katana*
Born in 1492
Father: Lord Seiroku Suzuki
Homes: Osaka, Edo, Tojo
　　　 Fukuchiyama
Died in 1530. Buried in Tojo.

Married: 1509
Family: a son, born 1512; 3 daughters

LADY MIKI SUZUKI

Born in 1515 as Miki Ikeda
Father: Ikeda-San
Home: Edo

LORD TOMISHIKI SUZUKI

Fifth master of *katana*
Born in 1512
Father: Lord Michio Suzuki
Homes: Osaka, Edo, Tojo
　　　 Fukuchiyama
Died in 1562. Buried in Osaka.

Married: 1533
Family: a son, born 1534; a daughter
　　　 and sons Sadao & Hirohisa

LADY KUNIKO SUZUKI

Born as Kuniko Itakura
Father: Viscount Itakura
Home: Edo

LORD SHIN SUZUKI
Sixth master of *katana*
Born in 1534
Father: Lord Tomishiki Suzuki
Homes: Osaka, Edo, Tojo
    Fukuchiyama, Karuizawa
Died ?

Married: 1555
Family: daughter born 1555 & Goto in 1558
a son Masatoshi born 1556

HARUKO SUZUKI

Born in 1553 as Haruko Nagata
Father: Lord Nagata
Home: Kishu area

LORD MASATOSHI SUZUKI
Seventh master of *katana*
Born in 1556
Father: Lord Shin Suzuki
Homes: Osaka, Edo, Tojo
    Fukuchiyama, Karuizawa

Married: 1575
Family: son Satoru born 1575, daughter
Nanami born 1576, son Shuji born 1577
Died 1600 at Sekigahara, son born
1579 died as a child

TAKAKO SUZUKI
Born as Takako Arai
Born in 1577

SATORU SUZUKI

Born in 1575
Died 1616

Family: son Masaharu born 1599

NORIKO SUZUKI

Born as Noriko Matsudaira

Born in 1602

LORD MASAHARU SUZUKI

Eighth master of *katana*

Born in 1599

Died in 1644

Married: in Osaka, 1616;
son Masanobu born 1620

AKEMI SUZUKI

Born as Akemi Kikuchi

Born in 1622

Home: Northern Kyushu

LORD MASANOBU SUZUKI

Ninth master of *katana*

Born in 1620

Married: 1640. Dau. Sachiko born 1641;
son Korekiyo born 1657

SACHIKO ASANO

Born as Sachiko Suzuki

Born in 1641

Home: Tojo

LORD NAGATOMO ASANO

Tenth master of *katana*

Born in 1643

Died 1675

Home: Ako Castle, on Biwa-ko

Married 1659. Son Naganori, born Edo 1667.

AKURI MIYOSHI

Born 1674

Born as Akuri Miyoshi

Father: Nagaharu Asano of Hiroshima

Became Yosen-in

Died 1714

LORD NAGANORI ASANO

known as Takumi-no Kami

Born in Edo, Sept. 28, 1667

Eleventh master of *katana*

Died: Seppuku March 14, 1702

Mistress: Satomi Hino

Dau: Lady Asano no Kinume

Born 1695

X

X

\|/

Ryoko Suzuki b.1661, married: Lord Hino b. 1654
Married 1678 at age 17   He the Daimyo of Nara
      Daughter Satomi Hino b. 1679. Became mistress to
       Lord Asano Takumi-no Kami in 1694.   X
                   \|/

Tosa no Hanshiro < - - - - - - - - - - - - - **Lady Asano no Kinume**
Born 1680; died 1754   Born 1695; died 1752
Twelfth master of *katana*
  |
  | Married 1710; son Tsuyoshi born 1712
  |
 \|/

TSUYOSHI HANSHIRO   **SUMIKO SASAKI**
Home: Tosa province, Shikoku   Home: Ogura, Kyushu
Born 1712   Born: 1708
Thirteenth master of *katana*
  |
  | Married 1729. Dau. born first, then son Michio b. 1734
  |
 \|/

MICHIO HANSHIRO   **YASUKO KASAI**
Home: Tosa province, Shikoku   Home: Mutsu Province
Born 1734   Born 1736
Fourteenth master of *katana*
 |
 | Married 1753. son Shokei born 1754
 |
 |
 | **MATSUSADA SUZUKI**   **MOMO MATSUKATA**
 | Home: Niihama, Shikoku   Kagoshima, Kyushu
 | Born 1730
 |
 | Son Tadoshi born 1751
\|/

LORD TADOSHI SUZUKI
Fifteenth master of *katana* on 3/14/1792
Home: Niihama, Shikoku
Born 1751

TAKAKO HOSOKAWA

Home: Kumamoto, Kyushu
Born 1755

Married 1778. Son Mondo born 3/14/1792

MONDO SUZUKI
Born 1792

XIX

YET ANOTHER CONFIRMATION

"*Ba-san*," he whined, "can you tell me the story of Momotaro-san again? Pleeeeeease?"

He knew that whining would sometimes get her immediate attention, and she would then sit on the couch with him snuggled close beside her, and he would have her absolute and undivided attention. And today, this was exactly what he wanted.

"Well, Akira-*chan*, what would you like to know about it? I'm sure you remember the story; it was not more than six months ago that we last read it."

She was on to his conniving ways by now, and knew there was something more that he wanted.

"Well, actually, I wanted to know about the family crest you have on your wall. It looks like it is made out of beads. But, I can't really tell what it is. Can you tell me about it?"

His grandmother felt that this was the actual question he wanted answered, so they walked into the living room and she took the small plaque off the wall.

"This is called a *kamon* in Japan, which means a particular family's crest. When we call it "*mon*," we just mean crest in general. The "*kamon*" identifies other members of the family. Many centuries ago, the generals of our warring armies would put their family crest on the clothing of all the warriors, from the top samurai down to the newest foot soldier. In some of the great battles where many families' armies were involved, there could be a dozen or two dozen different *kamon* on the battlefield at one time. From the earliest times, only noble families had a family name and a family *kamon*. But gradually, more and more families were allowed to take a last name and choose a crest that suited them."

"This *kamon* is from the Suzuki family, and it is a pagoda. This is the crest that my mother's family wears. And my father's family wears the wisteria *kamon*. That *kamon* is very common nowadays, as many families chose to use it. But the Suzuki *kamon* is still quite rare. Our friend Jean made this for us many years ago, as she is a talented artisan and was fascinated to meet someone from Japan. "

"Does this answer your question, Alex?" she asked patiently.

"It kind of does, but did the families also put their *kamon* on other things? Like, their dishes, or their houses, or on their swords?" He asked this in a singsong kind of whine, and he saw her stiffen slightly. Oops, he thought, maybe I went a little too far?

"That's exactly what they did. The castles would have large banners with the owner's *kamon* on it for all to see. And they put that *kamon* on most every other kind of personal item. Is this your real question, Akkun, or do you really want to know something else?"

"I'm really glad you told me about the Suzuki *kamon*, 'Ba-san. I've been wondering about it a lot, and every time I come to see you I want to ask you. Now I finally got my answer. In my Japanese school, we read about Asano, and how he had to kill himself. Do you know what *kamon* was on his clothing?"

"His family was a distant relative of my mother's family, the Suzukis. And I think his *kamon* was crossed feathers," she explained to him. "Is that what your teacher told you? I don't really remember any more."

"She didn't really say, so I was hoping you would know. I guess I can look in one of your books and try to find out."

With that, he snuggled close to her and buried his face in her sleeve, not wanting to say any more about Asano for fear he would blurt out something he had learned from *katana*.

You should know that our country was in a period of peaceful times; the samurai were put to work doing jobs that helped run the country, or the towns, or the villages. They still wore their swords, but there was very little fighting for them to do.

So, in a very happy spirit, the families of my two masters, the Suzukis and the Hanshiros, celebrated the marriages of their oldest sons on the 15th of April, 1816. My master, Mondo Suzuki, was 24 at the time he took as his wife the 17-year-old Yumiko Sakai. This family you have heard of before; they are a branch of the Matsudaira clan with their home in Yonegawa, to the north of Edo. Harunori Uesugi, the head of the family that had taken over the Hino estate, arranged this marriage. He also acted as *nakodo* for Torao Hanshiro, and on that same day he took as his wife young Etsuko Yumoto. She was from the famous *onsen* town of Hakone, again near to Edo. Torao at the time was but 20, younger than his friend and benefactor Mondo, but also four years older than his bride.

Onsen, you will recall, are the hot springs in Japan, and few are as well regarded for their healing powers as those at Hakone.

The family of Sakai was named a *fudai daimyo*, meaning "hereditary vassal," by the great war lord Tokugawa Ieyasu, after the battles at Sekigahara. This term simply means that they were part of the *Shogunate* administration and thus, were allowed to own a small fief.

Torao was the great grandson of Michio Hanshiro, who had given my mate and me to Mondo Suzuki's father, Tadoshi, on the occasion of Mondo's birth.

As you see, the Hanshiro family and the Suzuki family were very close, with the Suzukis assisting the Hanshiros with their orchard and with choosing their mates.

Directly after their weddings at the local temple, both young couples trekked to temple 61, named *Koon-ji*, of the 88 temples of Kobo Daishi on Shikoku Island. You know that this is the temple that Mondo's ancestor went to upon his marriage, asking the patron god of the temple to bless his marriage with children. The Sakai family accompanied Mondo and Yumiko on this journey, but my Lord Tadoshi had expired in 1809 and his wife Takako had passed three years earlier. So, my Lord Mondo celebrated with just the presence of other relatives.

The decades before and after these marriages, though they were peaceful within our nation, still had many incidents with foreigners coming to our shores. As I have told you, the *Shogunate* had decreed that no foreigners were allowed in Japan, and as a result, there were many altercations between the crews of these ships, mostly British and Russian, and our local samurai.

My Lord Mondo, though still a young man, carried my mate and me to Edo to speak with the *Shogun* about these continuing disturbances. It was at the time of Lord Tadoshi's death that Mondo was also admitted to the *Roju*, and it was in this capacity that he traveled to speak with Tokugawa Ienari, the reigning *Shogun*.

His statement was brief and pointed, saying that the country was losing an opportunity for trade. Since many Japanese were already studying the language of the British, why not also take British money?

But the *Shogun* was adamant: There would be no foreigners in Japan!

Others of the *Roju* supported the statements by my Lord Mondo, but the Shogun's argument made some sense to them. He reminded all who were present that the last time Japan did that – allowed foreigners into their towns – the Dutch, the Spanish, and the British created a terrible problem by exporting their various brands of Christianity to Japan and not just their goods. So, for the sake of the country's sanity, the *Shogun* stood firm in his denial.

Hence, it was not surprising to my Lord Mondo Suzuki when the *Shogun*, in 1835, ordered all coastal *daimyo* and all government authorities to drive away any foreign ships immediately upon sighting. They were not to be welcomed into Japan's coastal waters nor allowed to dock at any port. This policy, by edict of the *Shogun*, would have no exceptions, even for the health of the crews of these foreign vessels, nor for them to take on water, rations or other supplies.

Because of this edict, others in Japan were enhancing their coastal defenses, particularly the *daimyo* of Satsuma province in southern Kyushu. He, like some other *daimyo* of other areas, created battlements for cannon and placed floating mines in their harbors.

Torao had no interest in the politics of the country, and was having success in the raising and selling of fruits of his expanding orchard. Towards this end, he used the contacts of Mondo's family connections to create alliances with freight carriers in 1830 to move fresh fruits to the large markets in Osaka, Kyoto, Hiroshima and Nagasaki. In the Kyushu market, the family of Mondo's mother's, the Hosokawas, were instrumental in forging a relationship with the *daimyo* of Satsuma province, where they were growing an especially sweet orange, known to you as the Satsuma. Additionally, Mondo's wife's family, the Sakais, provided connections and support for distribution in the Osaka area.

The Suzukis earned a large return on the monies they had invested in the Hanshiro orchard enterprises.

After four years of marriage, Master Mondo, who had received my mate and me in 1806 upon the death of his mother, had a son whom they named Monzaemon, an ancient and revered boy's name. It seemed that the offerings at *Koon-ji* temple had been accepted, as they then welcomed two more sons and three daughters in the following ten years.

The Hanshiro family growth began some five years later, when son Kan'ichi was born, followed in a year by a daughter. Baby Kan'ichi's grandparents, Eiichiro and Saki, were both on hand for his birth, as they continued to live in a separate home at the edge of the orchards.

Learning about the ancient families of his grandmother made Alexander more curious about her immediate family. He knew of his great-aunt Michiko, who lived in California, as he had fond memories of visiting with Michiko's family, both in California when he had traveled there with his *'ji-san, 'ba-san* and father, and when his great-aunt had visited his grandparents' home, as well. And, he also remembered that he had a great-uncle in Japan: This was the uncle named Akira, the same as his middle name. But, were there other Japanese relatives?

When he asked his grandmother about this, she showed him the family tree that his grandfather had made. It showed the parents, aunts and uncles of his grandmother, and went back as far as ... Mondo Suzuki! Yes, before his eyes were the names of Mondo and his son Monzaemon. He dared not show his excitement at seeing these names, and calmly thanked his 'ba-san for sharing the family tree.

He was even more determined than ever to visit his ancestral homeland one day, for he was feeling more and more Japanese with each passing day and each continuation of the saga told him by *katana*.

That night he excitedly added the new information to his written history:

LADY TOSHIKO SUZUKI

Born in 1427 as Toshiko Matsudaira
Father: Marquis Matsudaira
Related to: Minamoto Chikauji

Homes: Izumo, Edo

LORD HIROSHI SUZUKI

for whom *katana* was made.
Born in 1425
Father: somebody Suzuki
Related to: Emperors Go-
    Shirakawa, Go-Daigo & Antoku
Homes: Osaka, Edo, Tojo
Died in 1476. Buried in Tojo.

Married: 1444
Family: two sons, born 1448 & 1450;
a daughter, born 1453

\|/

LADY MICHIKO SUZUKI

Born in 1452 as Michiko Takatsukasa
Father: Prince Takatsukasa
Home: Edo

LORD KIICHI SUZUKI

Second master of *katana*
Born in 1448
Father: Lord Hiroshi Suzuki
Homes: Osaka, Edo, Tojo,
    Fukuchiyama
Died in 1497. Cremated in Tojo.

Married: 1470
Family: twins. a daughter born 1471;
a son born 1471, hours later.

\|/

LADY MASAKO SUZUKI

Born in 1474 as Masako Tokudaiji
Father: Prince Tokudaiji
Home: Shizuoka

LORD SEIROKU SUZUKI

Third master of *katana*
Born in 1471
Father: Lord Kiichi Suzuki
Homes: Osaka, Edo, Tojo,
       Fukuchiyama
Died in 1498. Buried in Osaka.

Married: 1491
Family: two daughters and a son, born 1492

LADY TOMIKO SUZUKI

Born in 1493 as Tomiko Mitsui
Father: Mitsui-*sama*
Home: Namazue

LORD MICHIO SUZUKI

Fourth master of *katana*
Born in 1492
Father: Lord Seiroku Suzuki
Homes: Osaka, Edo, Tojo
       Fukuchiyama
Died in 1530. Buried in Tojo.

Married: 1509
Family: a son, born 1512; 3 daughters

LADY MIKI SUZUKI

Born in 1515 as Miki Ikeda
Father: Ikeda-San
Home: Edo

LORD TOMISHIKI SUZUKI

Fifth master of *katana*
Born in 1512
Father: Lord Michio Suzuki
Homes: Osaka, Edo, Tojo
       Fukuchiyama
Died in 1562. Buried in Osaka.

Married: 1533
Family: a son, born 1534; a daughter
       and sons Sadao & Hirohisa

LADY KUNIKO SUZUKI

Born as Kuniko Itakura
Father: Viscount Itakura
Home: Edo

LORD SHIN SUZUKI
Sixth master of *katana*
Born in 1534
Father: Lord Tomishiki Suzuki
Homes: Osaka, Edo, Tojo
        Fukuchiyama, Karuizawa
Died ?

Married: 1555
Family: daughter born 1555 & Goto in 1558
a son Masatoshi born 1556

\|/

HARUKO SUZUKI

Born in 1553 as Haruko Nagata
Father: Lord Nagata
Home: Kishu area

LORD MASATOSHI SUZUKI
Seventh master of *katana*
Born in 1556
Father: Lord Shin Suzuki
Homes: Osaka, Edo, Tojo
        Fukuchiyama, Karuizawa

Married: 1575
Family: son Satoru born 1575, daughter
Nanami born 1576, son Shuji born 1577
Died 1600 at Sekigahara, son born
1579 died as a child

TAKAKO SUZUKI
Born as Takako Arai
Born in 1577

SATORU SUZUKI

Born in 1575
Died 1616

Family: son Masaharu born 1599

\|/

NORIKO SUZUKI

Born as Noriko Matsudaira

Born in 1602

LORD MASAHARU SUZUKI

Eighth master of *katana*

Born in 1599

Died in 1644

Married: in Osaka, 1616;
son Masanobu born 1620

\|/

AKEMI SUZUKI

Born as Akemi Kikuchi

Born in 1622

Home: Northern Kyushu

LORD MASANOBU SUZUKI

Ninth master of *katana*

Born in 1620

Married: 1640. Dau. Sachiko born 1641;
son Korekiyo born 1657

\|/

SACHIKO ASANO

Born as Sachiko Suzuki

Born in 1641

Home: Tojo

LORD NAGATOMO ASANO

Tenth master of *katana*

Born in 1643

Died 1675

Home: Ako Castle, on Biwa-ko

Married 1659. Son Naganori, born Edo 1667.

\|/

AKURI MIYOSHI

Born 1674

Born as Akuri Miyoshi

Father: Nagaharu Asano of Hiroshima

Became Yosen-in

Died   1714

LORD NAGANORI ASANO

known as Takumi-no Kami

Born in Edo, Sept. 28, 1667

Eleventh master of *katana*

Died: Seppuku March 14, 1702

Mistress: Satomi Hino

Dau: Lady Asano no Kinume

Born 1695

X

X

\|/

Ryoko Suzuki b.1661, married: Lord Hino b. 1654
Married 1678 at age 17   He the Daimyo of Nara

Daughter Satomi Hino b. 1679. Became mistress to
Lord Asano Takumi-no Kami in 1694.   X
                                          \|/

Tosa no Hanshiro < - - - - - - - - - - - - - **Lady Asano no Kinume**
Born 1680; died 1754   Born 1695; died 1752
Twelfth master of *katana*

|
| Married 1710; son Tsuyoshi born 1712
|
\|/

TSUYOSHI HANSHIRO   **SUMIKO SASAKI**
Home: Tosa province, Shikoku   Home: Ogura, Kyushu
Born 1712   Born: 1708
Thirteenth master of *katana*

|
| Married 1729. Dau. born first, then son Michio b. 1734
|
\|/

MICHIO HANSHIRO   **YASUKO KASAI**
Home: Tosa province, Shikoku   Home: Mutsu Province
Born 1734   Born 1736
Fourteenth master of *katana*

|
| Married 1753. son Shokei born 1754
|
|
| **MATSUSADA SUZUKI**   **MOMO MATSUKATA**
| Home: Niihama, Shikoku   Kagoshima, Kyushu
| Born 1730
|
| Son Tadoshi born 1751
\|/

LORD TADOSHI SUZUKI   **TAKAKO HOSOKAWA**

Fifteenth master of *katana* on 3/14/1792

Home: Niihama, Shikoku   Home: Kumamoto, Kyushu

Born 1751. Died 1809   Born 1755. Died 1806

Married 1778. Son Mondo born 3/14/1792

LORD MONDO SUZUKI   **YUMIKO SAKAI**

Sixteenth master of katana

Born 1792   Born 1799

Home: Niihama, Shikoku   Home: Yonegawa

Married 1816. Son Monzaemon born 1820

2 sons, 3 daughters in next ten years

TORAO HANSHIRO   **ETSUKO YUMOTO**

Born 1796   Born 1800

Home: Niihama, Shikoku   Home: Hakone

Married: 1816. Son Kan'ichi born 1825, dau. born 1826

XX

JAPAN OPENS ITS DOORS

The years in which Monzaemon was raised were years of immense change for our people. Foment was everywhere as enlightened men argued for the return of the Emperor as the ruler of our nation. Discontent with the *Shogunate* brought small armies of men to battle, and saw the armies of the *Shogun* adopting the uniforms, weapons and military tactics of the Western world.

All of this came about as a result of the landing of an American fleet of warships in the harbor of Edo when Monzaemon was thirty-three years old. These ships, with their hulls painted a menacing black color, carried the American Commodore Matthew Perry and numerous sailors, intent on forcing the *Shogun* to open trade with the United States, the country that lay thousands of miles to the east of our land.

Despite the resistance of the *Shogun*, who took counsel from his closest advisors and from *the Roju*, of which my master, Mondo Suzuki, was an active member, the Commodore was convincing in his demands and in his threats of violence by the cannon aboard his four ships. In the year 1854, a treaty was signed by the *Shogun* with the American representative, allowing for trade between the two countries.

Lord Mondo Suzuki had embraced this treaty, and lived just another two years after its signing. My mate and I were passed to our next master, Lord Monzaemon, at that time and he took his father's place in the *Roju*, traveling frequently from his home in Niihama to the *Shogunate's* palace in Edo. As Lord Monzaemon traveled along the Tokaido Road towards Edo, he detoured so he could see the Black Ships, as they had become known to the Japanese people, anchored in the harbor of Shimoda, a small and sleepy fishing village at the tip of the Izu peninsula.

The presence of these ships signaled to all of Japan that our way of life was about to make a major change. Those among our *daimyo* and other important men who recognized this change as a positive thing were eager for the *Shogun*, Tokugawa Iesada, to step aside in favor of the Emperor Komei.

Many skirmishes took place in southern, central and northern Japan over the period of several years until finally, in January of 1868, the *Shogunate* was terminated and Emperor Komei was returned to power.

My master, Lord Monzaemon, was both saddened by the passing of his father and elated at the restoration of the Emperor. My Lord's life during that time had been further complicated by a great fire, which had burned our castle in Niihama. What remained was but a large house on the grounds, apart from the castle keep itself, and it was into that house that the Suzuki family moved. During that time, my Lord had also sold much of the large land holdings which had been under Suzuki control for centuries. Some of this land later became the city of Niihama, and some, including their holdings on Mount Ishizuchi, was to become a park owned by all the peoples of the province.

Despite his duties to his family and his country, my Lord Monzaemon found time to take a wife. His parents had used the service of a *nakodo*, as was the custom, and my Lord was married when twenty-five years of age to the youngest daughter of a cadet branch of the Yamamoto family, herself just two years younger in age. The Lady Keiko had a personality that matched her name, which means Katsura Tree Child. You should know that the Katsura tree is recognized in Japan for its extremely hard wood, and young Keiko was extremely hard headed. You should also know that Lady Keiko was born in the Year of the Horse, which, as you have been told previously, also means she was of a strong temperament.

Oh! thought young Alexander, I need to find out more about these Black Ships. Learning the history of Japan through the stories of *katana* is so exciting!

When he was next at his *Nihon-go* lessons, he talked with his classmates who were from Japan. Did they know about these Black Ships, he had asked. Not surprisingly, he found that this was common knowledge among the children who had attended Japanese schools. They were well aware, too, that over a hundred years earlier the Emperor had been returned to power.

"You are certainly learning a lot about Japan," said one of his schoolmates. "We think you know more about Japanese history than do most of us!" Alex responded quietly, "I'm lucky to have a grandmother who helps me learn things." He knew this was a little white lie, but he also know he could not tell anyone where he was really getting all his information.

At home, he told his parents over dinner all about the Black Ships, saying that his classmates had been discussing this. His father knew that history, and was delighted in Alexander's continued interest in his grandmother's homeland.

"Dad?" he inquired. "Could we go see the port where the Black Ships were allowed to anchor?" His father explained that, many years before Alexander had been born, Alex's grandfather had been in the Navy, and as a musician, had played for the annual Black Ship Festival in the small town of Shimoda. "So you see, Alex, our family is connected to what you are now learning. Perhaps the next time you see your grandparents you could ask about that festival. I'm sure your granddad has some stories he could tell you about it."

As was his habit, he promised himself that he would do exactly that. And he did.

Do not think that you should hear no more of the Hanshiro family, for Kan'ichi took as his wife the eldest daughter of the Matsui family, whose name means 'pine tree well' and was an old and respected family to the west of Lake Biwa. They were merchants who were not involved in the great battle at Sekigahara, but had supplied armaments to the forces of the winner, Ieyasu Tokugawa. As such, they were awarded the right to make a *kamon*, and chose a *kamon* which was similar in design to that of the famous *daimyo*, Date Masamune, from several hundred years before.

His wife, five years his junior, was named Kaoru, which means Fragrance. And, true to her family's *kamon*, which was a depiction of the *Tuta*, or tomato leaf, and to her own name's meaning, she was a lover of plants of all kinds, and kept a small garden of aromatic flowers planted all about the family home at the Hanshiro orchard. In all respects, she was a perfect mate for Kan'ichi, and she immediately became the close friend of Monzaemon's wife, Keiko, though these two women were completely different from one another.

The first son of Lord Monzaemon, named Masuhei, was born in 1849, just a year before Kan'ichi was married. As you now know, this was a period of increasing turmoil in our land, and Monzaemon was kept busy with his part in the affairs of state and caring for his family after the disastrous fire.

The momentous events that returned the Emperor to power made fundamental changes to our society, beginning, perhaps, with the pamphlets that an educator named Yukichi Fukuzawa began publishing and distributing; these pamphlets had names such as *"Seiyo Jijo"*, meaning "Conditions in the West", and *"Gakumon no Susume"*, which means "The Encouragement of Learning." The purpose of this literature was to help our people understand the value of some of the institutions of Occidental culture, including the education of all classes of people and not just the upper class. Already the Suzukis and the Hanshiros were engaged in the learning of English, as I have previously said, and they supported the distribution of these leaflets in their community of Niihama.

After the restoration of the Emperor, the national slogans changed from *Sonno Joi* to *Bummei Kaika*: Civilization and Enlightenment. The peoples were hungry for the benefits of education, and many schools opened to commoners and to girls, and schools for the teaching of English became more popular.

More changes in our national government came about, as well, including the change, in 1869, of the *daimyo*, to prefectural governors, working on behalf of the central government in Tokyo, as Edo was now called.

And only four years after the governorships were instituted, the Meiji government – the new Emperor had been Crown Prince to Emperor Komei - began allowing the practice of Christianity within our borders again. It was during this same year, 1873, that the government also changed our calendar to coincide with the Occidental way of recognizing dates. Just three years later, orders were given that samurai were no longer allowed to carry their two swords in public; that era was now put behind us, and most of these men had been put into government service anyhow, no longer needing to carry their weapons in public. The old class distinctions were being abolished.

Not all samurai could agree to this, however, and in the fall of 1877, samurai from the southwestern area of our country rebelled, attempting to take over the government and restore the *Shogunate* and their own elevated place in society. The government forces quelled this uprising, and many samurai lost their lives in this last, ill-fated, enterprise. This debacle was known as the Satsuma Rebellion, or the Southwestern Rebellion – *Seinan-no-eki* to the Japanese.

During this time Kan'ichi and Kaoru welcomed their son Takayasu, and in 1878, when he was twenty-two, he married Miho Higuchi, four years his junior. The Higuchi family, local to our island, were not of elevated background. Takayasu, desirous of gaining broader acceptance than the family name Hanshiro allowed for him, changed his name to Takayasu Maki on his eighteenth birthday. Name changing was not an unfamiliar custom in those days, and his wife became Miho Maki upon her marriage.

Takayasu was an energetic and intelligent man, and studied books about Western farming that had been made available by Finance Minister Matsukata. By this method, he was able to increase dramatically the yield of the orchards. This expansion allowed him to obtain a government contract for supplying his produce to the government's military bases in Shikoku, Kyushu and in southwestern Honshu.

My Lord's son Masuhei took as his wife Yasuko – meaning Peaceful Child – Hisamatsu. She was the middle daughter of the clan who owned Matsuyama Castle, known then as West Castle. The Suzuki and Hisamatsu families had had close ties for centuries, and this was a union of equals, unifying the island of Shikoku permanently. Their marriage, in 1870, when Masuhei was 21 and the delightful Yasuko was 20, was a joyous event, and their wedding was attended by family, by their friends the Makis, and by nobles and persons of wealth and rank from Shikoku, Kyushu and Honshu.

Masuhei's parents lived until the son, adopted by Masuhei in 1890, was about five years old. The adoption, you will remember, is called *Yoshi*. As Masuhei and Yasuko had been unable to have their own children, they adopted, first, a boy from the Kubo family, and then a girl from the Ito family in 1899. Their son they named Isematsu – meaning Pine of Ise – and their daughter they named Haruko, a name that you already know means "Spring Child." These two were intended to be raised together and then married, continuing the bloodline of the Suzukis by the joining of two important families of Japan, the Kubos and the Itos.

Just prior to the death of Monzaemon, in 1899, my mate and I were passed to Masuhei. The Katsura Tree-named Keiko lived just one year longer, and passed during the celebration of the new century, in 1900.

Alexander, accustomed as he was to momentous events in the saga being related by *katana*, was nonetheless struck by the quickness of the changes that had taken place in Japan. Just during the lives of these ancestors, he thought, Japan had left the feudal society and the *Shogunate* form of government and was now adopting western ideas of farming and education.

He remembered the name of Masuhei and Isematsu from his 'ba-san's family tree, and knew that *katana's* story would soon be drawing to a close, as these relatives were no longer ancient.

Completing the information in the family history he had been keeping, it looked like this when he was finished:

LADY TOSHIKO SUZUKI

Born in 1427 as Toshiko Matsudaira
Father: Marquis Matsudaira
Related to: Minamoto Chikauji

Homes: Izumo, Edo

LORD HIROSHI SUZUKI

for whom *katana* was made.
Born in 1425
Father: somebody Suzuki
Related to: Emperors Go-
    Shirakawa, Go-Daigo & Antoku
Homes: Osaka, Edo, Tojo
Died in 1476. Buried in Tojo.
    |
    |
Married: 1444 |
Family: two sons, born 1448 & 1450; |
    a daughter, born 1453 |
    |
    |
    \|/

LADY MICHIKO SUZUKI

Born in 1452 as Michiko Takatsukasa
Father: Prince Takatsukasa
Home: Edo

LORD KIICHI SUZUKI

Second master of *katana*
Born in 1448
Father: Lord Hiroshi Suzuki
Homes: Osaka, Edo, Tojo,
    Fukuchiyama
Died in 1497. Cremated in Tojo.
    |
    |
Married: 1470 |
Family: twins. a daughter born 1471; |
    a son born 1471, hours later. |
    |
    |
    \|/

LADY MASAKO SUZUKI

Born in 1474 as Masako Tokudaiji
Father: Prince Tokudaiji
Home: Shizuoka

LORD SEIROKU SUZUKI
Third master of *katana*
Born in 1471
Father: Lord Kiichi Suzuki
Homes: Osaka, Edo, Tojo,
     Fukuchiyama
Died in 1498. Buried in Osaka.

Married: 1491
Family: two daughters and a son, born 1492

LADY TOMIKO SUZUKI

Born in 1493 as Tomiko Mitsui
Father: Mitsui-*sama*
Home: Namazue

LORD MICHIO SUZUKI
Fourth master of *katana*
Born in 1492
Father: Lord Seiroku Suzuki
Homes: Osaka, Edo, Tojo
     Fukuchiyama
Died in 1530. Buried in Tojo.

Married: 1509
Family: a son, born 1512; 3 daughters

LADY MIKI SUZUKI

Born in 1515 as Miki Ikeda
Father: Ikeda-San
Home: Edo

LORD TOMISHIKI SUZUKI
Fifth master of *katana*
Born in 1512
Father: Lord Michio Suzuki
Homes: Osaka, Edo, Tojo
     Fukuchiyama
Died in 1562. Buried in Osaka.

Married: 1533
Family: a son, born 1534; a daughter
and sons Sadao & Hirohisa

LADY KUNIKO SUZUKI

Born as Kuniko Itakura
Father: Viscount Itakura
Home: Edo

LORD SHIN SUZUKI
Sixth master of *katana*
Born in 1534
Father: Lord Tomishiki Suzuki
Homes: Osaka, Edo, Tojo
      Fukuchiyama, Karuizawa
Died ?

Married: 1555
Family: daughter born 1555 & Goto in 1558
a son Masatoshi born 1556

\|/

HARUKO SUZUKI

Born in 1553 as Haruko Nagata
Father: Lord Nagata
Home: Kishu area

LORD MASATOSHI SUZUKI
Seventh master of *katana*
Born in 1556
Father: Lord Shin Suzuki
Homes: Osaka, Edo, Tojo
      Fukuchiyama, Karuizawa

Married: 1575
Family: son Satoru born 1575, daughter
Nanami born 1576, son Shuji born 1577
Died 1600 at Sekigahara, son born
1579 died as a child

TAKAKO SUZUKI
Born as Takako Arai
Born in 1577

SATORU SUZUKI

Born in 1575
Died 1616

Family: son Masaharu born 1599

\|/

NORIKO SUZUKI
Born as Noriko Matsudaira
Born in 1602

LORD MASAHARU SUZUKI
Eighth master of *katana*
Born in 1599
Died in 1644

Married: in Osaka, 1616;
son Masanobu born 1620

\|/

AKEMI SUZUKI
Born as Akemi Kikuchi
Born in 1622
Home: Northern Kyushu

LORD MASANOBU SUZUKI
Ninth master of *katana*
Born in 1620

Married: 1640. Dau. Sachiko born 1641;
son Korekiyo born 1657

\|/

SACHIKO ASANO
Born as Sachiko Suzuki
Born in 1641

Home: Tojo

LORD NAGATOMO ASANO
Tenth master of *katana*
Born in 1643
Died 1675
Home: Ako Castle, on Biwa-ko

Married 1659. Son Naganori, born Edo 1667.

\|/

AKURI MIYOSHI
Born 1674
Born as Akuri Miyoshi
Father: Nagaharu Asano of Hiroshima

Became Yosen-in
Died 1714

LORD NAGANORI ASANO
known as Takumi-no Kami
Born in Edo, Sept. 28, 1667
Eleventh master of *katana*
Died: Seppuku March 14, 1702
Mistress: Satomi Hino
Dau: Lady Asano no Kinume
Born 1695

X
X
\|/

Ryoko Suzuki b.1661, married: Lord Hino b. 1654
Married 1678 at age 17   He the Daimyo of Nara

Daughter Satomi Hino b. 1679. Became mistress to
Lord Asano Takumi-no Kami in 1694.   X
\|/

Tosa no Hanshiro < - - - - - - - - - - - - - - **Lady Asano no Kinume**
Born 1680; died 1754   Born 1695; died 1752
Twelfth master of *katana*
|
| Married 1710; son Tsuyoshi born 1712
|
\|/

TSUYOSHI HANSHIRO   **SUMIKO SASAKI**
Home: Tosa province, Shikoku   Home: Ogura, Kyushu
Born 1712   Born: 1708
Thirteenth master of *katana*
|
| Married 1729. Dau. born first, then son Michio b. 1734
|
\|/

LORD MICHIO HANSHIRO   **YASUKO KASAI**
Home: Tosa province, Shikoku   Home: Mutsu Province
Born 1734   Born 1736
Fourteenth master of *katana*
|
| Married 1753. son Shokei born 1754
|
|
| **MATSUSADA SUZUKI**   **MOMO MATSUKATA**
| Home: Niihama, Shikoku   Kagoshima, Kyushu
| Born 1730
|
| Son Tadoshi born 1751
|
\|/

LORD TADOSHI SUZUKI   **TAKAKO HOSOKAWA**

Fifteenth master of *katana* on 3/14/1792

Home: Niihama, Shikoku   Home: Kumamoto, Kyushu

Born 1751. Died 1809   Born 1755. Died 1806

|

|

|

\|/

Married 1778. Son Mondo born 3/14/1792

LORD MONDO SUZUKI   **YUMIKO SUZUKI**

Sixteenth master of *katana*   Born as Yumiko Sakai

Born 1792   Born 1799

Home: Niihama, Shikoku   Home: Yonegawa

Married 1816. Son Monzaemon born 1820

2 sons, 3 daughters in next ten years

TORAO HANSHIRO   **ETSUKO YUMOTO**

Born 1796   Born 1800

Home: Niihama, Shikoku   Home: Hakone

Married: 1816. Son Kan'ichi born 1825, dau. born 1826

KAN'ICHI HANSHIRO   **KAORU MATSUI**

Born 1825   Born 1830

Home: Niihama, Shikoku   Home: west of Lake Biwa

Married: 1850. Son Takayasu born 1856

\|/

LORD MONZAEMON SUZUKI
Seventeenth master of *katana*
Born 1820. Died 1899.
Home: Niihama, Shikoku

KEIKO SUZUKI
Born as Keiko Yamamoto
Born 1822. Died 1900.
Home: unknown

Married: 1854. Son Masuhei born 1849

LORD MASUHEI SUZUKI
Eighteenth master of *katana*
Born 1849
Home: Niihama, Shikoku

YASUKO SUZUKI
Born as Yasuko Hisamatsu
Born 1850
Home: Matsuyama, Shikoku

Married: 1870. No children.
1890: Adopted Isematsu from Kubo, born 1885;
1899: Adopted Haruko from Ito, born 1895

TAKAYASU HANSHIRO
Born 1856
Home: Niihama, Shikoku
He took family name of Maki 1874

MIHO HIGUCHI
Born 1860
Home: Shikoku Island

Married: 1878

XXI

CONFLICTS CONTINUE

The boy realized, after he had finished his notes on the Suzuki family genealogy, that *katana's* story was ending. Already the family was entering the 20th century, the same century in which he, Alexander, now lived. It excited him to know he would be finding out the last adventures of *katana* and its mate – its missing mate, he just thought – while saddening him that his own adventure was drawing to a close.

Young Isematsu Suzuki, to whom were given my mate and me upon his graduation of cavalry officer's school, was sent to the Yalu River area of the peninsula of Korea in 1904 to head a cavalry unit in Japan's fight with Russia over their mutual territorial rights. In preparation for carrying us into battle, a different kind of warfare than we had experienced before, his family had our original wormwood scabbards bound in leather. They then removed the many jewels that covered our hilts and wrapped our handles with a crisscross of cords so his hands would not slip when we were covered with blood. The new leather scabbard coverings contained metal rings that allowed us to be suspended from his belt, unlike the way we had been carried previously, thrust in the *obi*, by all of our masters before him.

The young officer, my new master, fought well during this very brief military campaign, earning the respect of both his men and fellow officers in the *Jobi* division's cavalry regiment, and being awarded several campaign medals for his valiant actions. He carried one of us at a time on the left side of his belt, and had an Army-issued revolver, plus a Carbine rifle, similar to what the accompanying infantry carried. The pistol, he often lamented, was balky and difficult to fire; it was a Nambu Model 1904 and its only positive feature was that it fired a heavy, enemy-stopping, 8mm round.

When returning home on the troop carrier, he ruminated on his name and how it reflected his performance in this battle setting. Isematsu, as I have previously said, is the Pine from Ise, which is revered for its strength and longevity. The peninsula of Ise, is, as previously described, considered the fount of Japanese civilization. Hence, his name is based on two strong Japanese traditions of the highest regard. The medals now pinned to his chest confirmed his being held in the same high regard.

And he, likewise, could be considered as springing from the fount of Japanese history, being the heir, as he was, to the revered Suzuki family name and *kamon*.

Since he was adopted by Masuhei, you should know that his father's family was Kubo, an old and respected name in Japanese history. His mother was from the Matsudaira family who, as you now know from the Asano story and before, owned the grounds upon which stood the temple where Lord Asano committed *seppuku*. You have been told previously that the Tokugawa dynasty originated as a part of the Matsudaira clan. Of his several siblings, the brother next to him, named Eitaro – second son – became a major governmental figure in transportation and, many years hence, would grant railway passes to Suzuki family members when transportation was difficult.

Another brother died in infancy, while a third brother became a wealthy business owner on the island of Saipan, which came under Japanese control in 1914. His sister, also named Haruko, married Kioshige Kasai, another important family name which you have heard before. A younger sister and her husband became the owners of the Gifu Trucking

Company, which was, for some years, the largest privately owned trucking firm in all of Japan.

His youngest sister, Fusako, married an intellectual who became a professor at Kyoto University.

Another war? thought Alexander. It seems that Japan has been a warring nation throughout the whole story *katana* is telling me. But then, he reasoned, this is a story told by a fighting sword! So perhaps I should have expected many battles throughout its history.

As soon as he returned home from school the following day, he asked his father about the sword.

"Dad, when you've told me about the sword before, you talked about its family history a little bit, but you never said anything about the sword itself. I mean, do you think it still has blood on it from any of the battles it has been in?"

His father took down *katana*, unsheathed it, and showed Alex the *tsuba*, the round metal hand-guard that protects the user's hand from the blade of his opponent.

"You see, Alex, how corroded this guard is? It's been covered in blood for so many centuries that it is all pitted, and the gems that were once in it are now long gone. If you look closely, though, you can still faintly see the pattern of a tiger lurking in the tall grass, and some flecks of gold. The *tsuba*," he continued, "is made of iron and it pits easily from the blood and the oxidation. That's the same as the hilt itself. I won't take the handle off now for you to see, but you can believe me, it, too, is heavily corroded from years of blood being soaked into it."

Again, the boy had to control the smirk that he felt; a smirk that might have let on that he already knew this answer. A smirk that could have led to questioning about things he was not yet permitted to discuss.

As you have been told, Lord Masuhei and his wife, Yasuko, adopted Haruko with the intention of marrying her to their adopted son, Isematsu. She, too, was from an old and important family, the Itos. Her mother, Kumeko Ito, had been a Suzuki, from a cadet branch of the family living in the Osaka area. Her great-uncle was Prince Kimmochi Saionji, who became a famous politician decades after Haruko's children were born. A distant cousin of hers was Prince Fumimaro Konoye, another well-known politician in later years. Her brother, younger by ten years, was Yoshitomo Ito, who became a Naval officer and married Hatsuko Takahashi, from the Takahashi family in the Senjo area of Shikoku. This is a mountainous region and home to many temples. Some of these temples are included in the 88 Temples of Shikoku, about which I have told you previously.

The Ito family had an illustrious background, and she could include amongst her relatives, near and distant, Hirobumi Ito, who had been Prime Minister in Japan prior to the Russo-Japanese War. At the end of that war, he became the first Resident-General of Korea, when it was a protectorate of Japanese rule

These two were married in 1910, which was the same year that Japan annexed Korea, hoping to assimilate Koreans into the Japanese empire. Soon the story was told that the Korean people were ignorant and could not read or write until the Japanese taught them a 'simplified' *kanji*. In fact, Korean script developed in the 15th century, about the time that my mate and I were made. But due to this false rumor, Koreans were looked down on by Japanese ever since then.

Upon my master's return from battle in 1904, he took the place of his father in the Privy Council, which had replaced the *Roju* group of councilors under the *Shogun*. The council had been established by edict of the Emperor in 1888, and, though it had no legislative powers, it was the Emperor's closest advisory body, since all who were part of this august group had no political gain in mind, but were bedrock families of our nation.

No sooner had the Emperor Meiji expanded our territory to include Korea than he suddenly died. His son, Yoshihito, became Emperor Taisho in 1915. But he was not strong, either physically or mentally, and in 1921 his son, Prince Hirohito, became "*sessho*" – Prince Regent – assuming control of the empire, and then became Emperor Showa in 1926 upon his father's death.

These were, once again, turbulent years for our nation, as the constitution allowed the military to operate separately from, and unrestrained by, the civilian government. Though all bowed in reverence to the Emperor, the military gave his wishes little weight in their decisions. So independent were the young military officers that some of the more hotheaded amongst them attempted to stage a coup in February 1936. They succeeded in killing Viscount Korekiyo Takahashi, a former Prime Minister and confidant of the Emperor, and several others. The Viscount was a distant relative of Hatsuko Takahashi, of whom you already know, and other Takahashis about whom you shall learn presently.

Concerned, as they were, that our country was headed into yet another war, in the late 1920s my Lord and his wife approached the leader of the Buddhists at a local temple – the people referred to him as *"Sensei"*, meaning Teacher – to inquire how they could help change the dynamic in the country from war to continued peace. The *Sensei*, sensing their deep conviction, told them that what they desired was a momentous feat, and would take much prayer and sacrifice on their part to help bring about.

"Ours is a poor temple," he told them. "We have little money to repair its roof, which requires continued maintenance. If you truly want to show your kind spirits and peaceful intentions, we would be honored by your gift of a new bronze roof."

Thus this small temple, in the hills above their home in Niihama, gained its bronze roof as a gift from Lord Isematsu and Haruko Suzuki in the year 1929. That roof is visible yet to all who worship there; a reminder of the inherent love of mankind embodied in this couple.

Lest you worry that you will not learn of the Maki family, let me tell you that after Takayasu and Miho were married in 1878, they produced a son, Sohei, in 1880. He was schooled locally, on farming techniques and mathematics, and also studied English reading and writing, intending to assume responsibility for the family's large orchard business. To that end, he married Noriko Sato in 1900 when they were both 20 years old. Her name means Law Child, or Exemplar Child, and she lived up to both meanings. She was a studious girl and became quite knowledgeable about law, seeking out books and men of the profession to learn all that she could. She became the source of advice to her husband on the running of the business, so he could attend to the production of the farm's fruits.

They, in turn, had a son they named Akira, which, as you already know, means Bright or Clear. As their family was a well-known merchant family of some wealth, Akira was able to marry the eldest daughter of the Okamoto family. Katsumi was two years younger than Akira, born in 1905 at the large family home upon a hill in Kobe. Their name actually means "Hill Origin," and the family were early residents of the hills around the port of Kobe. Their marriage in 1926 was a welcome social event on the island of Shikoku, weary as were its inhabitants of the continued fighting in China, the mounting national debt, the assassination of Prime Minister Takashi Hara and other national growing pains.

The birth of Akira in 1903 presaged both the marriage of Isematsu and Haruko in 1910 and the birth of their son, Kazuma, in 1915. It was the fervent hope of my Lord Isematsu, that their son would continue the family's proud tradition of service to the Emperor. Their second, and last, child, a daughter, was born in January 1922. Masako, whose name meaning you already know is Elegant Child, they sent to Tokyo to a girls' boarding and finishing school, determined that she would participate to the fullest possible extent in the country's future.

Weary though the boy was by this time, Alexander set to the task of including the new information on the sheets he had with the Suzuki, and now also the Maki, family histories.

When he had completed them, they looked like this:

LADY TOSHIKO SUZUKI

Born in 1427 as Toshiko Matsudaira
Father: Marquis Matsudaira
Related to: Minamoto Chikauji

Homes: Izumo, Edo

LORD HIROSHI SUZUKI

for whom *katana* was made.
Born in 1425
Father: somebody Suzuki
Related to: Emperors Go-
    Shirakawa, Go-Daigo & Antoku
Homes: Osaka, Edo, Tojo
Died in 1476. Buried in Tojo.

Married: 1444
Family: two sons, born 1448 & 1450;
a daughter, born 1453

LADY MICHIKO SUZUKI

Born in 1452 as Michiko Takatsukasa
Father: Prince Takatsukasa
Home: Edo

LORD KIICHI SUZUKI

Second master of *katana*
Born in 1448
Father: Lord Hiroshi Suzuki
Homes: Osaka, Edo, Tojo,
    Fukuchiyama
Died in 1497. Cremated in Tojo.

Married: 1470
Family: twins. a daughter born 1471;
a son born 1471, hours later.

\|/

221

LADY MASAKO SUZUKI

Born in 1474 as Masako Tokudaiji
Father: Prince Tokudaiji

LORD SEIROKU SUZUKI
Third master of *katana*
Born in 1471
Father: Lord Kiichi Suzuki
Home: Shizuoka Homes: Osaka,
    Edo, Tojo, Fukuchiyama
Died in 1498. Buried in Osaka.

Married: 1491
Family: two daughters and a son, born 1492

\|/

LADY TOMIKO SUZUKI

Born in 1493 as Tomiko Mitsui
Father: Mitsui-*sama*
Home: Namazue

LORD MICHIO SUZUKI
Fourth master of *katana*
Born in 1492
Father: Lord Seiroku Suzuki
Homes: Osaka, Edo, Tojo
    Fukuchiyama
Died in 1530. Buried in Tojo.

Married: 1509
Family: a son, born 1512; 3 daughters

\|/

LADY MIKI SUZUKI

Born in 1515 as Miki Ikeda
Father: Ikeda-San
Home: Edo

LORD TOMISHIKI SUZUKI
Fifth master of *katana*
Born in 1512
Father: Lord Michio Suzuki
Homes: Osaka, Edo, Tojo
    Fukuchiyama
Died in 1562. Buried in Osaka.

Married: 1533
Family: a son, born 1534; a daughter
    and sons Sadao & Hirohisa

LADY KUNIKO SUZUKI

Born as Kuniko Itakura
Father: Viscount Itakura
Home: Edo

LORD SHIN SUZUKI
Sixth master of *katana*
Born in 1534
Father: Lord Tomishiki Suzuki
Homes: Osaka, Edo, Tojo
    Fukuchiyama, Karuizawa
Died ?

Married: 1555
Family: daughter born 1555 & Goto in 1558
a son Masatoshi born 1556

\|/

HARUKO SUZUKI

Born in 1553 as Haruko Nagata
Father: Lord Nagata
Home: Kishu area

LORD MASATOSHI SUZUKI
Seventh master of *katana*
Born in 1556
Father: Lord Shin Suzuki
Homes: Osaka, Edo, Tojo
    Fukuchiyama, Karuizawa

Married: 1575
Family: son Satoru born 1575, daughter
Nanami born 1576, son Shuji born 1577
Died 1600 at Sekigahara, son born
1579 died as a child

TAKAKO SUZUKI
Born as Takako Arai
Born in 1577

SATORU SUZUKI

Born in 1575
Died 1616

Family: son Masaharu born 1599

\|/

NORIKO SUZUKI
Born as Noriko Matsudaira
Born in 1602

LORD MASAHARU SUZUKI
Eighth master of *katana*
Born in 1599
Died in 1644

Married: in Osaka, 1616; son Masanobu born 1620

AKEMI SUZUKI
Born as Akemi Kikuchi
Born in 1622
Home: Northern Kyushu

LORD MASANOBU SUZUKI
Ninth master of *katana*
Born in 1620

Married: 1640. Dau. Sachiko born 1641;
son Korekiyo born 1657

SACHIKO ASANO
Born as Sachiko Suzuki
Born in 1641

Home: Tojo

LORD NAGATOMO ASANO
Tenth master of *katana*
Born in 1643
Died 1675
Home: Ako Castle, on Biwa-ko

Married 1659. Son Naganori, born Edo 1667.

AKURI MIYOSHI
Born 1674
Born as Akuri Miyoshi
Father: Nagaharu Asano of Hiroshima

Became Yosen-in
Died   1714

LORD NAGANORI ASANO
known as Takumi-no Kami
Born in Edo, Sept. 28, 1667
Eleventh master of *katana*
Died: Seppuku March 14, 1702
Mistress: Satomi Hino
Dau: Lady Asano no Kinume
Born 1695

Ryoko Suzuki b.1661, married: Lord Hino b. 1654
Married 1678 at age 17   He the Daimyo of Nara
     Daughter Satomi Hino b. 1679. Became mistress to
      Lord Asano Takumi-no Kami in 1694.   X
                   \|/

Tosa no Hanshiro < - - - - - - - - - - - - - - **Lady Asano no Kinume**
Born 1680; died 1754   Born 1695; died 1752
Twelfth master of *katana*
  |
  | Married 1710; son Tsuyoshi born 1712
  |
 \|/

TSUYOSHI HANSHIRO   **SUMIKO SASAKI**
Home: Tosa province, Shikoku   Home: Ogura, Kyushu
Born 1712   Born: 1708
Thirteenth master of *katana*
  |
  | Married 1729. Dau. born first, then son Michio b. 1734
  |
 \|/

MICHIO HANSHIRO   **YASUKO KASAI**
Home: Tosa province, Shikoku   Home: Mutsu Province
Born 1734   Born 1736
Fourteenth master of *katana*
 |
 | Married 1753. son Shokei born 1754
 |
 |
 | **MATSUSADA SUZUKI**   **MOMO MATSUKATA**
 | Home: Niihama, Shikoku   Kagoshima, Kyushu
 | Born 1730
 |
 | Son Tadoshi born 1751
 |
\|/

LORD TADOSHI SUZUKI

Fifteenth master of *katana* on 3/14/1792
Home: Niihama, Shikoku
Born 1751. Died 1809

TAKAKO HOSOKAWA

Home: Kumamoto, Kyushu
Born 1755. Died 1806

Married 1778. Son Mondo born 3/14/1792

\|/

LORD MONDO SUZUKI

Sixteenth master of *katana*
Born 1792
Home: Niihama, Shikoku

YUMIKO SUZUKI

Born as Yumiko Sakai
Born 1799
Home: Yonegawa

Married 1816. Son Monzaemon born 1820
2 sons, 3 daughters in next ten years

TORAO HANSHIRO

Born 1796
Home: Niihama, Shikoku

ETSUKO YUMOTO

Born 1800
Home: Hakone

Married: 1816. Son Kan'ichi born 1825, dau. born 1826

KAN'ICHI HANSHIRO

Born 1825
Home: Niihama, Shikoku

KAORU MATSUI

Born 1830
Home: west of Lake Biwa

Married: 1850. Son Takayasu born 1856

\|/

LORD MONZAEMON SUZUKI
Seventeenth master of *katana*
Born 1820. Died 1899.
Home: Niihama, Shikoku

KEIKO SUZUKI
Born as Keiko Yamamoto
Born 1822. Died 1900.
Home: unknown

Married: 1854. Son Masuhei born 1849

LORD MASUHEI SUZUKI
Eighteenth master of *katana*
Born 1849
Home: Niihama, Shikoku

YASUKO SUZUKI
Born as Yasuko Hisamatsu
Born 1850
Home: Matsuyama, Shikoku

Married: 1870. No children.
1890: Adopted Isematsu from Kubo, born 1885;
1899: Adopted Haruko from Ito, born 1895

TAKAYASU HANSHIRO
Born 1856
Home: Niihama, Shikoku
He took family name of Maki 1874

MIHO HIGUCHI
Born 1860
Home: Shikoku Island

Married: 1878. Son Sohei Maki born 1880

SOHEI MAKI
Born 1880
Home: Niihama, Shikoku

NORIKO SATO
Born 1880
Home: Unknown

Married: 1900. Son Akira born 1903

AKIRA MAKI
Born 1903
Home: Niihama, Shikoku

KATSUMI OKAMOTO
Born 1905
Home: Kobe

Married: 1926

LORD ISEMATSU SUZUKI
Nineteenth master of *katana*
Born 1885
Adopted from Kubo family
Home: Niihama, Shikoku
Extended family includes:
Brother: Eitaro Kubo

Sister: Haruko Kasai: Gifu Trucking

HARUKO SUZUKI

Born 1895
Adopted from Ito family
Home: Unknown
Extended family includes:
Great Uncle: Prince Kimmochi
  Saionji
Cousin: Prince Fujimaro Konoye
Prime Minister Hirobumi Ito
Brother: Yoshitomo Ito, married to
  Hatsuko Takahashi

Married: 1910. Son Kazuma born 1915;
Dau. Masako born 1922

XXII

KATANA'S LONG TALE
CONCLUDES

Katana opened this session with a quote from Sir Walter Scott's epic poem, written in 1806 about the 1513 Battle of Flodden Field: "O, what a tangled web we weave when first we practice to deceive!"

With the civilian government having been in discussions with the Russian government prior to the Russo-Japanese War in 1904, the Japanese military struck its enemy prior to a formal declaration of war, securing a surprising upset against its larger foe.

The Japanese military leaders during the late 1930s and early 1940s, still ebullient over that victory, and believing that their might would again be victorious in all that it undertook, pushed their way into China, securing much territory and setting up a puppet government. Feeling even more invincible, they struck America, again prior to a formal declaration of war. This accomplished but one end, as the Commander-in-Chief of the Combined Fleet, Admiral Isoroku Yamamoto, intoned: It awakened a sleeping giant and filled him with a terrible resolve.

This war, known now as World War II, ensnared members of the extended Suzuki family in tragic ways.

Haruko Suzuki's brother, Yoshitomo Ito, a naval Captain at the end of the conflict, was aboard Japan's finest battleship, the Yamato, when it was sunk by American naval aircraft off the island of Okinawa. His wife, Hatsuko, planted a lock of his hair and some of his fingernail clippings under his grave marker in the family gravesite in Niihama, to commemorate his sacrifice for his country. His death was a valiant and useless gesture to turn the tide of war.

Lord Isematsu and Haruko's daughter, Masako, was married to an Army officer, Izumi Takahashi, whose uncle was the Viscount Takahashi who was murdered by rogue Army officers in the attempted coup of 1936. Izumi was five years senior to Masako, and had been educated in Tokyo, as well. He was able to survive the war and afterwards became an accountant and an active member of Rotary International. His parents, whose *kamon* was the pagoda, were quite wealthy and left to him a large estate near Niihama, an estate he lost to a local bank, as he had pledged it as collateral for a loan made to an Army friend. The loan was for the friend's business, which failed, causing the Takahashi family estate to be sold.

Their son, Kazuma, was an officer in the Imperial Japanese Navy, and worked on many advanced projects during the early years of the war. One of these projects was the development of the BAKA 'human torpedo,' which saw nominal action. Towards the end of the conflict, he was transferred to Northern Manchuria to help organize the military resistance to Russian troops that moved into that territory in the waning days. He carried with him the *wakizashi* that was my mate, and had it taken from him when he was captured by Russian soldiers.

At the end of the war, when his body was not identified in Manchuria, the family had word that he had been in Hiroshima when the atomic bomb was dropped on that city by American B-29 bombers. Izumi, having returned home recently, and Isematsu, his father-in-law, traveled to that destroyed city not a week after its destruction to look for the missing Kazuma. He was not to be found, as he had actually been taken prisoner and spent time until his repatriation in a Soviet prisoner-of-war camp in Siberia.

As the Japanese government was collecting all items of metal during the war years, Haruko had buried me with a *wakizashi* from another pair of swords so they could not be found and melted for the war effort. Hence, I survived the war, as well.

This news was almost more than the boy could bear, or understand. Yes, he knew of the famous battleship Yamato, as his father had made a scale model of it, saying that it, along with its sister ship Musashi, was the largest battleship ever made. But to learn that a family member had lost his life on that huge ship stunned him.

And yes, he had heard from his 'ba-san of his great-grandfather, Izumi, but knew nothing of his life during the war years. He was happy to finally know the family connection between his great-grandfather and the famous Takahashi he had learned about previously.

So that's why there is no wakizashi mate to katana, he thought. Most likely, it is hanging on some Russian family's wall right now, and they have no idea of its history. No idea than I'm here, with its mate, and longing to see it for myself.

Upon his return home, Kazuma, who had served his country brilliantly in so many ways, was shunned by his father. Shunned, because he had allowed himself to be taken prisoner and had not committed *seppuku* as he was expected to do. Tired, as he was, from the ordeals of the long war and his captivity, Kazuma opened a garage for the repair of vehicles, avoiding contact with his parents. It was not until after his father passed away, in 1957, that he was able to reunite with family and be welcomed back into their care.

Both Isematsu and Izumi, as a result of their exposure to the effects of the bomb in Hiroshima, developed forms of cancer for which there was no cure, and each of them succumbed to its effects.

But Kazuma was not to have a life of ease for long, as the newly constituted Japan Maritime Self Defense Force – no longer was the country allowed to have an army, a navy or an air corps that had the capability to invade another country – tapped him to join the senior staff of the Naval academy, not far from their former navy base in Yokosuka. That base was now a major naval station for the American Navy. After some years in that capacity, and after many years serving his country as a naval officer, he retired as a Vice-Admiral, flying a three-star flag from the guidon posted on the front bumpers of his vehicle.

Lord Isematsu was the last male member of the Suzuki family honored as a member of the Imperial Family. In failing health for several years, Isematsu died in 1957, at which time Emperor Hirohito sent an emissary in full morning coat to deliver a condolence gift. The local temple's high priest and a contingent of over 40 lesser priests also came. Prime Minister Ikeda was present, as well as many ranking military and civic dignitaries. After the service, the whole group walked to the crematorium carrying his body. The following day, the family went back and took his bones.

Upon the death of his father, Lord Isematsu, who had traveled frequently between his home in Niihama to the Emperor's side during the war, Kazuma carried on the tradition of making annual trips to the Imperial Palace in Tokyo to meet with the Emperor as part of the Privy Council. He met originally with Emperor Hirohito, who had officially declared the surrender of Japanese forces in 1945, and later with his son, Emperor Akihito, who assumed the Chrysanthemum Throne in 1989. Thus, despite the Suzuki family having lost its castle and much of its wealth – their many homes outside of Niihama were taken by the post-war government – honor continued to be bestowed on this family and its *kamon* by the Imperial monarchy.

Kazuma and his wife, Yaeko, from the Sasaki clan, had two sons upon his return from captivity. The boy Masatoshi died shortly after birth, but Tetsuo married a woman named Yasue.

Izumi and Masako Takahashi built two smaller homes in Niihama, using land that was the last of the Suzuki estate. In one home lived Kazuma, his wife and family and his mother Haruko; in the other lived Izumi, Masako, and their family.

Masako and her husband had three children, starting with a daughter, Sachiko – who was called Nina by her mother from the very start – born in January, 1944. Her birth was followed in three years by the birth of their son, Akira, and two years after that by the birth of their daughter, Michiko, whose name means Beautiful Wise Child.

Daughter Nina enjoyed several years of her childhood in the old Suzuki family compound where her grandfather spent his final years, prior to the construction of the two smaller homes in which the family grew up. Though much had changed for the family, due to the losses of this war, their area of Niihama was still called Tojo Izumigawa-cho, or East Castle, in honor of the family's status. This practice continued until the death of Haruko, who was considered the last of the pre-war nobility. At the passing of her grandmother, Nina, by then living in America, was contacted by the Japanese consulate and told to relinquish her non-expiring diplomatic passport. She was given a regular passport that no longer showed her as a part of Japan's previous nobility.

Isematsu Suzuki often told granddaughter Sachiko a little rhyme: "Mukashi wa reki reki; Ima wa kire gire." Loosely translated it means: In older (better) times, everything was high and mighty; now, it is torn to shreds. By reversing the order of "re ki" to "ki re", he has also reversed the meaning. His commentary was on the fortunes of the Suzuki family.

When Nina was very young, she swam in the river nearby her home and peed in it. Her mother's friend, a worshipper of the god Fudo, said she had angered the river gods, who then gave her a bad ear infection. As the war had deprived the country of its medical doctors, she was taken to a veterinarian who cut the skin behind her ears, drained the fluid, and sewed her up. With no medication, however, the infection persisted, and her mother's friend told her to go to the river each morning for a week to ask forgiveness. Nina went with her grandmother, Haruko, as instructed. After one week of this act of penance, the infection was cured and did not return.

This same friend of Masako's, during the war, predicted Japan's defeat, and for espousing this, she was imprisoned for much of the war. In 1955, as Isematsu was nearing death, Aunt Ito visited this friend and asked her for two more years of life for Grandpa Suzuki. As I have told you previously, he lived until 1957.

Izumi Takahashi's sister, Itoko Nagata, is from the Kishu section of Honshu. Her family is related to the Abe and Asano families, and uses the same crossed feathers as its *kamon*. Itoko's son was a 'Nomura man', meaning he was a stockbroker in Japan's most prestigious brokerage firm. When Nina was, herself, in college in Tokyo, he often drove her around in his chauffeured Chevrolet. Such were the perquisites of wealth in the days after nobility had left their families.

You should now know of the Takahashi's three children. Of course, your grandmother married an American and they had two children; a son they named Richard Rei and a daughter they named Kristina Kei. Their son, as you know, is your father, and their daughter is your aunt who passed away recently. While your grandparents were living on the Navy base at Yokosuka, Masako and Haruko visited them, hiding me in their luggage. There, they handed me to your grandmother, entrusting her to spirit me out of Japan and to the safety of America. After hiding me in the lining of the sofa the Navy shipped back to San Francisco for her, she then handed me to your father, on whose mantle I have resided for some years.

We do not know what actually happened to my mate, the *wakizashi*, but we do know this: In the early 1980s, your grandparents made friends with several people who were studying psychic phenomena. Having just met these folks, they accepted an invitation to meet a person who practiced psychometry, that is, the ability to gain psychic information by touching an object. All who attended, and there were some twenty people that night, brought something for this woman to touch and then try to relate something about the object.

Your grandfather took a ring made of Alaska gold and Alaskan black diamond. When the psychic held this ring, she said, "There is another ring, just like this one but having a malachite stone, on the finger of a relative in Japan." All in attendance were amazed when your grandfather said, "Yes, when I bought this ring some years ago, I purchased one with malachite and gave it to my mother-in-law, Masako, who still resides in Japan!"

Then, your grandmother sat in front of this woman, handing me to her. Nina had wrapped me, still in my scabbard, in a fine cloth covering. None of the people there, excepting your grandparents, knew anything of my existence or my history. The young woman unwrapped the covering and held me, still in my scabbard.

"This is a Japanese samurai sword," she said quietly. When she tried to pull me from my scabbard, she said, "It is telling me that, as a woman, I cannot touch it until you, Nina, say it is all right." This your grandmother allowed, and the woman continued, "But I have the very strong feeling that there is some connection with Manchuria. The sword cries out for its mate. Please tell me, has this sword been in Manchuria?"

Your grandmother then related, to the psychic and to all who were there that evening, that my mate, *wakizashi*, had accompanied her uncle to Manchuria during World War II, and there, had been taken from him after his capture by the Russian army. The short sword was not returned with him at the end of the war.

The loss of my mate was so traumatic that this practitioner of psychometrics, this woman who could divine the unknowable, could feel my pain through the wood and leather scabbard. "From this sword I sense, I have a vision of, someone begging this sword to deliver the final blow and stop his pain, his misery. But I cannot tell you when this took place."

But you, continued *katana*, you know that I was used by your ancestor to kill his uncle in the castle at Fukuchiyama. It was to this event that she likely referred.

This was surely an auspicious evening for your grandparents.

The Takahashi son, Akira, married a woman of the Morita family, Nanami, and they eventually sold the family homes in Niihama and built their new home in Takamatsu. You will recognize that city's name as being the locale of the Momotaro-san story. Nanami had a brother, Ichiro, who was also married to a Sachiko. Her uncle, Akio, was co-founder of Sony Corporation, which is now world famous for its many products.

Their three children are a daughter, Masami, whose name uses the *kanji* for "masa" from Masako and for "mi" from Nanami, a son Koki, and a second son, Yuji. This last child was adopted into the Maki family upon his marriage to their youngest daughter. As her parents had only daughters and no sons, they continued their family line through their adopted son, who is now *yoshi*. He will be heir to the family's large orchards.

So, as you can see, the Suzukis and the Makis are, again and still, joined together.

The oldest daughter, Nina, was not the only one to marry an American, however.

Youngest child, Michiko, lived with Nina's family in Yokosuka after her graduation from high school, and met an American Navy man. They married and, after his retirement from the naval service, live in California with their two sons.

Thus ends the illustrious history of my mate and me, and the Suzuki family lineage from the date of my making until now. I have told you all there is to tell.

It is now up to you, at long last, to tell this story to the world, however you want to do it and whenever you are prepared to do it.

For the last time, he realized, he set aside *katana*, read over all that he had written, and prepared to complete the family genealogy that he had been faithfully keeping all this time.

When he was finished, it looked like this:

LADY TOSHIKO SUZUKI

Born in 1427 as Toshiko Matsudaira
Father: Marquis Matsudaira
Related to: Minamoto Chikauji

Homes: Izumo, Edo

LORD HIROSHI SUZUKI

for whom *katana* was made.
Born in 1425
Father: somebody Suzuki
Related to: Emperors Go-
    Shirakawa, Go-Daigo & Antoku
Homes: Osaka, Edo, Tojo
Died in 1476. Buried in Tojo.

Married: 1444
Family: two sons, born 1448 & 1450;
    a daughter, born 1453

LADY MICHIKO SUZUKI

Born in 1452 as Michiko Takatsukasa
Father: Prince Takatsukasa
Home: Edo

LORD KIICHI SUZUKI

Second master of *katana*
Born in 1448
Father: Lord Hiroshi Suzuki
Homes: Osaka, Edo, Tojo,
    Fukuchiyama
Died in 1497. Cremated in Tojo.

Married: 1470
Family: twins. a daughter born 1471;
    a son born 1471, hours later.

LADY MASAKO SUZUKI

Born in 1474 as Masako Tokudaiji
Father: Prince Tokudaiji
Home: Shizuoka

LORD SEIROKU SUZUKI

Third master of *katana*
Born in 1471
Father: Lord Kiichi Suzuki
Homes: Osaka, Edo, Tojo,
    Fukuchiyama
Died in 1498. Buried in Osaka.

Married: 1491
Family: two daughters and a son, born 1492

LADY TOMIKO SUZUKI

Born in 1493 as Tomiko Mitsui
Father: Mitsui-*sama*
Home: Namazue

LORD MICHIO SUZUKI

Fourth master of *katana*
Born in 1492
Father: Lord Seiroku Suzuki
Homes: Osaka, Edo, Tojo
    Fukuchiyama
Died in 1530. Buried in Tojo.

Married: 1509
Family: a son, born 1512; 3 daughters

LADY MIKI SUZUKI

Born in 1515 as Miki Ikeda
Father: Ikeda-San
Home: Edo

LORD TOMISHIKI SUZUKI

Fifth master of *katana*
Born in 1512
Father: Lord Michio Suzuki
Homes: Osaka, Edo, Tojo
    Fukuchiyama
Died in 1562. Buried in Osaka.

Married: 1533
Family: a son, born 1534; a daughter
    and sons Sadao & Hirohisa

LADY KUNIKO SUZUKI

Born as Kuniko Itakura
Father: Viscount Itakura
Home: Edo

LORD SHIN SUZUKI
Sixth master of *katana*
Born in 1534
Father: Lord Tomishiki Suzuki
Homes: Osaka, Edo, Tojo
     Fukuchiyama, Karuizawa
Died ?

Married: 1555
Family: daughter born 1555 & Goto in 1558
a son Masatoshi born 1556

HARUKO SUZUKI

Born in 1553 as Haruko Nagata
Father: Lord Nagata
Home: Kishu area

LORD MASATOSHI SUZUKI
Seventh master of *katana*
Born in 1556
Father: Lord Shin Suzuki
Homes: Osaka, Edo, Tojo
     Fukuchiyama, Karuizawa

Married: 1575
Family: son Satoru born 1575, daughter
Nanami born 1576, son Shuji born 1577
Died 1600 at Sekigahara, son born
1579 died as a child

TAKAKO SUZUKI
Born as Takako Arai
Born in 1577

SATORU SUZUKI

Born in 1575
Died 1616

Family: son Masaharu born 1599

239

NORIKO SUZUKI

Born as Noriko Matsudaira

Born in 1602

LORD MASAHARU SUZUKI

Eighth master of *katana*

Born in 1599

Died in 1644

|

Married: in Osaka, 1616; |

son Masanobu born 1620 |

|

\|/

AKEMI SUZUKI

Born as Akemi Kikuchi

Born in 1622

Home: Northern Kyushu

LORD MASANOBU SUZUKI

Ninth master of *katana*

Born in 1620

|

|

Married: 1640. Dau. Sachiko born 1641; |

son Korekiyo born 1657 |

|

\|/

SACHIKO ASANO

Born as Sachiko Suzuki

Born in 1641

Home: Tojo

LORD NAGATOMO ASANO

Tenth master of *katana*

Born in 1643

Died 1675

Home: Ako Castle, on Biwa-ko

|

Married 1659. Son Naganori, born Edo 1667. |

|

\|/

AKURI MIYOSHI

Born 1674

Born as Akuri Miyoshi

Father: Nagaharu Asano of Hiroshima

Became Yosen-in

Died 1714

LORD NAGANORI ASANO

known as Takumi-no Kami

Born in Edo, Sept. 28, 1667

Eleventh master of *katana*

Died: Seppuku March 14, 1702

Mistress: Satomi Hino

Dau: Lady Asano no Kinume

Born 1695

X

X

\|/

Ryoko Suzuki b.1661, married: Lord Hino b. 1654
Married 1678 at age 17   He the Daimyo of Nara
        Daughter Satomi Hino b. 1679. Became mistress to
        Lord Asano Takumi-no Kami in 1694.   X
                                                \|/

Tosa no Hanshiro < - - - - - - - - - - - - - **Lady Asano no Kinume**
Born 1680; died 1754   Born 1695; died 1752
Twelfth master of *katana*
    |
    | Married 1710; son Tsuyoshi born 1712
    |
   \|/

TSUYOSHI HANSHIRO   **SUMIKO SASAKI**
Home: Tosa province, Shikoku   Home: Ogura, Kyushu
Born 1712   Born: 1708
Thirteenth master of *katana*
    |
    | Married 1729. Dau. born first, then son Michio b. 1734
    |
   \|/

LORD MICHIO HANSHIRO   **YASUKO KASAI**
Home: Tosa province, Shikoku   Home: Mutsu Province
Born 1734   Born 1736
Fourteenth master of *katana*
  |
  | Married 1753. son Shokei born 1754
  |
  |
  | **MATSUSADA SUZUKI**   **MOMO MATSUKATA**
  | Home: Niihama, Shikoku   Kagoshima, Kyushu
  | Born 1730
  |
  | Son Tadoshi born 1751
 \|/

LORD TADOSHI SUZUKI
Fifteenth master of *katana* on 3/14/1792
Home: Niihama, Shikoku
Born 1751. Died 1809

TAKAKO HOSOKAWA
Home: Kumamoto, Kyushu
Born 1755. Died 1806

Married 1778. Son Mondo born 3/14/1792

LORD MONDO SUZUKI
Sixteenth master of *katana*
Born 1792
Home: Niihama, Shikoku

YUMIKO SUZUKI
Born as Yumiko Sakai
Born 1799
Home: Yonegawa

Married 1816. Son Monzaemon born 1820
2 sons, 3 daughters in next ten years

TORAO HANSHIRO
Born 1796
Home: Niihama, Shikoku

ETSUKO YUMOTO
Born 1800
Home: Hakone

Married: 1816. Son Kan'ichi born 1825, dau. born 1826

KAN'ICHI HANSHIRO
Born 1825
Home: Niihama, Shikoku

KAORU MATSUI
Born 1830
Home: west of Lake Biwa

Married: 1850. Son Takayasu born 1856

LORD MONZAEMON SUZUKI
Seventeenth master of *katana*
Born 1820. Died 1899.
Home: Niihama, Shikoku

KEIKO SUZUKI
Born as Keiko Yamamoto
Born 1822. Died 1900.
Home: unknown

Married: 1854. Son Masuhei born 1849

LORD MASUHEI SUZUKI
Eighteenth master of *katana*
Born 1849
Home: Niihama, Shikoku

YASUKO SUZUKI
Born as Yasuko Hisamatsu
Born 1850
Home: Matsuyama, Shikoku

Married: 1870. No children.
1890: Adopted Isematsu from Kubo, born 1885;
1899: Adopted Haruko from Ito, born 1895

TAKAYASU HANSHIRO
Born 1856
Home: Niihama, Shikoku
He took family name of Maki 1874

MIHO HIGUCHI
Born 1860
Home: Shikoku Island

Married: 1878. Son Sohei Maki born 1880

SOHEI MAKI
Born 1880
Home: Niihama, Shikoku

NORIKO SATO
Born 1880
Home: Unknown

Married: 1900. Son Akira born 1903

AKIRA MAKI
Born 1903
Home: Niihama, Shikoku

KATSUMI OKAMOTO
Born 1905
Home: Kobe

Married: 1926

243

LORD ISEMATSU SUZUKI
Nineteenth master of *katana*
Born 1885. Died 1957
Adopted from Kubo family
Home: Niihama, Shikoku
Extended family includes:
Brother: Eitaro Kubo

Sister: Haruko Kasai: Gifu Trucking

HARUKO SUZUKI

Born 1895
Adopted from Ito family
Home: Unknown
Extended family includes:
Great Uncle: Prince Kimmochi
    Saionji
Cousin: Prince Fujimaro Konoye
Prime Minister Hirobumi Ito
Brother: Yoshitomo Ito, married to
    Hatsuko Takahashi

X
X
X
X
X
X
X
X

Married: 1910. Son Kazuma born 1915;
Dau. Masako born 1922

X **KAZUMA SUZUKI**
X Born 1915
X Home: Niihama, Shikoku
X
X
X
X

YAEKO SUZUKI
Born as Yaeko Sasaki

Son: Masatoshi, who died young
Son: Tetsuo who married Yasue

X **MASAKO TAKAHASHI**
X Born in 1922
X Born as Masako Suzuki
X

IZUMI TAKAHASHI
Born in 1917

X X X X X X X X >Dau. Sachiko (Nina) Takahashi
| Born: 1944
| Married
\|/

Son RICHARD REI
Twentieth master of *katana*
Son: Alexander Akira
Dau. Kristina Kei

Son: Akira Takahashi
    Born: 1947
    Home: Takamatsu, Shikoku
    Married: Nanami Morita
    Dau. Masami
    Son: Koki
    Son: Yuji adopted into Maki family

Dau. Michiko Takahashi
    Born: 1949
    Married
    Two sons

XXIII

THE END JUSTIFIES
THE MEANS

They all sat in his grandparents' living room: his mother and father, his *'ba-san* and his *'ji-san*. Expectantly, they waited for him to say what he had gathered them to tell.

"I'm not quite sure how to tell you all of this," he haltingly began. "But I have been holding the sword – *katana* – for the past several months and it has been talking to me. As it spoke, I wrote all that it told me. And what it told me was the history of how it was made, and the history of the family – no, the families – who held it as its master."

He paused as he looked at each face, absorbing their level of interest in what he had said, and in particular, absorbing their level of belief in what he had said.

"During all this time, I have become extremely curious about all things Japanese. And I have asked so many questions of my teachers, Hata *Sensei* and Miss Haversham, and you, too, *'ba-san*, that I'm sure I've become such a pest!"

He smiled, and they all smiled with him.

"So today, I wanted to share that story with all of you. When *katana* first spoke to me, I was admonished to not tell what I had been told until the sword permitted me to do so. It has now done that, so here is the story."

And with that, he very quickly shared what he had been told: The making of the sword by the famed swordsmith, Seki no Magoroku, the use of the sword during centuries of battle, the passing of *katana* from father to son, and the transfer of the blades to the Asano family as a gift from the Suzukis to the Asanos when one of their daughters married an Asano son.

He told them, also, of how the short sword, the *wakizashi*, was taken by the Russians at the very end of World War II, and how the long sword, *katana*, has mourned its loss.

Finally, he told them of the passing of the single blade to his grandmother from her grandmother, who had held it in safe keeping all through the war and, in respect for her husband's wishes, had not passed the sword to her own son, but gave it instead to their oldest grandchild.

He showed them the many pages of family history he had written, as further proof of his incredible story.

When he had finished, the sun was beginning to set behind the trees in the yard. Several times during his long monologue, his grandmother had brought out coffee and tea for the others, and for him, a large glass of milk.

There was a long silence. Each person who had heard this incredible tale was mulling over these events. No one knew quite what to say.

Then his grandfather, never one to be shy about speaking his mind, said to him, "Alexander, this is a fabulous story. We all knew you were on to something, as we saw great changes in you over these past months.

"Not only are we so pleased that you shared it with us, but for myself, I think it's a story that needs to be shared with the world.

"So, I think I'll make your story into book."

And he did.

The photo below is from "The Arts of the Japanese Sword" by B.W. Robinson, London, Faber and Faber Limited, 1961. Plate 12. The narrative under the photos reads, "(a) *Katana* blade attributed to Seki Magoroku Kanemoto [131, 15] (early 16th century); the tang has been shortened, and *of Seki in Mino province* is all that remains of the signature. Presented to Queen Victoria in 1860 by the Shogun Iyemochi. 3 ft. VAM, 262-1865". Of the ten blades of this design by this sword smith, only two blades are known to exist.

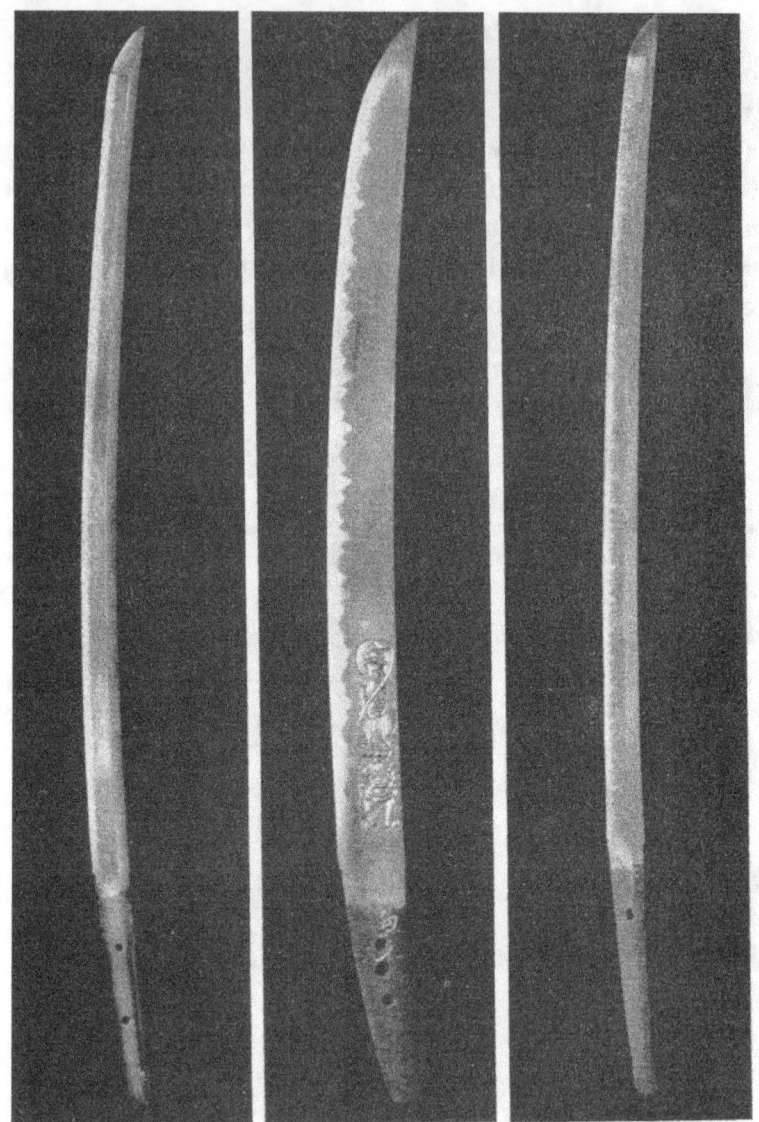

12. THE FIVE TRADITIONS (v) *SEKI-DEN* (*MINO-DEN*)

(a) *Katana* blade attributed to Seki Magoroku Kanemoto [131, 15] (early 16th century); the tang has been shortened, and *of Seki in Mino province* is all that remains of the signature. Presented to Queen Victoria in 1860 by the Shōgun Iyemochi. 3 ft. VAM, 262–1865.

(b) *Tantō* blade signed *Kanemoto* [131, 15] (early 16th century) with later engraving of the divinity Monju on the lion. 1 ft. 6¼ in. VAM, M.28–1912 (ex Dobree Coll.).

(c) *Katana* blade signed *Kanemoto* [131, 15] (16th century). 3 ft. 1½ in. Author's Collection.

The author's nephew, when in London, was able to request a viewing of the blade noted above, and sent these two photographs to the author.

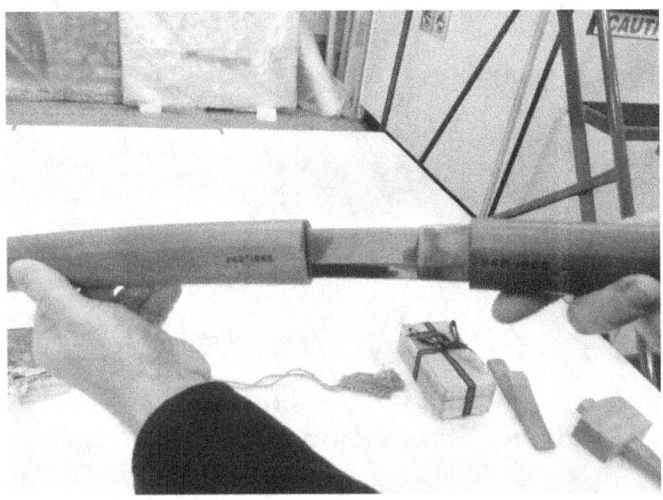

Katana at the Victoria & Albert Museum, London. (Photo courtesy of Alex K. Brown, nephew of the author.)

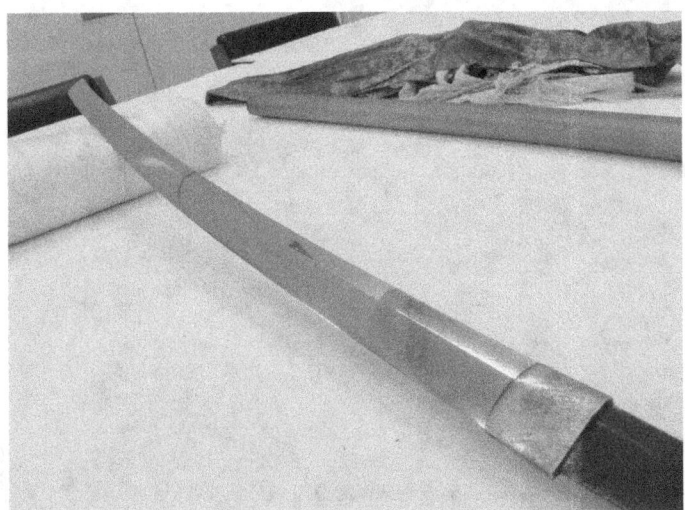

Katana at the Victoria and Albert Museum, London (Photo courtesy of Alex K. Brown, nephew of the author.)

Ako Castle remains.
(Photo courtesy Wikipedia: Ako Domain)

Aso Castle (aka: Ako Castle Restored)
(Photo courtesy: KobeJournal.com)

(Photo: http://aroundtokyo.net/blog/wp-content/up-
loads/2014/08/IMGP6095.jpg)
Lord Asano's gravesite at *Sengaku-ji* Temple. Note the *kamon*
of crossed feathers to the left of the steps.

Battleship Yamato during sea trials, 1941.
(Photo courtesy: https://www.facebook.com/battleship.
yamato.7?fref=ts&ref=br_tf)

BIBLIOGRAPHY

The following books and web-sites were valuable resources used in the preparation of this book, and are recommended reading for those who wish to learn more about any specific era, place or event covered by this story, or about Japan in general.

Alletzhauser, Albert J.: The House of Nomura: The Inside Story of the Legendary Japanese Financial Dynasty

Allyn, John: The Forty-Seven Ronin Story

Axiom: The Religion of the Samurai

Basho, Matsuo (trans. Corman, Cid & Susumu, Kamaike): Back Road to Far Towns (Oku-No-Hosomichi)

Bellan, Robert Neelly: Tokugawa Religion: The Cultural Roots of Modern Japan

Bryant, Anthony J. & McBride, Angus: Elite Series 23: The Samurai
          : Men-at-Arms Series 86: Samurai Armies 1550 – 1615
          : Warrior Series 7: Samurai 1550 – 1600

Clavell, James: Shogun
          : Tai-Pan
          : King Rat
          : Noble House
          : Whirlwind

Cleary, Thomas: The Japanese Art of War: Understanding the Culture of Strategy

De Mente, Boye Lafayette: Japan Encyclopedia

Dollinger, Hans: The Decline and Fall of Nazi Germany and Imperial Japan

Hakusui, Inami: Nippon-To, The Japanese Sword

Henderson, Harold G. (Trans.): An Introduction to Haiku

Hotta, Eri: Japan 1941: Countdown to Infamy

Ishinomori, Shotaro: Japan Inc.

Ito, Masanori, with Pineau, Roger: The End of the Imperial Japanese Navy

Japan Travel Bureau: History of Japan

Kadohata, Cynthia: The Floating World

Kanai, Madoka: Japan – A History in Art

Kikuchi, Charles: The Kikuchi Diary

Kogawa, Joy: Obasan

             : Itsuka

Lebra, Takie Sugiyama, Ed.: Japanese Social Organization

Leckie, Robert: Okinawa: The Last Battle of World War II

Leonard, Jonathan N.: Early Japan: Great Ages of Man series, Time-Life Books

Metropolitan Museum of Art: A Shoal of Fishes

Mitford, A. B.: Tales of Old Japan

Musashi, Miyamoto: A Book of Five Rings: The Classic Guide to Strategy

Olden, Marc: Dai-sho

Pascale, Dr. Richard Tanner & Athos, Dr. Anthony G.: The Art of Japanese Management: Applications for American Executives

Perrin, Noel: Giving up the Gun

Piggott, Juliet: Japanese Mythology

Pitts, Dr. Forrest R.: Japan In the Global Community

Reischauer, Dr. Edwin O.: Beyond Vietnam: The United States and Asia

             : The Japanese

Reischauer, Haru Matsukata: Samurai and Silk: A Japanese and American Heritage

Roberts, John G.: Mitsui: Three Centuries of Japanese Business

Robinson, B. W.: Hiroshige

             : The Arts of the Japanese Sword

Robson, Lucia St. Clair: The Tokaido Road: A Novel of Feudal Japan
Sadler, M.A., A. L., (trans.): The Ten Foot Square Hut and Tales of the Heike
Schlossstein, Steven: Kensei: A Novel of Computer-chip Rivalry and the Trade War on America
Shikibu, Murasaki (trans. by Seidensticker, Edward G.): The Tale of Genji
Skimin, Robert: Chikara! A Sweeping Novel of Japan and America from 1907 to 1983
Statler, Dr. Oliver: Japanese Pilgrimage
Stern, Harold P.: Birds, Beasts, Blossoms, and Bugs
Suetsugu, Bobby: Samurai Sushi: A Field Guide to Identifying and Appreciating the World's Most Unique Wraps, Rolls, and Sashimi
Turnbull, Dr. Stephen: The Samurai and the Sacred
                    : Samurai Warriors
Tsunetomo, Yamamoto (trans. Wilson, Wm. Scott): Hagakure: The Book of the Samurai
Utamaro, Kitagawa: A Chorus of Birds
Vaccari, Oreste & Enko: Complete Course of Japanese Conversation-Grammar (the story of Chushingura was taken from this publication.)
Waddell, Dr. Norman (trans.): Wild Ivy: The Spiritual Autobiography of Zen Master Hakuin
Wikipedia: multiple pages
Yokota, Yutaka (with Harrington, Joseph D.): Kamikaze Submarine
Yumoto, John M.: The Samurai Sword: A Handbook
Miscellaneous publications:
        Grafton, Carol Belanger: Treasury of Japanese Designs & Motifs for Artists & Craftsmen
        Ministry of Foreign Affairs, Japan: The Japan of Today (1964)

ABOUT THE AUTHOR

Photo: Alexia Manson

Gene Brown grew up in Anchorage, Alaska, and is a retired musician, having been a lead trumpet instrumentalist in U.S. Navy unit bands during the early Viet Nam era. He lived nearly five years in Japan, where he met his wife, the former Sachiko (Nina) Takahashi of Niihama. His writing endeavors have also produced a collection of autobiographical short stories, many of which have been featured on the blog www.growingupanchorage.com. Brown lives in Seattle, Washington.

www.ingramcontent.com/pod-product-compliance
Lightning Source LLC
Chambersburg PA
CBHW070330260626
47160CB00003B/1004